Praise for *Shine Annie*

Annie Ruth Watson is the daughter of one of the most successful black farmers in Tobacco County, Georgia. She is a senior in high school and excellent student who plans to attend college in the Fall. Her boyfriend Raymond, is one of the most popular boys in school and a star athlete. Annie Ruth's future is bright.

Her life is suddenly rocked to the core, when she learns that Raymond's feelings for her were not quite as they appeared. Suddenly without a prom date, she accepts an invitation from a longtime classmate named Curtis, who has secretly had a crush on her for years. The pain of Raymond's rejection, coupled with the unwise decision to drink alcohol lead to some poor decision making that will change the course of Annie Ruth's life for good. It is then up to her to make the most of the new path she finds herself on, embracing the love and good things in her future while getting over the past.

Shine Annie is a story that deals with issues of race, the color-complex, class, domestic violence, the realization of dreams, and so much more. Though written with a charming simplicity, the story is complex and richly layered. The characters are well thought out and endearing. Most important, *Shine Annie* highlights the importance of making a life for oneself when things don't go quite as planned. First-time novelist Betty Oglesby Payne has crafted a tale that is timeless, thought-provoking and satisfying. — Stacey Seay, *RAWSISTAZ Reviewers*

Shine Annie

SHINE ANNIE

Betty Oglesby Payne

NEWSOUTH BOOKS
Montgomery | Louisville

NewSouth Books
P.O. Box 1588
Montgomery, AL 36102

ISBN-13: 978-1-60306-004-2
ISBN-10: 1-60306-004-9

Design by Randall Williams
Printed in the United States of America

To my family

CONTENTS

1

Senior Year, 1960

The crepe myrtle trees were still in bloom in southeast Georgia that September. Blazing star and goldenrod flourished. Scuppernongs hung ripe and ready for picking on their vines. Summer had a few weeks left on its tail. The heat and sweat were as sure as breath.

In Tobacco County, near Rail City, seventeen-year-old Annie Ruth Watson lived with her parents in a large white farmhouse. The yard of their well-cared-for home was covered with a thick, lush, neatly groomed lawn. The rich sandy humus soil of the yard also nurtured big bunches of pampas grass, Confederate roses, and chrysanthemums.

Annie Ruth was awake early that morning, but she stayed in bed and listened to her mother's footsteps approaching her bedroom.

"It's five-thirty. Get up, Annie Ruth." Mama walked briskly into the room and flicked on the light. Then she went out again in her blue-flowered house dress. A light, gentle breeze from an opened window blew into the already warm room.

Annie Ruth got up. The pleasant odor of Mama's dusting powder floated in the air. The sweet fragrance brought pleasurable thoughts to her mind—Raymond, the first day of school, seven hours of being on the same premises with the good-looking boy who called her "My Lady."

She straightened the pink chenille bedspread over its matching sheets, slipped on her bathrobe and bedroom slippers and headed to the bathroom.

She knew she shouldn't waste time, but she liked having Raymond in her thoughts. So, in the comfort of a soapy bath, she looked into the wishing well of her mind.

Armed with college degrees and good jobs, she and Raymond would be ready to begin their marriage. The most radiant of brides, she stood by her handsome groom during a wedding of splendorous beauty. She admired his perfectly sculptured jawline, a nose and a mouth that a lover could never forget. His tall athletic physique and dark brown eyes were additional elements of his captivating handsomeness. She was overcome with delirious happiness when he declared, "I do."

"Annie Ruth, hurry up in there," Mama commanded outside the door.

Annie Ruth's lovely fantasy blew away like a soap bubble. "Yes, ma'am," she replied. She finished her bath and got dressed. She was looking in the mirror on her wardrobe and combing her hair when Mama came into her bedroom again. Annie Ruth turned to face her.

"How this outfit look, Mama?"

Mama surveyed the homemade avocado skirt and white blouse. "It look real nice on you."

Annie Ruth turned back to the mirror and added the final touches to her hair. She glanced at Mama's image.

Her eyes looked thoughtful. "Mama, why are you staring at me?"

Mama did not break her stare. "I was thinking about how much you look like them Watsons."

Annie Ruth peered at herself in the mirror. She didn't share Mama's golden brown skin, medium height, and full hips. Her smooth ebony skin and tall, slim but well developed frame were from Daddy's side of the family.

Mama straightened the collar on Annie Ruth's blouse. "Child, you the spitting image of your Aunt Angela. She was so pretty and smart." Mama's voice saddened. "She made a dumb mistake, though, marrying that no-account Ray Rodgerson. That mistake cost her her life. Annie Ruth, study your books, get an education, and—"

"Don't let some sweet-talking, good-looking boy fool you," Annie Ruth finished. She had been hearing the first part of that sentence from her parents since the first grade. Mama had started saying the last part when she turned sixteen and fell in love with Raymond Baldwin.

"Yes, don't let some good-looking and sweet-talking boy fool you," Mama said.

Annie Ruth put her comb in the opened purse on top of her dresser. She wiped her hands on her damp bath towel and started to take it to the bathroom. Mama reached out for the towel. Mama wanted to keep her in the bedroom to continue the conversation. Their eyes met.

"Mama, why don't you just go ahead and say Raymond's name, instead of saying some good-looking, sweet-talking boy?"

Mama smiled, "So, good-looking and sweet-talking means Raymond Baldwin?"

Annie Ruth averted her eyes and stifled the annoyance flaring within her. "I know he's who you talking about. Mama, you always putting Raymond down."

Mama folded the towel. "I just don't want you to get too carried away with him. Getting an education oughta come first. You got plenty of time for boys."

Annie Ruth got a notebook out of the dresser drawer and put it under her purse. She looked at her mother carefully. "You fell in love with Daddy when you were sixteen. Y'all got engaged when you were seventeen."

"That was a different time and a different day," Mama replied sternly. "I was a good student, but I wasn't an A-student with scholarship opportunities. And I didn't have parents who were financially able to send me to college. My poor parents had to sacrifice and pinch pennies just to get me through high school."

In spite of her mother's stern reply, Annie Ruth was feeling quite brave. "Suppose you had had the opportunity to go to college, what would you have done?"

Mama's voice was strong with conviction. "I woulda went to college, kept my head together, and my frock tail down, and married your father after my graduation."

Annie Ruth's voice didn't waver, either. "I can be in love with Raymond and finish college too, Mama."

"I hope you can, Annie Ruth. I sure hope you can." Mama turned to leave the room. "You want a glass of lemonade to go with your grits and eggs? It's so hot."

"Yes, ma'am," Annie Ruth replied. She picked up her notebook and purse, her thoughts wistfully racing ahead to a time when Mama would think such talks unnecessary.

While Annie Ruth was eating breakfast in the large kitchen, Mama wiped the yellow oilcloth on the table. She whisked away any stains that might have fancied resting on her stove and counter tops. And she straightened the yellow curtains that were struggling to shade the room from the morning sun. Annie Ruth observed her admiringly. *I'll show her. I'm gonna be a schoolteacher. And I'm also gonna be a good housewife just like she is.*

Annie Ruth could hear Daddy outside on the back porch. She knew he was scrubbing his hands and arms thoroughly and brushing the dust of early morning farm chores off his overalls before coming into the kitchen.

He sauntered in. "Good morning, daughter."

"Good morning, Daddy." Annie Ruth watched Daddy pull out a chair from the table. He adjusted his muscled six-foot-nine frame on it. "I need to do some figuring for the cotton harvest," he declared and from the breast pocket of his overalls pulled out a small writing pad and pen.

Annie Ruth smiled to herself. Big Sid Watson, the biggest, blackest farmer in Tobacco County, was what the Negro community called Daddy. Annie Ruth watched Daddy do his figuring. He was a good farmer because he worked with his brain as well as his body. Yeah, Daddy sure believed in educating the brain too. Annie Ruth glanced at the wall clock. She had at least twenty minutes before the school bus came. *Shoot, I hope Daddy don't start preaching about education this morning.*

Daddy looked at Annie Ruth. "First day of your senior year, this is an important year. Keep your grades up."

I knew it was coming. "Yes, sir," she said. "I'm gonna keep them up."

Mama put mugs of coffee on the table for herself and Daddy.

"Tell her about it, Sid," she said sitting next to her husband. "She and I done already talked about how she don't need to get too carried away with that Baldwin boy."

"Aw, Mama, you act like I'm gonna get pregnant or something!"

Mama took a sip of her coffee without saying anything.

Daddy glanced at each of them. "Annie Ruth, we ain't trying to give you a hard time, but education has always been the best chance in life for a Negro. Times are getting better for our race. Young Negroes need to get the best education that they can. We wanna see all of our children with college degrees."

Annie Ruth smiled weakly, knowing Daddy was trying to ease the awkward moment between her and Mama.

Daddy went on. "We'd love to see your cousin, Billie Lee, with a degree, too. She ain't got her mind on going to college, though. She got her mind on Lenny Wright and getting married. Annie Ruth, try to talk her into going to college with you next year."

Mama nodded in agreement. "If we could get her to go to college, maybe that would be enough to get Lenny out of her system. With him out of the picture, I think she could make it. I got some real misgivings about her marrying that Wright boy."

Annie Ruth was grateful when the school bus horn brought an end to her parents' lecture. "Bye!" She grabbed her notebook and purse and headed outside.

"Bye! Study hard!" Daddy called.

"I always study hard," she muttered softly. Then she ran to the safety of the school bus.

Annie Ruth's day brightened when she boarded the bus and

saw that the seat next to Billie Lee was vacant.

Billie Lee grinned. "I bet Uncle Sid and Aunt Maybelle gave you a good talk this morning." She recited in exaggerated seriousness: "You better study your books and get an education."

"And don't let some good-looking sweet-talking boy fool you," Annie Ruth added sardonically. "Billie Lee, I get so tired of Mama putting Raymond down. This morning, after she finished talking about Raymond, I couldn't eat my breakfast in peace for Daddy preaching about how he hope I make it in college and how education is the best chance a Negro has. And—"

Billie Lee finished Daddy's comments for her. "Times are getting better for our race. Young Negroes need to get the best education that they can."

Annie Ruth shared her laughter. It was nice having Billie Lee to talk to.

Billie Lee's eyes were full of empathy. "Don't forget. I done heard Uncle Sid's sermon a few times myself, Annie Ruth. Every chance Granny, Uncle Sid, and Aunt Maybelle get they be telling me to consider going to college instead of getting married right after graduation." The wind from the opened window blew Billie Lee's long hair in her face. She pushed it back. "Granny told me this morning to study hard this term so my grades will be good enough just in case I change my mind about going to college.

Annie Ruth adjusted her purse and notebook on her lap. "Daddy and Mama told me to try to talk you into going to college with me next fall."

Billie Lee shook her head and turned toward Annie Ruth. "I always be quiet and listen to the grown folks, but I ain't listening to that jive from you. I don't see why you let what they say bother you. You going to college anyway."

"I know. It's cause I really love Raymond. And it irritates me when Mama talks down my love for him. It's like she wants to push our courtship aside, like it don't matter," Annie Ruth said. "I don't like the way Mama and Daddy are always preaching to me about college when they know I'm planning to go." Annie Ruth felt a pang of irritability toward her parents. "They act like I ain't got sense enough to make it to college like my brothers."

Billie Lee pushed her hair back again. "Annie Ruth, you know you gonna make it. Our parents are like most grown folks. They think young folks ain't got sense and don't know anything about life and love."

Annie Ruth thought about what Billie Lee had said for a moment and then replied, "Yeah, you right."

Curtis Lynch was sitting several seats back. He had been reading before Annie Ruth boarded the bus. After she got on, he was unable to keep his eyes on his book. His eyes took in every movement of her shoulder-length hair and the side of her face as she looked at Billie Lee. But watching her was not enough; he decided to move closer.

The old bus shook and rattled noisily on the bumpy dirt road. Curtis clutched the backs of the seats to keep his balance while he moved up to the empty seat directly in front of the girls. He swiveled in the seat and faced them. "Hey, Annie Ruth. Hey, Billie Lee."

"Hey, Curtis."

"I can hardly believe we're finally seniors," Curtis said. "I'm glad this is our last year."

Annie Ruth smiled. "Yeah, I'm glad to be a senior, too."

"I certainly ain't got any regrets," Billie Lee added.

Curtis focused his attention on Annie Ruth. He loved the movement of her lips, the flash of her teeth as she laughed, and the glint of her earrings against her dark skin and hair. Her eyes were like sunbeams on a chilly afternoon, warming him with the joy of her attention. He had to take advantage of the time on the bus to enjoy Annie Ruth, because once they arrived at school Raymond Baldwin would overshadow him.

As the bus driver slowed and prepared to enter the school driveway, Annie Ruth looked out and saw Lucinda Mills, one of their close friends. Lucinda was wearing patent leather high-heeled shoes and a blue dress with a tight waist and cropped jacket. She nudged Billie Lee. "There's Lucinda. Ain't her outfit saying something."

Billie Lee looked out the window and nodded. "She is sharp."

Lucinda was waiting for them when they got off the bus "Hey! Lord, have mercy! The sun done about cooked y'all out there in the country. Curtis, your eyes and teeth are about all I can see of you!"

Curtis shot back, "Watch your mouth, Lucinda. Don't come over here talking down to us hard-working farm children. We weren't all as lucky as you, to be born with a silver mop in your hand ready to go to work in Miss Anne's cool house."

Annie Ruth joined the others in a good-natured laugh.

"Y'all know I was only teasing," Lucinda said sheepishly.

"Yeah, we do. But you know Curtis likes to have the last word," Annie Ruth replied. "Lucinda, you looking good."

Lucinda smiled graciously. "Thank you."

"Hey, everybody."

Annie Ruth beamed at the approaching couple. "Hey, Dwight and Edwina, y'all getting an early start on courting?"

Dwight took Edwina's hand. "Yeah, we starting this school term off right."

The smell of freshly mopped and waxed floors filled the air.

Annie Ruth searched through the students for Raymond. When she caught sight of him, he was talking to a pretty sophomore, Hootie Simpson. He was so engrossed that he didn't see Annie Ruth. But Hootie saw her. Her eyes flickered on Annie Ruth and then looked up at Raymond adoringly. The bell for homeroom rang. Since Annie Ruth and Raymond weren't in the same homeroom, she had to wait until homeroom was over to talk to him.

Raymond was waiting for her after homeroom. She glared at him. "What were you and Hootie talking about this morning?"

"My Lady, don't start that jive. We were only talking. I'm allowed to be friendly to my schoolmates, ain't I?"

Annie Ruth's voice softened. "Yeah, I was just disappointed cause I didn't get a chance to talk to you before homeroom."

"Don't let something as little as that bother you," Raymond said. "Shoot, there ain't a chick in this school that can beat your time. You're as foxy as they come. I'm the top athlete. You're the top student. The best deserves the best."

Raymond shifted his notebook to his left hand and put his right hand gently on her elbow. "We'll be seeing a lot more of each other now that school done started. Maybe your daddy will relax those rules of his, and we can start going out. You think he'll let me take you home Friday night after the game?"

"I hope so. I'll ask Daddy and Mama tonight. Billie Lee and Lenny will probably have to go along with us." Annie Ruth smiled inwardly at the disappointment on Raymond's face.

"Well, that's better than no date at all," Raymond said. "I'll talk to Lenny about it. I was hoping to be able to have some time alone with you. But Lenny is buying a car this week, so I won't have to ask my dad about using his."

Annie Ruth took out her schedule. "Let's compare schedules."

They studied their assigned classes and Raymond said, "Looks like we got the same academic classes like we did last year."

Annie Ruth was glad. She loved being in the same class with Raymond.

By the time they reached their first period class, Annie Ruth had forgotten Hootie Simpson. She sat down next to Raymond. Billie Lee and her close friends, Lucinda, Curtis, Dwight, and Edwina sat nearby.

Their teacher, Mr. Clayton, quickly checked his roll handing each student a book when he called his or her name.

Annie Ruth looked in the front cover of her textbook. "Susan Flanders" was written there, but the unfamiliar name did not provoke her curiosity.

Dwight looked in the front of his book and frowned. "I thought these were new. Who is this Sarah Boatright?"

Annie Ruth looked more interestedly at the unfamiliar name in her book but didn't say anything.

Edwina looked in her front cover. "Who's Jack Taylor?"

"White people. I know both of them," Raymond said.

He probably knows them from working at Sinclair's Grocery. He meets a lot of white people there, Annie Ruth thought.

"White people." Dwight closed his book. "That figures. We always get old books from the white school."

"And whenever we do get new books," Lucinda added, "there

usually ain't enough of them to go around."

"That's right," several other students added.

"Aw, stop complaining," Raymond chided. "It was nice of the white folks to give us books. They better than no books at all."

Curtis frowned at Raymond. "Man, that's ridiculous! Our parents work hard and pay taxes just like white people."

Raymond threw Curtis a disgusted glare. "Curtis, you walk around reading and running your mouth all the time. Why don't you go to Atlanta with Martin Luther King and those other trouble-making Negroes?"

Curtis smiled. "If I had the opportunity, I would be honored to do that."

Some others chuckled.

Dwight looked at Curtis approvingly. "Tell him about it, man."

"Y'all need to hush all that jive about getting books from the white school," Raymond said. "So what. Y'all Negroes ain't learning what's in the *old* books!"

"If we've learned that we're Negroes, and we've got nothing to be ashamed of, then we've learned more than you'll ever know!" Curtis cried.

Annie Ruth felt a wave of embarrassment. She looked at Raymond defensively.

Raymond scowled and stood up. "Step over here and run off that mouth of yours!"

Curtis stood up, his fists clenched.

Annie Ruth stared anxiously at them.

"Sit down both of you!" Mr. Clayton ordered.

When the boys obeyed, Annie Ruth breathed a sigh of relief.

Mr. Clayton wasn't a real big man, yet he loomed over the boys like a disapproving giant and demanded their respect. He spoke in a crisp voice. "I want you to think and discuss issues. But this isn't a battleground for fighting about racial inequalities. This is a classroom—a preparation for life and for battles against the injustices that exist in our segregated world. And, young Negro *brothers*—" His penetrating eyes flashed at Curtis and Raymond. Curtis looked down. Raymond looked out the window. "And, young Negro *brothers*, the battles should be nonviolent. And not against each other!"

After class was over, Annie Ruth and Raymond watched as other students expressed their approval to Curtis for his speaking out. She touched Raymond's arm tenderly. "Don't let it bother you. Curtis is too race conscious. He took what you said too seriously. I know you were just teasing."

When Annie Ruth got on the school bus that afternoon to go home, the first thing she saw was Billie Lee's troubled face.

"What's wrong?" Annie Ruth asked, sitting down beside her.

Billie Lee wiped her eyes with the back of her hand.

"It's the same old story. Hootie Simpson and her friends started picking at me on the way to the bus. She told me, 'I didn't know that Tobacco County High done integrated. I ain't ever seen any colored girls with hair like that.'"

Annie Ruth touched her cousin's hand. Both she and Billie Lee were tall, slim, and well-developed, but Billie Lee's copper-colored hair was longer and softer. Her extremely light skin, thin lips, and gray eyes were definitely not part of her Watson heritage. "Don't pay Hootie and her friends any mind, Billie Lee," Annie Ruth said. "She probably picking on you cause she don't like me. She wants Raymond."

Billie Lee wiped her eyes again. "Hootie said, 'Yeah, Billie Lee ought to borrow some of Annie Ruth's blackness. Lord knows, she got more than enough. I don't see what a good-looking light-skinned boy like Raymond see in that tall, black country girl.' Then Racine Evans spoke up. 'He just like going with her cause she the best student in the twelfth grade. She got long hair, pretty clothes, and her daddy's the biggest colored farmer in Tobacco County. I ain't studying either one of them, Annie Ruth or Billie Lee. They think they so much.'"

Annie Ruth waved her hand with annoyance. "Why you worried about what they said? It's like Mama always says, you can do your very best and people are still gonna talk bad about you." Annie Ruth took a long look at Billie Lee. "Are those girls buying your food and clothes? Are they providing you a place to live? When you die is God gonna judge you by what people said about you?"

"Of course not, Annie Ruth."

"Then what you worrying about them for?" Annie Ruth declared, handing her a handkerchief.

Billie Lee swallowed and wiped her eyes. She was looking down and twisting the damp handkerchief in her hands. "It ain't that simple. I done been called everything—mulatto, half-breed, white man's bastard, high yellow, and red bone. Sometimes I get to thinking about that. I wouldn't mind being a mulatto or a half-breed if I was born out of love. But you know my mother got pregnant when her husband caused her to be used for sex by a white man."

Billie Lee's voice caught. "If only I was born out of love. I wouldn't care what people called me." She looked up sadly. "*If*, that's the problem, Annie Ruth, *'if'*. Cause I was born out of a betrayal. Who am I? What's my *real* last name?

Annie Ruth stilled the twisting handkerchief. Her voice was firm. "You here, Billie Lee. That's what Daddy always tell you. Granny, Daddy, Mama, my brothers, our cousins, and me, we love you. That's what matter. You a Watson. You're Billie Lee Watson, niece of Big Sid Watson, the biggest, blackest farmer in Tobacco County!"

Annie Ruth was glad to see the sadness gradually fade from Billie Lee's face. Billie Lee gave her a grateful look and smiled weakly. "Annie Ruth, you always know what to say to make me feel better! I'm glad you my cousin."

"That makes two of us," Annie Ruth said. "Now, let's put our heads together and figure out how we gonna convince Daddy to let us ride home with Raymond and Lenny after the game Friday night."

Billie Lee's face brightened. "You really think Uncle Sid will let us go?"

"You get Granny to bring you over to our house after supper tonight," Annie Ruth said. "We'll ask him together. Shoot, Billie Lee, we're seniors. It's time for them to stop treating us like little girls."

2

First Date

The evening sun shone on the Watsons' kitchen table. Crickets were serenading with their evening song. Annie Ruth sat directly in front of her father who was considering her and Billie Lee's plea to be allowed to ride home with Raymond and Lenny on Friday night. Anxiety was doing the twist between Annie Ruth's throat and stomach. She glanced at Billie Lee, sitting next to her. Her cousin looked just as anxious.

Daddy opened his mouth.

Oh please say we can go, Annie Ruth cried silently.

"Maybelle, may I have a piece of cake?" Daddy asked.

Annie Ruth swallowed a sigh.

Lord, have mercy, look like Daddy could go ahead and make up his mind!

Mama gave him a slice of cake. "Annie Ruth get some knives for you and Billie Lee," she said. "Y'all need to help your Granny and me peel the rest of these pears."

Annie Ruth got two knives and handed one to Billie Lee. "What you gonna make with these pears, Mama?"

"Preserves."

24

"They some nice pears, too," Granny said. "I put up a dozen quarts yesterday."

Annie Ruth's thoughts drifted to making preserves as she peeled. Mama would take the peeled, sliced pears and put them in a large pot with a little water and plenty of sugar and cook them slowly. When it was ready, the slices would be brown and the juice sweet and syrupy.

Why was it so hard for her parents to see that her love for Raymond was like preserves in the making? Her and Raymond's love was raw and pale, but after years of careful simmering, their love, like her parents', would be preserved and ready to last a lifetime.

A few minutes later, Annie Ruth focused her attention on Daddy again. He seemed to have finished his cake and arrived at a decision at the same time.

"I'm gonna allow y'all to go Friday night," he said. "Mind you, this ain't gonna be a weekly thing. You both can continue having Raymond and Lenny visit you on Sunday evenings at home where y'all can be chaperoned, but any going out or riding with boys will have to be cleared with me first."

Annie Ruth squeezed Billie Lee's hand under the table. "Thanks, Daddy."

"Thanks, Uncle Sid."

Mama added a final note of advice, "Y'all better keep your frocks down and remember what you been taught."

"That's right. Y'all better not let them boys fool y'all," Granny added.

Annie Ruth and Billie Lee smiled and rolled their eyes. "Yes, ma'am."

That night Annie Ruth went to sleep thinking about her date

with Raymond. She was on his mind, too, but thoughts of her did not cause him to sleep easily. Clad only in a pair of boxer shorts, Raymond stretched his long legs. He was tired, but the too-warm air in his bedroom kept him from sleeping. He was tempted to discard his shorts and lie nude on top of his sheets, but he resisted that temptation out of respect for his mother who looked in on him every morning to make sure that he got up on time.

His father believed that no decent person should be caught in bed after six a.m., no matter what day of the week it was. So since he had been a small boy, he and his mother had a non-verbal agreement that she would make sure that he did not have to endure his father's wrath for not being an early riser.

Raymond grinned slyly. *I wish I coulda been a fly on the Watsons' wall when Annie Ruth asked Mr. Sid to let me take her home Friday night. He probably said yes. Mr. Sid ain't a fool. He knows Annie Ruth is crazy about me. Trying to keep her away from me would probably make her want me even more. Yes, sir, he'll probably agree to try to keep her from getting too carried away with me.*

Colored folks call him the biggest, blackest farmer in Tobacco County. They think he's a big shot. Even the white folks respect him. That's what I like. I like being known as the boyfriend of that big shot's daughter.

Raymond sighed when he thought about Annie Ruth's smooth dark skin. She was pretty if a fellow found very dark skin attractive, but, for him, her only attractive features were her tall, shapely figure and her thick shoulder-length hair. Raymond yawned. Billie Lee came closer to the desires of his heart, but closer was all, because the real desires of his heart were found in only one person—Gabrielle Sinclair, pretty, sweet, blond, and very white.

Raymond decided he had spent enough time thinking about Annie Ruth and her father. He closed his eyes and eased into a pleasurable ivory-colored haze of Gabrielle fantasies.

The football game that Friday looked like the beginning of a successful season for Tobacco County High's team and for Raymond. The game ended with the home team winning by twenty-one points and Raymond had run four touchdowns.

Annie Ruth felt like she was gliding on a cloud of happiness as she walked hand-in-hand with Raymond to Lenny's car.

Billie Lee and Lenny were waiting inside the car. Lenny checked his watch while Annie Ruth and Raymond were getting in. "Mr. Sid slipped a little. We still got almost an hour before we gotta have y'all girls home."

"He gave us the extra time cause he thought the coach was gonna keep the team a long time after the game like he usually do," Annie Ruth explained.

Raymond chuckled. "I'm sorry Coach's wife didn't feel well, but I'm glad he let us go early." He draped his arm around Annie Ruth's shoulders. "Man, let's go by the Blue Light Inn."

Annie Ruth pulled away. "You know Daddy don't want Billie Lee and me going to a juke joint!"

"I know that's the truth!" Billie Lee added.

"We can just sit in the parking lot and drink some Cokes and listen to the music. I'll park way back so nobody will see us," Lenny suggested. "As long as y'all don't go in, Mr. Sid won't find out."

"I-I don't know," Annie Ruth said.

Raymond hugged her close and kissed her cheek. "Come on, My Lady, Mr. Sid ain't gonna find out."

Annie Ruth's reluctance melted in the warmth of her happiness. "Well, okay. What you think, Billie Lee?"

Billie Lee looked at Lenny. "I don't think Uncle Sid will find out."

Annie Ruth leaned her head against Raymond's. *Shoot, she rationalized. What choice we got? There ain't any nice late night restaurants or drugstores where Negroes can sit and talk and have refreshments. A juke joint is the only place available. Besides, Edwina and Dwight, and Lucinda and her boyfriend go to juke joints all the time.*

When they got to the Blue Light Inn, Lenny parked as far back as possible. Raymond went inside alone and bought their Cokes.

When he came back, Raymond convinced Annie Ruth to sit alone with him for a few minutes in the back seat of the car of one of his teammates.

Annie Ruth took a sip of her drink. "Raymond, we shoulda sat in the front seat."

"Naw, there's more room back here."

When Raymond kissed Annie Ruth, she could feel herself tingle with excitement. He followed with a deeper kiss. She was surprised by the sexual excitement she felt when he squeezed her breast.

"Don't pull away, My Lady."

"I gotta." He tried to slip his hand under her skirt. "Raymond, stop that, and get hold of yourself. I ain't going all the way until I get married!"

Raymond took his hand away. "Shoot, that'll be years from now!"

Annie Ruth sat up straight. "I'm still gonna wait. I wanna be a virgin on my wedding night. Raymond, don't you want things to be perfect for us?"

"I can think of a lot more exciting things. Heck, we gotta get outta here and get y'all home, anyway."

On the way home, Annie Ruth looked out at the dark night.

Raymond had his arm around her shoulders and held her hand. She leaned her head closer to his. She felt so good being close to him. *I wouldn't dare sit this close to a boy at home. And Raymond never kissed me as passionately as he did tonight. I never felt like I did tonight before either! What if they had had more time? How would she have felt if he had continued to kiss her? Would she have had the strength to stop him?*

Annie Ruth had asked Billie Lee to spend the night with her. Raymond and Lenny said a quick goodbye on the Watsons' front porch. Annie Ruth and Billie Lee said good night to her parents and went to her bedroom.

Billie Lee dressed for bed slowly. "I know we gotta get up early in the morning, but I could lie in bed all night and think about Lenny."

"That ain't a good idea. You know we gotta pick cotton in the morning. And the hot sun is a killer if you don't get enough rest the night before."

Billie Lee chuckled and then looked at Annie Ruth intently. "Annie Ruth, you act like you thinking about something. You didn't say much after you and Raymond came back to the car at the Blue Light Inn."

"Billie Lee, do you ever think about going all the way?"

"All the way to where?"

"Now, Billie Lee."

"Oh, my gosh! Shoot! Well, Lenny talks about it a lot. He even asked me tonight. He said he'd get you and Raymond to stay in Alfred's car a little longer. I told him we gonna wait until we're married."

"Y'all ain't got long to wait. But it'll be years before Raymond and I get married."

"Don't wait so long. Get married after graduation like me."

"I wanna go to college."

"Get married and then go to college."

Annie Ruth finished undressing and put on her nightgown. "How we gonna afford to do that? Besides, I ain't even sure Raymond wants to get married that soon. He ain't ever ask me." She folded her clothes and put them in a laundry basket. "He got his heart set on playing ball in college and trying to be a professional. We just gotta wait."

Billie Lee put her clothes in her overnight case and climbed into bed. "Yeah, that's the best thing to do."

"Good night, Billie Lee."

"Good night."

A half-hour later, Annie Ruth was awakened by Billie Lee shaking her gently. "Annie Ruth, I done thought of the perfect solution for your problems."

"You discovered a gold mine and a birth control method with one hundred percent effectiveness."

"No, it ain't that great, but it's a good one."

"Child, please, tell me, so I can go back to sleep."

"Okay, forget about Raymond and start going with Curtis Lynch."

Annie Ruth tried not to show her irritation. "Curtis goes with Elizabeth Collins. Didn't you see them together at the ball game?"

Billie Lee pressed her point. "They just date sometime. I done heard them both say they're only friends. Besides, everybody knows he's crazy about you. I bet *he'd* wait for sex."

When the full meaning of Billie Lee's suggestion sank into Annie Ruth's sleepy brain, she cried, "Forget about Raymond? Start going with Curtis Lynch? Billie Lee, I can't believe you been wasting your time thinking about something like that!"

3

Sweet Memories

By noon Saturday, Annie Ruth and Billie Lee had each picked more than a hundred pounds of cotton. Tired and relieved to be through with field work for that day, they headed to their respective homes.

After Annie Ruth ate her dinner, Mama took her to her cousin Aldonia's beauty shop for a hairdo. Annie Ruth was glad that Aldonia had only two other customers ahead of her and no one else was waiting. Aldonia was the daughter of Aunt Florence, Daddy's sister. Although Aldonia was several years older than Annie Ruth and Billie Lee, the three were close friends. Annie Ruth looked forward to the two of them having time to talk. Aldonia's tallness was her only Watson attribute. Her full hips, petite waistline, mahogany skin, and round face were characteristics of her father's family, the Days.

Aldonia told Mama she would take Annie Ruth home when she finished her hair, so Mama left. Annie Ruth waited on the inexpensive maroon vinyl sofa while Aldonia quickly finished with pressing and curling the other two customers' hair. They were alone when Aldonia started preparing Annie Ruth's hair for shampooing. She turned Annie Ruth's face in her direction. "How come you being so quiet?"

"I was thinking about Raymond."

"You don't say. Well, who woulda thought?"

Annie Ruth giggled. "Aw, come on, am I that bad?"

Aldonia adjusted her head on the shampoo bowl and started washing her hair. "Child, you got one of the worse cases of lovitis I ever seen."

Annie Ruth was quiet while her hair was being shampooed. She started talking again when Aldonia started preparing her hair for drying. "Daddy finally broke down and allowed Raymond and Lenny to take Billie Lee and me home after the football game last night."

Aldonia stopped her large comb in midair. "Really! You mean to tell me Uncle Sid allowed you and Billie Lee to be in a car alone with some boys?"

Annie Ruth turned toward Aldonia. "I'll be graduating from high school this spring and going to college next fall. I need to learn about life."

Aldonia resumed combing and sectioning Annie Ruth's hair. "I know, but you know how strict Uncle Sid is," Aldonia said. "How's Billie Lee? Granny and Uncle Sid ain't talked her outta getting married, yet?"

"No, I doubt they will."

Aldonia motioned Annie Ruth to sit in a dryer chair. "I hope she making the right decision. Lenny got too much of a roving eye to suit me."

Annie Ruth moved to the dryer chair. "Why you say that?"

Aldonia shrugged. "Don't pay me any attention. Lenny's a

young man. He probably just sowing his last wild oats before he settle down."

"Aldonia, you beginning to sound like Mama. Lenny love Billie Lee. And he been working real hard on his new job on the railroad."

"I hope you right," Aldonia said. "I wanna see Billie Lee happy."

Aldonia didn't seem to be in a hurry to finish, so Annie Ruth continued the conversation. "So, what you gonna do, Aldonia?"

"Do about what?"

"About marrying—you ain't thinking about it?"

Aldonia smiled lightly. "I'm thinking about it."

"What you waiting on? Claude Mitchell or Daniel Parker would marry you in a heartbeat. The last time I saw Claude, he said 'Annie Ruth, when Aldonia walks, she got a million-dollar-swing!'"

Aldonia's laughter was as smooth as a silk scarf. "I ain't ready to settle down. I still got some unfinished business in my life."

"Tobacco County High's Homecoming Queen for school term 1960-61 is Miss Annie Ruth Watson!" The principal made that announcement on what Annie Ruth considered a beautiful October morning. She replayed the announcement several times in her mind and touched her chest. She felt like she was going to explode with happiness.

Although Raymond, Billie Lee, and her friends had predicted that she would win, she hadn't expected to. The queen was chosen from the three senior girls with the highest averages for the previous school terms. Annie Ruth was glad to be one of the top students. She knew that even if she did not get the

most votes and become queen, she would still be part of the
Homecoming Court. She would have liked being part of the
court, but she loved being queen. She felt like laughing and
shouting joyously. Annie Ruth Watson, Homecoming Queen,
1960-61! Life was wonderful!

Raymond was Annie Ruth's boyfriend, and Annie Ruth was
the homecoming queen, but it was not her ebony beauty or
regal appearance as she sat on the royal blue and gold decorated
float that magnetized his eyes the afternoon of the homecoming parade.

No, Raymond's innermost thoughts were being increasingly
dominated by the delicate ivory beauty of his first love—Gabrielle Sinclair. Raymond stood beside some other football players
and smiled proudly when the queen's float went by. Annie Ruth
did look like a queen. But Raymond's attention was directed
across the street. Many of the white merchants and store clerks
had come outside to watch the parade. A group of white teenagers was also watching. His eyes darted back to the group of
teenagers. Another float passed by and blocked his view.

He could feel his heart speed up. Could it really be her?
His view cleared again. Man, it was her! Gabrielle was standing
across the street in front of him. The band marched by playing
loudly. One of his friends nudged him and said, "Man, those
majorettes are sho nuff foxy!" All of his friends laughed loudly.
Their laughter and talk jarred him back to reality and reminded
him that it was not proper for a colored boy to be staring at a
white girl. His glances became furtive. She gestured as she was
talking to the others. Her slender fingers took his mind back
to the summer when he was fifteen years old.

That summer he had worked as the personal servant for

her grandfather, Elder Sinclair. The old man was the father of his father's boss man. Raymond had not been pleased when he learned he had to spend the hot, humid summer days being the personal servant of the old man. When he voiced his displeasure, his father looked at him like he was a fool.

"Boy, you crazy? Most of the colored boys around here gotta work hard in the fields. You gonna have it easy taking care old Mr. Sinclair. He ain't bedridden or anything. You ain't gonna have to empty slop jars." He stuck out his chest proudly. "All these white folks around here know my name. They know what good workers me and my young'uns are. That's why they asked you."

Raymond knew better than to try to argue more. So that summer he started work for the rich old white man who liked fast driving on dirt roads, drinking cold beer in local white honky tonks, and fishing all afternoon on a hot summer day. Raymond had learned to drive at the wheel of a tractor at the early age of twelve. Since the old man still had a valid driver's license and Raymond had a learner's permit, he drove Mr. Sinclair to his various pastimes.

He surprised himself by really liking the job and the old man. But the greatest and most pleasurable surprise for him was Miss Gabrielle, the daughter of Mr. Sinclair's youngest son, a rich businessman in Atlanta.

Miss Gabrielle came to visit her grandfather after Raymond had been working for Elder Sinclair for several weeks. He had just finished washing the truck when she came out with her grandfather.

"Good morning, Raymond," Mr. Sinclair said. "I'm glad you went ahead and washed the truck."

Raymond put the water hose in the garage and turned

around. "Good morning, Mr. Sinclair." He was glad he had replied before he saw the girl, because he was not sure he could have spoken if he had seen her first. *Man, she the prettiest girl I ever seen.*

"This is my granddaughter, Gabrielle. She's going to be spending some time with me this summer," Mr. Sinclair said. "Yep, she's always loved to hang around me since she was a little bitty thing."

Raymond looked at Miss Gabrielle shyly. *Long straight blond hair, white-gold jewelry, light blue dress, small, and very pretty!*

"Come on, Raymond, I want you to drive us over to Cousin Susan's place," Mr. Sinclair said.

"Yes, sir!" Raymond headed toward the truck.

Raymond drove Miss Gabrielle and her grandfather to many places that summer. He laughed to himself when he remembered his initial displeasure about having to take the job. *Man, I'm sure glad Dad made me take this job. I wouldn't have wanted to miss being around Miss Gabrielle.*

Raymond was surprised when Miss Gabrielle accompanied them on their first fishing trip after her arrival. "She ain't going to fish. She just want to go along and draw," Elder Sinclair said.

Raymond nodded. It didn't matter to him what she did as long as she went.

Later Miss Gabrielle even accompanied them on a swamp excursion. She came out of the house with her drawing pad while Raymond was helping her grandfather load the truck with their fishing supplies and a picnic lunch.

Raymond looked at her. "Miss Gabrielle, you sure you wanna go to the swamp with us? It ain't like a lake."

Miss Gabrielle laughed. "I know what a swamp is, Raymond. Are you trying to get rid of me?"

Raymond quickly shook his head. "No, I ain't." He wished he could tell her how much he liked being with her. "I was just thinking you'd be uncomfortable."

"I told her the same thing, Raymond. The swamp's no place for a girl." Elder Sinclair looked around. "I'll be right back. I left my insect repellent inside."

Elder Sinclair went inside the house. Raymond was glad to have a few minutes alone with Miss Gabrielle. He smiled at her. "I guess it will be okay for you to go, Miss Gabrielle. We ain't going real deep in the swamp anyway."

"That's exactly what I think," Miss Gabrielle replied. She took a picture out of her drawing pad. "Look, Raymond, I drew this picture of you and Granddaddy last week while you all were fishing."

Raymond examined the drawing. "Man! That really look like us. Miss Gabrielle, you got talent."

Gabrielle giggled. "Thank you. I'm going to paint a larger version later. It will be a lot prettier in color."

Raymond was still looking at the picture. "You even drew the trees and flowers."

"Yes." Gabrielle pointed with a perfectly manicured pink fingernail. "I drew pines, magnolias, crepe myrtles, weeping willows, azaleas . . ." She paused and looked at Raymond. "Southeast Georgia is beautiful, isn't it?"

Raymond handed the picture back. "I ain't ever thought about it. I been here all my life."

Gabrielle put the picture back in her pad. "I've traveled a lot with my parents. This area has a natural beauty that's hard to beat. That's why I want to go to the swamp with you and Granddaddy. It's supposed to be full of wildflowers and extraordinary plants."

Raymond heard every word she said, yet, he could not force his lips to make an audible response. It seemed like her beauty had put his brain in slow motion. *Man . . . she . . . so-o pretty!*

Mr. Sinclair came out of the house with the insect repellent. "Let's go, young'uns!"

Raymond turned and headed toward the truck. He smiled happily. He thought he had the best job a colored boy could ever want.

Elder Sinclair settled down to serious fishing soon as they reached the swamp. Raymond baited his hook and dropped in his line. The fishing held only half of his mind. Gabrielle held the other half.

The swamp seemed to magnetize Miss Gabrielle. She busied herself sketching a bunch of rose begonia.

Raymond forced himself to watch his fishing line. *Don't look at her too much. You don't wanna make Elder Sinclair suspicious.* He allowed what he judged to be at least thirty minutes to pass before he rewarded himself with another look at her. He turned his eyes toward Miss Gabrielle slowly . . . and froze. Then his brain utilized the same sharpness that he displayed in tough situations during a tight game. *Be cool. Take it easy. Make your move.* His body moved with athletic finesse. He grabbed the loaded gun that Elder Sinclair always kept nearby on their fishing trips and fired twice.

Miss Gabrielle screamed, dropped her drawing pad, and ran to her grandfather. A large alligator lay dead on the edge of the water with blood flowing from its mouth. It had barely missed sinking its sharp teeth into Miss Gabrielle's leg.

"Praise God, Raymond, I'm sure glad you're as fast with a gun as you are with a ball," Elder Sinclair said.

"Thank you, Raymond, I'll never forget this," Miss Gabrielle added nervously.

Raymond grinned and looked at the alligator. "Miss Gabrielle, that old gator knew he'd make you a nice pair of shoes and a purse. That's why he crawled up here."

Miss Gabrielle looked at the alligator and laughed nervously.

Raymond picked up her drawing pad and handed it to her. Elder Sinclair chuckled and poked the alligator several times with a long stick, then he hit it on the head hard. "Yeah, he's a goner, all right. He might as well be put to good use. Raymond, let's load him on the truck."

Raymond smiled to himself. He figured if pride could illuminate a person, he would have looked like a tall Christmas tree light helping Elder Sinclair load the alligator. He assessed the situation with pleasure. *Man, look how Miss Gabrielle is looking at me. She looking like she think I'm special. She make me think of those stories Mom used to read to me about beautiful princesses being saved from dragons by knights in shining armor. Well, this old foolish gator look like an ugly monster. And Miss Gabrielle is definitely a pretty princess. And man! She looking at me like I'm a hero!*

After the incident with the alligator, they restricted their fishing to the lakes that were on the Sinclair land. Raymond pretended he was engrossed in the fishing, but his mind and his cautious glances were always on Miss Gabrielle. Before she returned to Atlanta, she gave him a painting of the picture she had drawn of him and her grandfather fishing. He framed the picture and hung it on his bedroom wall, keeping his love for her in the secrecy of his thoughts.

Tobacco County High won the homecoming game that Friday night after the parade. Raymond was happy because he had continued to shine as quarterback, but football left his mind as soon as he took off his uniform and began to shower. He ignored a small pang of guilt when he thought of Annie Ruth's disappointment with him for not asking her father for permission to take her home after the game again. *Shoot, he rationalized. It's like I told her, I didn't need to infringe on their family celebration. It was more appropriate for her to ride home with her family since all of her brothers were home. Anyway, I'll visit her at her house Sunday evening. But, tonight I want to go home and think about Miss Gabrielle.*

Raymond was getting ready for bed when his father came into his bedroom and sat on top of a large trunk. "Won another one, eh!" Dad said.

Raymond laid his pants and shirt on a chair. "Yeah, the team's looking good."

Dad chuckled proudly. "My son's looking good. At the rate you going you'll have your pick of the Negro colleges in this state. I wish you could go to a big time white college. But Mr. Sinclair thinks you'll make it in professional sports even if you go to a Negro college."

Dad leaned forward and rested his elbows on his knees. "Things are really opening up for Negroes in professional sports. I believe you can break into it and make some big time money."

Raymond nodded and decided he'd better put on some pajamas. "Yeah, Dad, that's exactly what I'm hoping. All the coaches think I got a chance, too."

"Yeah, Coach Phillips talked to me about it tonight after the game. He said Fort Valley, Savannah, Albany, and even Tuskegee Institute over in Alabama have been calling about you."

Raymond pulled a pair of pajamas out of the dresser drawer and put them on. "Well, I'm gonna go to the college that offers me the most scholarship money."

"Yeah, that's right." Dad paused. "If I'd been like Jackie Robinson and had a chance to play on one of those white professional ball teams, maybe I would've tried to finish high school and go farther with sports." Dad looked thoughtful for a moment. "I was good. That's why everybody call me Ballgame, cause I could play so good. I was like you. I could play it all, football, basketball, and baseball. All a person had to do was name his game, and I was ready. But I was way down South here. So the only thing that seemed possible to me was playing on one of those colored teams. Shoot, you know a nigger can't run anything."

Raymond pulled back the covers and got into bed, propping himself up with pillows.

Dad turned the topic to Annie Ruth. "I figure you just fooling around with that Watson gal. When you get to college, I know you gonna get yourself a pretty yellow girl like your mama. Shoot, your mama's about as light as some of the white women around here."

Raymond grinned. "Yeah, I'm gonna have to change that situation one day."

Dad frowned. "What I ain't been able to figure is how a gal as black as Annie Ruth got to be homecoming queen. Now, I can see Billie Lee being queen."

Raymond stifled a yawn and rubbed his eyes. "They do the choosing by grades. Annie Ruth, Elizabeth Collins, and Adella Tyson were the three girls with the highest grades." He stretched and yawned. "They all dark-skinned, but Annie Ruth look better than the other two."

"Uh-huh, well, I imagine Annie Ruth's got plenty smarts. She get it from her daddy. I done heard a lot of white folks say he got a head on him."

Raymond agreed with the white folks. Mr. Sid was a smart man. "He got something going for himself. He got all that land. His farm is bigger than some of the white folks' farms around here."

"Yeah, but he need to act livelier around white folks. They say he ain't much for joking and funning with them. He oughta think about that cause he might need the white folks' help one day." Dad beamed. "Take me, I always joke and have fun with them. All the white folks around Rail City know my name. They know I'm a hard worker, too. Old Mr. Sinclair gave me this house and the acre of land it's sitting on just for staying on his place and working for him."

Raymond wondered if his father had ever stopped to consider that he had been working for the Sinclairs for well over thirty years. The rambling wood frame house covered with grey imitation brick and the acre of land had long since been worked out in the sweat of his father's body as he cleaned the offices and toilets of the Sinclair Mill and other businesses. He also knew his mother had made many payments on their home with her labor in the Sinclair mansion. His older brothers and sisters had worked real hard, too, before they were grown enough to go off to lives of their own choosing.

After his father left, Raymond closed his eyes and enjoyed his fantasies about Gabrielle.

Raymond had worked several hours on his usual Saturday job

at Sinclair's Grocery before he got up enough nerve to mention Miss Gabrielle to Mr. Owen, the white head clerk. Raymond was putting soft drinks in the drink box near the front counter when he finally spoke. "I saw Miss Gabrielle watching the parade yesterday. Mom told me that Mrs. Sinclair said she gonna be here for a long visit."

Mr. Owen spat tobacco juice in a can he kept behind the counter. "Yep, she's doing a little more than visiting, though. She's going to finish out the school term down here. This is her last year, but you know how busy her rich folks are. They got a lot of traveling to do, so she came down here with her aunt and uncle."

Excitement at Miss Gabrielle living in Rail City swirled in Raymond's chest. *Man, oh man! Miss Gabrielle's gonna be living right here in Rail city! Hot dog!* He pretended to be looking out the store window to see if a customer who had driven up needed gas. He used the time to steady himself. *Cool it man, cool it, he warned himself.*

Raymond was restocking some shelves when he saw Mr. Sid Watson get out of his pick-up truck and start walking toward the store. Confidence and courage shone on him like oil on a preening muscle builder. His freshly starched and ironed overalls and matching jacket adorned his body like a tailor-made suit on a successful businessman.

Curtis's father, Mr. Andrew Lynch, was getting ready to leave the store. He put his purchases in his truck and then turned to greet Mr. Sid. Mr. Sid stopped in front of Mr. Andrew. They shook hands and exchanged a few words. Then Mr. Andrew got in his truck and left. Mr. Sid greeted several other Negroes who were in the store's parking lot before entering the store.

Raymond directed his attention back to his work. When

Mr. Sid came into the store, Raymond could sense his presence although his eyes were on the large boxes of washing powder that he was putting on the shelves. Mr. Sid spoke to Mr. Owen. "Good morning."

"Good morning, Sid. How's your family and farm?" Mr. Owen asked.

"Fine, thank you, how's your family?"

"They all fine."

The white meat cutter greeted Mr. Sid as he moved about the aisles picking up coffee, tea, flour, and other items. He reached for a gallon of bleach at the same time Raymond began stocking that area. Their eyes met.

"Good morning, Mr. Sid."

"Good morning, Raymond."

Raymond decided to extend the moment with a little showboating in his favor. "Annie Ruth was sure beautiful yesterday on that float."

Mr. Sid's strong black jaw softened. Pride surfaced in his brown eyes. His thick moustache followed his large lips in a wide smile. His ebony head nodded unbashfully in agreement. "I thought she was quite beautiful myself. But that ain't new for me. I've always known I have a beautiful daughter."

Raymond smiled.

"She was the most beautiful girl in that parade. Have a good day, Mr. Sid."

"Same to you, Raymond. Say hey to your daddy and mama for me."

Raymond watched as Mr. Sid paid for his purchases and left with the same sureness and ease he'd entered the store with.

Mr. Owen's eyes squinted when the door closed. "That's one smart colored man," he said to the meat cutter. "His daddy left him about two hundred acres of land, and now he's got close to six hundred. He's a darn good farmer, too. The county agent said that he reads and understands farm books and reports as well as any white man."

The meat cutter threw a slab of bacon on the cutting table and cut it into thin slices with an electric slicer. "Yeah, he's smart. But he can be a little touchy, sometimes. He got huffed with me one time cause I called him 'boy.' I didn't mean any harm."

Mr. Owen spat tobacco juice in the can again. "That sounds like him. He's always stood up for himself. And he ain't gonna get back any farther than you can push him. And as big as he is, that ain't far."

Raymond listened to the white men with awe. It didn't matter whether the white folks talked about Mr. Sid with like or dislike, respect always tinged their words. "His daughter is my girlfriend," he said.

Mr. Owen looked at him approvingly. "That's good thinking. It's wise to choose a girl with a strong yoke."

The meat cutter began unpacking a box of prime cut steaks. "Yeah, always choose the girl with the strongest yoke."

Raymond would feel pride stretching itself on his face. The hands of his ego hung the image of a black girl on its egotistical shelf. The image was of Annie Ruth, daughter of Mr. Sid Watson, the biggest, blackest farmer in Tobacco County.

4

Euphoria

The Sunday night after homecoming, Annie Ruth went to bed in a state of euphoria. The joy of being homecoming queen and having Raymond come for a Sunday evening visit was draped around her like a luxurious robe.

In keeping with what had become a Sunday night ritual, Lenny put Raymond out on the main road. Raymond walked home with his hands in the pockets of his jacket to protect them from the chilly late October air.

When the headlights of a car flashed on him, he moved farther from the side of the road. A large car passed him. As he neared the Sinclair mansion, the same car passed him going in the opposite direction. He stared at the huge house, wishing he could see Miss Gabrielle. "Raymond!"

Raymond shook his head. He thought he had heard a fantasy voice.

"Raymond!"

He focused his eyes on the lighted porch. It was really Miss

Gabrielle. "Miss Gabrielle," he murmured.

She walked to the edge of the porch. He took his hands out of his pockets and went over to her.

"Hello, Raymond."

"Hey, Miss Gabrielle."

She threw her head back and laughed, her silky blond hair cascading down her back. "Raymond, it's time for you to stop calling me Miss Gabrielle, just call me Gabrielle."

Raymond smiled. "I'd like that." He gazed at her perfect nose and pink mouth. Her lovely face was accented with white-gold jewelry. He felt like he had been dying of malnourishment and was being brought back to life by her elegant ivory beauty. "I saw you at the parade yesterday."

Gabrielle blushed. "I saw you, too. I couldn't believe . . .uh . . .how much taller you've gotten."

"Really? I didn't notice you looking my way."

Gabrielle looked at her penny loafers. "I wanted to talk to you. But I thought it wouldn't look proper."

Raymond could hardly believe she was being so open with him. "I know. That's why I didn't say anything to you." He pushed his hands in his pockets nervously. "Miss, I mean Gabrielle, you sure are pretty. I mean you always been pretty, but you don't look like a little girl anymore."

"You don't look boyish any more, either." Gabrielle gazed into his eyes. "You're very handsome, Raymond."

Raymond hoped he saw the sparkle of romance in her blue eyes. "I better be going home, Gabrielle. Your aunt and uncle will be wondering why you ain't in the house."

Gabrielle smiled. "You're right. I just got back from a date with an old friend. I saw you when we passed in the car. I didn't want to go inside without saying hello."

Raymond turned to leave. He didn't want to spoil their reunion by making the Sinclairs suspicious of them. "I better go. I'm glad you waited to talk to me."

Raymond walked away a few steps. Gabrielle turned and walked to the door.

Raymond turned around. "Gabrielle?"

She turned around. "Yes, Raymond."

"I'm really glad you gonna be staying here."

She beamed. "So am I, Raymond."

Raymond headed down the lane to his house, thinking how glad he was that he lived so close to the girl of his dreams. For Gabrielle, her conversation with Raymond added excitement to a boring evening. She'd gone out with the son of one of her uncle and aunt's rich friends strictly to please them. That night in the darkness of her pretty room, she contemplated the events which preceded her being sent to Rail City.

Her mother had hired a new housekeeper. She stood beside her mother, watching the neatly dressed Negro woman leave.

"She'll start to work tomorrow. She's highly recommended." Her mother chortled softly. "Her name is Precious Sharita Davis. Somebody ought to spank her mother for naming that child that. I certainly have no plans of calling a nigra girl 'precious.' We'll call her Sharita. That's good enough."

Precious Sharita was a very efficient maid. Except for the spotlessness of their huge home and the competent management of the meals and service for the Sinclairs' many parties, her presence was hardly noticed. She was a woman of few words, and a master at taking care of domestic tasks.

Because she was as quiet and low-key as she was capable,

Father and Mother congratulated themselves on hiring an efficient person and went on with their busy lives.

Gabrielle noticed that Precious Sharita always took the time to read the newspaper. Being an avid reader herself, she considered that commendable. She started asking her questions about various articles, particularly those about the Civil Rights Movement. Those questions led to interesting conversations and discussions.

It wasn't long before Gabrielle knew that Precious Sharita was a high school graduate, a member of the First African Baptist Church and the NAACP, and the fiancee of a Negro brick mason named Otis.

Gabrielle appreciated the way Precious Sharita seemed to keep her room in picture-perfect order more out of kindness than duty. She also appreciated Precious Sharita's admiration of her drawing and painting talents. It made her feel good for Precious Sharita to praise her for the long periods of time she spent drawing, painting, and listening to Nat King Cole records (which they both loved).

Gabrielle was glad that Precious Sharita understood that although her parents loved her deeply, she was sometimes lonely amidst the big business deals, charity banquets and balls, and being on the society page.

Gabrielle really liked having Precious Sharita work for her family. A deep respect for each other developed between them. In time, Gabrielle suspected that respect would have turned into a sisterly friendship if it had not been for the attitudes of her parents.

Mother's attitude was the first to surface. Upon hearing that Martin Luther King, Jr., had been arrested in DeKalb County on a charge of driving without a driver's license, Mother declared directly in Precious Sharita's presence, "Somebody ought to slap that nigger down. He's trying to overstep his bounds!"

Mother didn't notice Precious Sharita's scowling face or her stiffened back. Beads of sweat sprang up on her forehead like tiny soldiers ready for battle. Mother's prejudices veiled her eyes from the angry response. She didn't sense the inner turmoil that Gabrielle believed was raging within Precious Sharita, whether to show her anger and risk losing her job or to keep her hurt feelings hidden. Gabrielle knew passiveness won, because Precious Sharita left the room mumbling something about needing to go check on dinner.

Mother's beliefs made her insensitive to the feelings and thoughts of a Negro; however, Gabrielle felt the embarrassment her mother was incapable of. Although the incident invited a dark cloud to hang itself on a pretty May day, nothing could compare to the darkness that descended on a July afternoon.

Gabrielle received a red 1960 Ford Falcon for her birthday. While she was driving around one day, she saw her father's car at one of his businesses. She decided to stop at the used car lot and tell him how much she was enjoying the car.

She opened the side door and took a couple of steps inside. She stopped when she heard loud voices. Her father was arguing with Precious Sharita's fiancé, Otis. They didn't hear the side door open or see her standing near the tall file cabinets.

"Mr. Sinclair, your manager told me the truck I bought was in good shape. But it ain't," Otis said. "It's already put me down. I'm getting behind in my brick laying work."

"Otis, you bought that truck on your own accord," Father said firmly.

"Yes, sir, but your manager promised me you'd make it good if anything went wrong right away!" Otis replied.

The manager shook his head. "No, sir, Mr. Sinclair, I didn't promise him any such thing."

Father sat on top of the desk. "Otis, you're wasting my time and yours. Now you heard my manager. He said he didn't make any promises. Go on!"

Otis stood erect and firm. "No, sir, I'm not going until you make good on the deal your manager promised."

Father's face turned fire-red. "My manager didn't make any such promises to you!"

"Yes, sir, he did."

"No, he didn't."

Otis shook his head.

Father hit him in the face with his fist. Otis punched him back. Father doubled over. The manager and a white mechanic who rushed in from the back door quickly came to help Father. The three men beat Otis unmercifully.

When it was over, Otis lay in a pool of blood. Before she ran out of the side entrance, Gabrielle saw her father brush some of Otis's broken teeth off of his expensive suit. The men in the room never noticed Gabrielle's presence or departure. That fact wrestled with her conscience. If she had stepped into her father and his helpers' view, would Otis have been saved from the beating?

There was no police investigation, no newspaper editorial, or NAACP protest. Gabrielle suspected that Otis remained silent because he feared her father's influence. A few negative words from a rich white business man to some key business people and a small struggling Negro-owned business like Otis's could be ruined.

Precious Sharita walked away from her job as the Sinclair's housekeeper without a day's notice. Gone were the quiet moments after her dates when Gabrielle and Precious Sharita would talk. Gone was Precious Sharita's never-too-busy-to-listen ear. Gone was the picture-perfect room kept that way without reminders or corrections. Gabrielle missed Precious Sharita, but she was glad not to have to face her Negro friend after what her father had done to Otis.

It's my fault. If I had let my father see me he wouldn't have beat Otis. I could've stopped the beating by just stepping into Father's view. Her feelings of guilt transformed her from a studious, responsible teenager to a mercurial wildflower who didn't respect curfews or do well in school and who shunned the "right" friends and spent time with beer drinkers and seekers of fast cars, wild parties and anything called fun. She stopped drawing and painting. To prove her defiance, she lost her virginity in the back seat of a car to not only the "wrong" boy, but to a boy she didn't even like.

After her parents recovered from their shock at their only child's behavior, they took her in October to her father's brother's house and the safety of Rail City.

That Sunday night after talking to Raymond on the porch, Gabrielle lay in her bed and thought about the preceding events. The quietness and slow pace of life in Rail City had made her decide to return to her studious habits, but it had not taken away the shame and guilt she felt about what her father had done to Otis. There was no one for her to talk to. Precious Sharita had disappeared into Atlanta's Negro community. Talking to her mother would have been like trying to defend the North to the wife of a Confederate soldier. So, Gabrielle was alone with the pain of a disturbing memory.

Her talk with Raymond made that Sunday night different

from previous times when the pain, confusion, and guilt fused into one disreputable shadow which took pleasure in blocking out the sun, darkening bright skies, and bittering her sweet moments. That Sunday night when the shadow attempted to pass over her dreamy eyes while she lay on the brink of sleep, she turned over and brushed it away with thoughts of Raymond Baldwin, a tall, handsome boy with a complexion that made her think of a coffee-and-cream colored tan.

As far as Raymond's color was concerned, that was about all Gabrielle saw—a coffee-and-cream tan. It was certainly nothing she allowed to prevent her from talking to him every chance she got when he passed the Sinclair mansion on his way home. It didn't squelch her desire to share her feelings, her opinions, her past enjoyment of drawing, painting, and Nat King Cole's singing or the events of her day with him during the few minutes of time they snatched together. It didn't stop her from arranging to meet him at late night for a few stolen moments in the Sinclair cabin.

The first time Gabrielle met Raymond at the cabin he brought the picture she painted of him and her grandfather. Gabrielle looked at the image of the beloved old man who had passed away less than a year after she painted the picture. She touched the drawing of the boy who had grown into a captivating suitor and then slipped into his coffee-and-cream colored arms.

He seems to understand me so well, always knowing what to do and say to make me feel good.

He looked down at her lovingly. She could feel her growing affection for him stir within her.

Raymond tightened his embrace. "I love you, Gabrielle."

"I love you, too, Raymond." The love and security she felt

in his arms helped her to reveal her secret. She told him about what her father had done to Otis.

Raymond listened intently. His eyes seemed to overflow with compassion. "It wasn't your fault. Even if your father and his helpers had seen you, he probably woulda just sent you home. The beating woulda still happened, if not then maybe later." He wiped her tears with his hands. "They were all angry men. They the ones you should be blaming, not yourself. Let it go."

His words and the concern and love on his face brought on a sense of relief that washed over her like a cool rain on a hot day. She remembered the day he had protected her from the alligator in the swamp, and she savored his protectiveness.

He hugged her. "Racism can be very mean. That's why we gotta be very careful." He then advised her about the racism that could destroy their love.

He told her about exact times to call him. Times when he was sure he would be at home and near the phone. He encouraged her to act as though he was only a Negro worker whenever she went into Sinclair Grocery and he was there. In public, they must stay in "their places." She would stay in the proper place of a decent Southern white girl. He would stay in the place of a good Southern colored boy. For appearances, she would continue to date the white boy her family had chosen for her. He would continue dating a Negro girl named Annie Ruth. He also advised her to keep a certain distance from his mother while she worked in the Sinclair mansion. A lot of familiarity between the two, he feared, might arouse the suspicions of her family.

Raymond had many fantasies about Gabrielle, but there was one particular fantasy he never thought would become reality until the first Saturday night in December. His parents went to

Atlanta for an overnight visit with relatives. Raymond stayed home in order to work in Sinclair's Grocery.

Gabrielle's uncle and aunt went to Jacksonville, Florida, for an overnight visit. She was left with her cousin who was home from college. Her cousin made two decisions: number one, she was grown enough to go on an out-of-town date with her fiancé. And number two, Gabrielle was mature enough to be alone in the huge house for several hours. Gabrielle encouraged her cousin in her decisions with confirmations of having no fear of being alone in the house and promises of watching television and going to bed early. The night stepped in soon after her cousin and her fiancé left. It reached out seductively and covered the evening with its lightless cloak. She went to Raymond's house.

Raymond was waiting for her dressed in a maroon shirt and khaki pants. He hugged her as soon as she walked in. She relaxed in his embrace and enjoyed the feel of his strong body against hers. She could smell the pleasant odor of his bath soap. *Oh, he smells so good. It feels wonderful being in his family's home. It makes me feel so much closer to him, like I'm part of him.* Gabrielle pulled back and looked up at his face. "I love you."

"I love you, too," he said, kissing her.

Raymond guided her to his bedroom. Gabrielle sat on the bed while he put "Come Closer To Me" by Nat King Cole on the record player. He fixed the machine so the record would play over and over. Then he joined her on the bed. He started kissing her as soon as he sat down.

Gabrielle was enjoying his kisses, but she began to tremble when he started undressing her. He squeezed her gently. "Gabrielle, darling, don't be scared. I won't ever hurt you. I love you so much."

She looked at him and smiled. He was her first love. *I believe he loves me. He's always so nice and gentle with me. His voice is always so loving and caring when he talks to me.* She was trembling from excitement, not fear.

"I'm going to use a condom. Relax, I know the score," Raymond reassured her.

She didn't reply. She responded by returning his passionate kisses and allowing herself to be lovingly and gently led down the passionate road of intimacy. When he penetrated her, she flinched and dug her fingernails in his back uncontrollably. *It feels like I never had sex that one time before! I'm glad, because in my heart this is my first time!*

Never had she experienced such lovemaking. She slipped into a sweet euphoria where only the two of them existed in unimaginable ecstasy that climaxed into an even more wonderful love!

Raymond continued to hold her close after their lovemaking. His lips brushed against her cheek as he spoke. "One day, Gabrielle, I'll be a rich professional ball player. I'll be able to afford to give you anything you want. Will you marry me then?"

Gabrielle felt no need to think over his proposal. She loved him dearly. "Yes, oh, yes, I will!"

After her evening with Raymond, Gabrielle was glad he had advised her to keep her distance as much as possible from his mother. Their intimacy provoked a shyness within her whenever she was near Mrs. Baldwin. Although she was declaring joyfully in her mind, *I love Raymond! I love Raymond!,* she was careful that her measured "good mornings and good evenings" to the almost-white woman didn't expose any warmth for the mother of her lover and fiancé.

Their love stimulated her creativity. She became receptive to her muse again, and her enjoyment of long periods of listening to Nat King Cole while drawing and painting was revived.

Sometimes her love for the handsome coffee-and-cream young man would envelope her. She would stare out of the window of her bedroom at the Baldwins' rambling old-fashioned house. She felt like walking through her uncle and aunt's elegant home, singing and dancing and strewing rose petals. Sometimes, the thought of society's disapproval would overshadow her happiness. She would gasp as the sharpness of reality gazed at her—she was in love with a Negro! When those times emerged, she would imagine herself drinking sweet coffee and cream on a cold morning while resting in Raymond's loving arms.

5

Disappointment

After homecoming Annie Ruth's life settled back into its usual routine. The month of November and its two-day break from school for Thanksgiving passed. December brought colder weather and the promise of Christmas. She and Billie Lee both got part-time jobs. Annie Ruth started helping Aldonia in her beauty shop. Miss Gertrude, one of their grandmother's friends, hired Billie Lee to help her while she was ill.

Annie Ruth was more than happy to help Aldonia on Friday afternoons and Saturdays. The job not only provided extra money, it also required her to be in town and increased her opportunities to see Raymond.

Time seemed to pass quickly. After school was out for Christmas vacation, Annie Ruth started helping Aldonia all day. Business was good. Aldonia took advantage of the lucrative opportunities by keeping her shop open until noon on Christmas Eve.

While Aldonia finished fixing their last customer's hair, Annie Ruth went up town on Christmas Eve to buy Thelma, her brother Carl's wife, a pink sweater. While she was waiting in line at the cash register, Raymond walked past the store window. She craned her neck to watch him cross the crowded street and turn the corner. Aldonia was supposed to meet her after she finished the customer's hair in front of Bostic Department Store. She sighed impatiently. She wanted to hurry so she'd have enough time to follow Raymond.

Raymond walked through the busy street of Christmas shoppers quickly. He was hurrying back to work after running an errand for Mr. Owen. He smiled inwardly as he maneuvered through the festive groups of Negroes. *Y'all Negroes acting like y'all being in town on Christmas Eve is just as exciting as Christmas Day. I bet some of y'all ain't been to town since the summer or early fall when y'all came to spend that blueberry, tobacco, and cotton picking money.* His thoughts about the Negro shoppers evaporated when he turned a corner and went down a back street.

Gabrielle would like the charm he'd bought her. The first time he saw the white-gold girl and boy connected by a tiny heart, he knew it was the perfect gift for her. He'd worked every day of the Christmas vacation to be able to afford it. Annie Ruth's gift hadn't dipped nearly as deep in his pocket or his heart. He'd bought her a not-too-cheap locket from Bostic Department Store. He figured she'd cherish it. And that was what he wanted. The more Annie Ruth looked like his girlfriend, and the more he looked like her perfect boyfriend, the better the cover he had for his and Gabrielle's love.

We gotta be careful. The last thing we need is for her family to find out about us. But how can we meet during the holidays? I wanna give her her present. Plus, I'm dying to see her. Man, I'll be glad when I'm rich and famous. Then we won't have to sneak around.

Gabrielle had managed to avoid going back to Atlanta for Christmas by pretending to want to stay in Rail City so she could be with her local friends. She figured her parents went along with her desires due to their elation over her having reverted to her previous studious, creative self.

That Christmas Eve she was enjoying a drive in the red Falcon her parents had given her for good behavior. She could feel the excitement and Christmas spirit of the shoppers. Nat King Cole's "Christmas Song" was being played on the radio. Though it was cold outside, the car was warm.

She thought of Raymond and relaxed. Happiness covered her like a shiny Christmas wrapping. She turned onto a back street. She smiled when she saw the back side of a well-built young Negro man. *There's Raymond.* She glanced in her rear view mirror and to both sides cautiously. She saw no one and no cars. She slowed the car to the pace of a boat floating on calm, romantic waters.

Raymond looked over and saw her. He looked all around, too, then walked quickly over to her. They grabbed only a few moments. Just enough time for her to tell him that she would meet him at the Sinclair cabin Christmas night after her parents left for Atlanta.

The elation of being able to see her on Christmas caught Raymond and sent him sailing in a holiday euphoric mind. He leaned into her car window and kissed her. Then she drove away. He continued walking. A ray of southeast Georgia winter sun reflected on the rear of the bright vehicle. He considered making love to her to be his first Christmas present and now he had just been given another wonderful Christmas gift!

Annie Ruth turned the corner just in time to see the red Falcon, the white girl, and the kiss. She suppressed her gasp with her hand. Clutching Thelma's gift to her chest she could feel disappointment and sadness covering her heart. She struggled to hold back the tears welling in her eyes as she watched Raymond walk down the street and turn the next corner. She looked around at the deserted street. She felt deserted, too. *Why was Raymond kissing that white girl? Who was she anyway? Is he going with her? No, no, he can't be. I love him! Lord, please, let him love me!*

Slow, discouraged steps took her back to Main Street. Aldonia was standing in front of Bostic Department Store sharing laughter and a cheerful conversation with a group of Negro shoppers. Annie Ruth wiped her eyes and greeted everyone. She was relieved when Aldonia said goodbye and excused herself. They headed to Aldonia's car.

Aldonia looked at Annie Ruth. "You okay?"

Annie Ruth looked down. "Yeah, I'm fine."

"You looked upset when you first walked up. Your eyes are red."

"It's just the cold weather getting to them," Annie Ruth said.

"Take care of yourself. They say the flu is going around."

"I will," Annie Ruth said.

They got into Aldonia's car. "If you ain't in a hurry, I got an errand to run before I take you home," Aldonia said.

"Go ahead," Annie Ruth replied. "I ain't in a hurry." *Seeing Raymond with that white girl took all my Christmas spirit. I ain't in a hurry to go home.*

"You sure? Ain't all your brothers home?"

"Yeah, they all there. James and Jerry came yesterday around noon, and Carl and his family came last night. I had time to visit with them." Annie Ruth shrugged. "They all gonna be home for awhile. I'll have plenty of time to be with them. Don't worry about me. Go ahead and run your errand."

Aldonia drove several miles out of town and turned onto a dirt road. A blue Buick was waiting in a clearing nearby. She drove over and parked beside it. Annie Ruth was astonished. "Mr. Bailey!"

"Be cool, child," Aldonia warned.

Mr. Bailey, the high school music teacher, frowned when he saw Annie Ruth, but Aldonia laughed. "Harold, Annie Ruth wouldn't tattle on her own cousin. Relax, she knows what to talk about and what not to talk about."

When Annie Ruth blushed and looked away, Aldonia got out of the car. She and Mr. Bailey walked to the other side of his car. Annie Ruth was not sure how long she waited in the car alone. Her mind was filled with her own problems.

But it all went back to one thing. She loved Raymond. There had to be a reason for what she'd seen. Maybe she just *thought* he'd kissed the white girl. Raymond knew a lot of people, white and Negro. He got to meet a lot of people working at Sinclair Grocery. Perhaps he was consoling the girl for some reason. Some reason, yes, there had to be a reason. She couldn't even imagine giving up her love for Raymond.

Aldonia was carrying a large gift-wrapped package when she returned to the car. Mr. Bailey opened the car door for her. She put the package in the back seat and got in. She closed the door and rolled down the window. He leaned over and kissed her. Mr. Bailey looked at Annie Ruth and smiled. "You've always been a smart girl, Annie Ruth. I hope you keep quiet about this."

He flashed her another smile. "Congratulations on winning homecoming queen. Have a Merry Christmas."

"Thanks, Mr. Bailey I wouldn't say or do anything that would hurt Aldonia."

Aldonia beamed. "Bye, Baby."

"Bye."

As they drove away, curiosity about Aldonia's relationship with Mr. Bailey pulled Annie Ruth's mind away from her own problems. She turned. "I knew you and Mr. Bailey were high school sweethearts, but I sure didn't know y'all still had a thing going on."

Aldonia nodded. "It's kind of a long story. Harold and I went together all through high school. He was two grades ahead of me, though. By the time I got to Savannah State, he was a junior. After I couldn't afford to go back to college my second year, I decided to become a beautician. Harold and I made plans to get married as soon as he graduated and found a job."

"What happened?"

Aldonia blinked and wiped her eyes. "You know how men are. Harold got lonely while he was away at college and fooled around with Natalie Brown." Aldonia's voice sounded angry. "I think she saw her chance to get him after I didn't go back to college. When she got pregnant, her parents put pressure on his parents, so they got married. And I was left standing in the cold."

"How did y'all start back going together?"

"Right after he graduated, Harold got the job as the music teacher and band director at the high school. As soon as he and Natalie moved back here, he started calling me and begging me to see him. I couldn't tell him no. We just wound up going together again."

Annie Ruth frowned. "Ain't you afraid of his wife or the school board finding out?"

"We been extra careful." Aldonia shrugged. "We ain't fools. We know how to take care of ourselves."

"I hope y'all know what you doing," Annie Ruth said. "If it was to get out, both of y'all would have problems."

Aldonia gripped the steering wheel. "Annie Ruth, I know you don't approve of what I'm doing. And you right. I shouldn't be going with a married man. But, Harold says he's gonna marry me as soon as he can make a break and divorce Natalie."

Aldonia glanced at Annie Ruth. "Anyway, Natalie knew Harold and I were going together. She shouldn't have gotten pregnant. She tricked him into marrying her."

Annie Ruth looked out of the window, blinking back tears. "Aldonia, you don't have to keep trying to explain things to me. It ain't my business. Just make sure you don't come up with the short end of the stick."

Aldonia patted her hair anxiously with her left hand. "Child, I love the man. I done dated other men. I even flirted around and teased the other boys in high school, but Harold was my first love. He's still my only love. You don't know how it feels to have to give up the man you love to another woman. It hurts. It hurts like hell."

Annie Ruth didn't answer. *She did know,* she thought, holding back her tears. *She knew too well.*

That evening, Annie Ruth kept herself busy by helping her mother with the cooking and holiday preparations. The next morning she did the same thing. When everything was done, she took a seat in the living room. She turned the television on, but her mind replayed the scene of Raymond and the white girl again and again.

"Enjoying TV, Annie Ruth?"

"Huh?" Annie Ruth frowned and looked up.

Carl, her older brother, was staring at her thoughtfully. He turned off the television and sat down beside her. "What's on your mind?"

"Nothing," she answered.

Carl raised his eyebrows. "That's surprising. You're one of the top students, this year's homecoming queen, and even a working girl, and nothing is on your mind."

She forced a weak smile. Carl glanced around the room. "Man, Christmas cheer never comes up short in the Watson household. Mama's got enough food cooked to feed an army, the house and tree decorated, nice gifts, relatives coming and going. Daddy's strutting around like a proud peacock." Carl's voice trailed off. He looked at Annie Ruth knowingly. "Boy troubles, eh?"

Surprised by her brother's intuition, Annie Ruth quickly looked away. *I better not let Carl know about Raymond and the white girl, cause knowing him, he be wanting me to quit Raymond.* She answered him carefully. "I'm just tired from helping Aldonia and keeping up with my chores."

"I see," Carl said. "Mama and Daddy told me you're kind of wrapped up in that Baldwin boy."

That Baldwin boy. Carl is as bad as Mama. She stifled a sigh. "His name is Raymond, Carl."

"Thelma and I saw him yesterday. We were picking up a few things for Mama in Sinclair's Grocery. I hear he's a good athlete," Carl said. "He's what you girls consider good-looking. Yeah, he's got what it takes to mess with a young girl's mind."

"Ain't nobody messing with my mind, Carl."

Carl stared at her intently. "I hope not, Annie Ruth, because you're young and smart. You've got your whole life in front of you."

Annie Ruth smiled. *Lord have mercy, Carl's gonna start preaching about education like Daddy.*

"We get a chance to participate in and see more about the Civil Rights Movement in Atlanta than you all do down here," Carl said. "President Kennedy is going to bring about a lot of changes in this country."

Ain't no preachers in our family. I think that's cause Daddy and Carl done missed their calling. They get to talking about civil rights and education and they don't know when to quit.

"A better day is coming," Carl declared. "Negroes are going to have more opportunities, better jobs, better pay, chances to live and work wherever we want to."

Carl looked at Annie Ruth intently. "The Negro race's lights of intelligence, abilities, achievements, contributions, and so forth have previously been ignored, dimmed, and extinguished. The day is coming for our lights to shine."

Carl patted Annie Ruth's hand. "Young lady, you've got the potential to shine. Don't limit yourself. Put your education first. You'll have plenty of time to fall in love and get married."

Thank God, he's finished. Annie Ruth nodded. "I hear you, professor."

Carl chuckled and relaxed on the sofa. "Remember Isabella Carwford?"

"Yeah, your old girlfriend."

"We went together all through high school, but when we got to college we both decided we wanted to date others." Carl smiled. "Let's see, I was infatuated by several beautiful young ladies before I met my wife."

Annie Ruth giggled. "Carl, you been around."

Carl laughed, and then his expression became serious again. "No, they were all nice young ladies. But we put our educations first." Carl sighed. "Annie Ruth, what I'm trying to tell you is that the world is big. Don't limit yourself. There's no need to get hung up on one person so early."

"Christmas gifts! Christmas gifts!" Granny cheered bursting into the house like a whirlwind of Christmas spirit. Annie Ruth was glad Carl ended his talk with her and got up to greet Granny, her sister from Savannah, Aunt Geechee, and Billie Lee.

Christmas was always a "big day" at the Watson household. Everybody was there including Aldonia and all of her family. If Annie Ruth hadn't been thinking about seeing Raymond with the white girl, she would have been just as happy and joyful as the rest. *Raymond, Raymond, I wish I was thinking about how you love me instead of do you love me?*

Since it was Sunday, Raymond and Lenny arrived around four o'clock for their usual house dates. Lenny took advantage of Daddy's jovial mood by asking for permission to take Billie Lee and Annie Ruth for a ride. They drove to the colored park in town and strolled in the chilly afternoon air.

"You like your gift?" Raymond asked Annie Ruth as they walked in the opposite direction of Billie Lee and Lenny.

Annie Ruth touched the tiny locket around her neck. "It's lovely, thank you."

"I'm gonna enjoy the shoeshine kit you gave me. You know how I like to keep my kicks sparkling." Raymond frowned. "What's the matter, My Lady? You ain't been yourself all evening. Billie Lee's been drooling all over Lenny, and you keep looking at me like I'm a stranger."

Annie Ruth stopped walking and looked at him. "Raymond,

how do you really feel about me?"

"Annie Ruth, we been going together for almost two years. Why you ask something like that?"

Annie Ruth stared at him. "You still ain't answered me."

"I'm crazy about you . . ." Raymond finished with a deep kiss. Annie Ruth held him tightly. She wanted so much to believe him.

6

The Way Things Were

Friday, February 17, 1961, Annie Ruth got on the school bus and sat down beside Billie Lee. "Here's an application for college. I promised Daddy I'd give it to you."

Billie Lee's face twisted in exasperation. "Y'all mean well, but I love Lenny. Ain't no way I could leave him and be happy." Billie Lee took the application and put it in one of her books. "I'll keep this although I know I won't be using it."

Annie Ruth shrugged. "It's up to you."

Billie Lee stared at Annie Ruth. "I still love you, cousin, but I liked being around you better in 1960 than in 1961. You been quiet and moody since Christmas."

Annie Ruth began to pick at her fingernails. "I saw Raymond downtown on Christmas Eve while I was buying a Christmas gift for Thelma. I followed him down a deserted street. He met a white girl down there in a red car. They talked a little." Annie Ruth's voice trailed off. Blinking back tears, she said, "Then he kissed her."

Billie Lee leaned closer. "You sure it was Raymond?"

Annie Ruth wished she wasn't sure. She nodded sadly. "I'm positive."

Billie Lee leaned back. "How did he explain?"

Annie Ruth stopped picking her fingernails. "He ain't ever explained cause I ain't ever told him I saw him. He doesn't call me like he use to. He didn't come to school yesterday, and he didn't call to tell me why. Sometimes when we're together he seem so cold and far away. Whenever I ask him what's wrong, he just smile and say, 'My Lady, I'm fine.'" She looked at Billie Lee. "I want to believe him so much. I'm so scared, though. I keep hoping that everything will get better during basketball season since he been playing so well and all, but it ain't."

Billie Lee frowned. "Raymond and a white girl, that's hard to figure."

Annie Ruth sighed. "You figure it out, Billie Lee, then you explain it to me."

Annie Ruth was getting her books out of her locker that morning at school. Hootie Simpson walked up. "Well, Annie Ruth, look like we can both give up on Raymond. Look like he prefer vanilla, not chocolate."

Annie Ruth closed her locker. "Hootie, what you talking about?"

"I'm talking about Raymond being crazy about a white girl. Mr. Sinclair shot him cause he was trying to sneak up to her bedroom."

Annie Ruth gasped. "Raymond's been shot!"

Billie Lee, who had been standing nearby, moved closer and touched her arm gently.

Hootie laughed vindictively. "Look at you! Getting all upset cause Raymond's been shot. Child, you crazy, caring about a boy who dumped you for a white girl."

Annie Ruth straightened. "Hootie, you don't know what you talking about. Raymond can't be shot!"

"He got shot Wednesday night," Hootie insisted. "I found out last night when Mama got home from work. If we had a phone, I woulda called you. Mama said the white folks been trying to keep it hush-hush. But she overheard her boss talking to another white man. He just got shot. He ain't dead." Hootie shifted her books. "But, she said her bossman said if he get caught trying to mess with that white girl again, he gonna get himself killed."

Annie Ruth didn't answer. She could feel her eyes filling with tears. She stared at Hootie.

Smiling smugly, Hootie walked away.

Billie Lee nudged Annie Ruth. "Come on, we gotta get to class before the tardy bell rings."

Annie Ruth took a handkerchief out of her purse and wiped her eyes. Her heart cried sadly while she followed Billie Lee to class. *Raymond, why you get yourself in such a mess? I love you so much. Ain't my love enough for you?*

Raymond eased up from the hospital bed and drank several sips of water. He placed the glass on a nearby table and sank back on the bed. He had a shattered knee, a broken heart, and he could kiss not only his future with Gabrielle good-bye, but also his future in professional sports. Depression soaked him like the sweat from the fever he had developed. How could a night that had started out so beautiful turn into such horror?

He and Gabrielle had thought they were being so careful. They had limited themselves to secretive telephone conversations and one short rendezvous at the Sinclairs' cabin during the month of January. But when the month of February came they succumbed to their romantic yearnings and met on the Wednesday night after Valentine's Day. They declared their love for each other, made love quickly and left.

In keeping with their practice, Raymond waited in the dark cabin for at least twenty minutes after Gabrielle drove away before he slipped out in the night and made his way home. He felt the excruciating pain in his knee immediately after hearing the shot. His mind got lost in a painful unconsciousness when something blunt struck his head. When his mind found reality again he was lying in a bed in Rail City's Colored Hospital.

He looked at his mother sitting near the bed. She leaned forward. "Son, you need me to get you something?"

Raymond shook his head. "You need to get some rest. You look tired. Why don't you go home? You gonna have to go back to work Monday."

Her face hardened. "I ain't studying about going back to work until I know you done mended."

Raymond was surprised by her answer. "You know Dad won't agree with that."

"I ain't studying about what your dad thinks," she said.

Mrs. LaDora Baldwin watched as Raymond went back to sleep. *No, Son, this is one time I ain't studying about what your dad thinks. I reckon it's the first time in a long time that I ain't been studying about what he thinks.* She leaned back in the chair and began to ponder.

Raymond was the youngest of her and Ballgame's five children. She had thought her childbearing days were over, and had been looking forward to the carnal pleasure of aging—lovemaking without fear of unplanned fruit. But, she was Ballgame's woman. He liked to win, and so, just before her fertility race was completely run, she bore Raymond, a perfect baby boy who made his father spry and proud. Actually, all of their children had made Ballgame spry and proud. She was sure that he cherished her and their children. He was proud of that which he believed came from himself—his family and the labor of his body.

He really valued his labor for the white man. She could not count the times he'd said to her, "If you work hard, the white folks will help you out." And they both had worked hard. Ballgame could always see a specialness in what she now knew was just being a loyal Negro worker.

He'd say, "You work for rich Old Mr. Sinclair until the day he died. Now you working for his rich son. They don't want anybody else working for them. All those other colored women around here ain't dependable. Plus, they half-do their work. Look how Mrs. Sinclair talks to you and gives you all of her expensive clothes when she's through with them."

LaDora closed her tired eyes. Yeah, she continued to ponder, I used to believe Ballgame. I imagined the rich Sinclairs thought we were their special Negroes. I know better now. White folks think they're better than Negroes no matter what. You either white or black—ain't no in between. My daddy was a white overseer, and my mama was high yellow, but in the eyes of white folks I'm still a Negro.

Yeah, Mrs. Sinclair let me know what she thought of Negroes. I wasn't thinking about nothing that morning except cleaning their bedroom bathroom until I walked in that pretty place and saw that smooth cool looking bathtub. I'd seen that tub plenty of times, but that morning I felt extra hot and sweaty after walking up the lane to work. It seemed like it was begging me to get in and refresh myself. I couldn't resist it. I wasn't used to a bathtub. All we got is a toilet in a used-to-be-closet. I thought about what Ballgame always said about us being special, then I filled the tub with water and added some bath oil. I took my clothes off and got in. It felt like heaven.

LaDora winced in embarrassment at the memory. Well, Mrs. Sinclair let me know I'd overstepped my bounds when she came in and saw me in that tub. She looked like I was some nasty dog soaking in her bathtub. She told me off in good fashion. That taught me a lesson. I just let Ballgame talk from then on, cause I know we ain't nothing special to them.

LaDora looked at her sleeping son. Maybe that was what had brought Raymond to the hospital bed and taken away his dreams of being a big-time ball player. Had he believed his dad's talk about the white folks seeing them as special? Could that belief have caused him to fall in love with Miss Gabrielle?

"I woulda never thought that boy woulda been such a fool," Ballgame said when he found out about Raymond's relationship with Gabrielle. "He know better than to try to slip up to her bedroom."

"He said he wasn't trying to slip up to her bedroom. He said they met at the cabin out by the lake, and that's where he got shot. I believe him cause he did have a lot of dirt and grass on his clothes."

Ballgame glared at her. "That's just as bad. If Mr. Sinclair hadn't known me and how I raised my young'uns to work and stay in their place, he woulda been dead."

"He said that he and Miss Gabrielle are in love. They were planning to get married as soon as he made it big as a ball player," LaDora said.

Ballgame waved his hand like he was brushing away an annoying insect. "That's foolish! It's against the law for a Negro to marry a white person in the state of Georgia."

"Things may change one day," LaDora replied softly. "Maybe they weren't counting on marrying or living in Georgia anyway."

Ballgame ignored LaDora's reply. "If Raymond had been courting a pretty high yellow girl like you instead of fooling around with that black Watson gal, he wouldn't have gotten so carried away with Miss Gabrielle." Ballgame drew in his breath. "You can keep hanging around this hospital and letting your work go if you want to. I see I can't stop you. But that boy's gonna be all right. He won't be a big-time ball player, but he'll still be able to work and make a living. I got work to do. Mr. Sinclair is counting on me to have his buildings clean."

"You mean we gonna go back to work for those people?"

Ballgame's voice was firm. "Those people, woman? You letting foolishness get in your mind. Where else we going? What other jobs we got? The white folks know you and I are good people."

Gabrielle had gone home that Wednesday night, took a bath, and put on a silky ivory-colored nightgown and went to bed with loving thoughts of Raymond. She awoke a few hours later from a terrorizing nightmare. She had dreamed about Otis's beating, but it wasn't Otis who was being beaten. It wasn't Precious Sharita's fiancé. It was hers—Raymond. She got up and looked out of her bedroom window. She could see Raymond's family's house. She squinted her eyes as the bright lights of a car that was coming up the lane flashed on her window and turned and headed toward the main road. She stood at the window and continued to stare out at the still night. It offered no explanation of the nightmare that had roused her from her sleep. After a while she went back to bed and dozed off and on until morning.

Her mother walked in the next morning while she was getting ready for school. She was surprised to see her. "Mother, what are you doing here?"

Mother's eyes flashed angrily. She took off her mink coat and laid it on the bed. "It's not for a pleasant visit, thanks to you, Missy!"

"What's the matter, Mother?"

Mother stepped closer. Gabrielle couldn't remember seeing her that angry before, not even when they had considered her a behavior problem.

"A more sensible question would be what is wrong with you? Your father and I didn't raise any white trash girl! How dare you come down here and stoop so low as to get involved with a nigra boy!"

Her mother's words lashed out at her. *Oh, my! I've got to think of something. I wonder how she found out about Raymond and me.* Gabrielle couldn't look into Mother's furious eyes.

Mother sat on the foot of the bed. "Don't bother to deny it. Your uncle and aunt have already told your father and me about you lying to them about going over to your friend Lisa's house to do some homework. Marvin said he decided to go to the cabin and see if there was any fire wood there about an hour after you left. When he saw your car parked at the cabin he figured you and that white boy you've been dating were in there. He figured he'd sneak up on you all and give you both a good 'dressing down' for doing something that could lead to disgrace. So, he parked his truck in the woods and walked over to the cabin."

Mother stood up. "Well, you know what he saw when he looked in the cabin window. Even though you all had only a small lamp on, he still saw you and that nigra sitting close on the sofa and talking. He said he turned around immediately and went back to his truck to get his hunting rifle. You left before he got back."

Gabrielle was thankful that her uncle had not seen them making love or kiss good-bye.

Mother's eyes gleamed with anger. "That nigra better be glad that your uncle is a Christian man, and he took pity on LaDora and Ballgame, because otherwise Marvin would have given him more than a warning!"

Gabrielle was suddenly struck by fear for Raymond. "What do you mean by Uncle Marvin giving Raymond a warning?"

"I mean that after you left, your uncle shot him in the knee and knocked him unconscious. Then he took him to the nigra hospital."

Gabrielle started crying and grabbed several tissues out of a box on her dressing table to wipe her tears.

Mother signed irritably. "My goodness, Gabrielle, that nigra isn't dead. But he will be if you continue to carry on with him. You're lucky your uncle stopped you before you made a foolish mistake like you did in Atlanta with that low-class white boy." She threw up her hands in exasperation. "Honestly, I don't know how you could have done such a thing. Suppose you had had sex with that nigra? You could have gotten some nasty nigra disease or wound up pregnant and having to go to some quack for an abortion!"

Gabrielle pressed the tissues to her eyes.

I have not gotten any disease, and I'm not pregnant. Raymond was always careful about using a condom. He always tried to protect me. He loves me, and I love him. Now, you're trying to destroy our love.

Gabrielle threw a wet wad of tissue in the trash can and grabbed a fresh handful.

Mother took one of Gabrielle's suitcases out of the closet and then turned to her again. "What I understand, Missy, is that you're damn lucky that your uncle caught you and not some other white person. As it is he saved your name. He's told everybody that he caught that nigra trying to sneak up to your bedroom, and he didn't kill him out of pity for his parents." Mother's eyes narrowed. "If you get branded as a nigger lover no decent white man will touch you with a ten-foot pole. What white man do you think will marry you if he learns that you've taken up with some nigra?"

Gabrielle shook her head. "Mama, you don't know Raymond. He loves me, and he's going to be a professional ball player one day. He'll be rich."

"What difference would that make? He would still be a nigra! No daughter of mine is going to be a nigra lover! Besides, he can forget about sports now that he's been shot in the knee." Mother took another suitcase out of the closet. "Gabrielle, start packing. You're going back to Atlanta and get in school there and behave yourself. You're going to forget about that nigra and be glad your uncle was decent enough to drop him on the porch of that nigra hospital."

Gabrielle threw her tissues in the trash can and went to her window. The rambling old-fashioned house at the end of the lane looked like a helpless shelter. It wasn't strong enough to protect her coffee-and-cream romance. Her and Raymond's glowing love had been dampened from exposure to the coldness of society.

When she turned around, her mother's stern eyes met hers. "What's it going to be? Are you going to go back to Atlanta and behave yourself or are you going to keep up this circus behavior? Will it take seeing that nigra dead to shake some sense into your head?"

Raymond dead! Gabrielle winced at the thought. She didn't want to think about Raymond being dead. She would rather live without him than have their love cause his death.

Gabrielle turned her back to the window and the rambling old-fashioned house at the end of the lane. Her mother finished getting out her luggage. Gabrielle started packing. She placed her love for Raymond and all its beautiful memories in the white-gold vault of her heart.

That Friday night Annie Ruth avoided looking at the picture of Raymond that she kept by her bed. After she lay down she closed her eyes and tried not to think about Raymond. Her bedroom door opened. Mama walked in guided by the light flooding in from the hallway. "Annie Ruth?"

"Yes, ma'am."

"You mind if we talk?"

Annie Ruth sat up. "No, ma'am. Turn on the light."

Mama flicked on the light and sat on the edge of the bed. "Heard any news about Raymond while you were working at Aldonia's?"

Annie Ruth shook her head. "Not much more than what I heard at school."

Mama looked at Raymond's picture. "Um, um, Sid and I were talking about it earlier this evening. It's a blessing from God that Mr. Sinclair felt pity for LaDora and Ballgame and didn't kill the boy. It's a wonder he wasn't killed like that Emmett Till over in Money, Mississippi, a few years back."

Annie Ruth took a deep breath. "That's what everybody keep saying. The white folks beat and killed Emmett Till, but they say Raymond wasn't beaten. Nobody's seen him though other than his family and the hospital workers. I heard that Mrs. Baldwin has refused to let him have visitors. And she even insisted that he have a private room."

"I don't blame her," Mama said. "You know how careless some people can be with other people's feelings. If it was a son of mine, I wouldn't want folks making a spectacle of him." Mama looked at Annie Ruth compassionately. "Did you try to visit him?"

"No, and I ain't gonna try to."

Mama stood up, then sat back down. "Annie Ruth, when I first heard about what had happened to Raymond I thought, 'Well, at least Annie Ruth will realize that he ain't the right person for her.' Then later on I got to thinking. Sid was my first real love. Raymond is your first love. I fell in love with Sid when I was sixteen. You fell in love with Raymond when you were sixteen. If something like this had happened with Sid, it woulda broke my heart."

Annie Ruth squeezed her mother's hand. "From what they say, I'm the opposite of everything she is. I'm black. She's white. I'm tall. She's short. My hair is black. Her hair is blond. But most of all," Annie Ruth's voice quivered, "she's got Raymond's love. I don't."

When Annie Ruth began to cry, Mama hugged her. "Everybody's got to lose sometime with love. That's the way it is. It don't matter whether you lose to somebody who's opposite or someone who is similar. Either way it's a loss."

Time went on. Annie Ruth's eighteenth birthday passed. The month of March had blown in and was half over the Saturday morning a tall young man walked into Aldonia's shop and asked to see Annie Ruth. He introduced himself as Raymond's cousin and said Raymond was outside waiting to see her. When Annie Ruth followed him out, Raymond's cousin pointed to a car that was parked near the street and then went to a nearby store. Annie Ruth went over to the car. She was shocked by Raymond's slimmer face and lackluster eyes.

Raymond smiled weakly. "My Lady, you acting like you scared or something."

Annie Ruth moved a little closer to Raymond. "I'm surprised to see you. I had heard you were living over in Jesup."

"I have been." Raymond averted his eyes. "You probably heard that the Sinclairs have forbidden me to be on or near their property. So I couldn't go back home. My parents took me to my aunt's house in Jesup after I got out of the hospital."

In spite of her resentment toward him, Annie Ruth felt a pang of pity. "I'm sorry you can't go back home, Raymond." She looked at his knee. "Your knee healed?"

Raymond touched his knee lightly. "I'm still getting around on crutches. So far, it looks like I'll never have proper use of it again. So, I can forget about a professional career in sports."

In spite of her previous pity, anger and humiliation were still dragging on Annie Ruth. "I'm sorry about that. I know it's not easy having to kiss something that you love good-bye."

Raymond shifted uncomfortably in the seat. "I know you mad at me."

Annie Ruth frowned. "Raymond, how do you expect me

to feel? You never loved me. You just fooled me into thinking that you did. Then you got yourself shot trying to sneak into that white girl's bedroom."

Anger flared in Raymond's eyes. "That ain't the way it was!"

Annie Ruth crossed her arms. "Well, a lot of colored folks are saying that ain't the way it was. They say that the two of you were in love, and y'all were caught kissing."

Raymond drew in a sharp breath. "Her name is Gabrielle. We became friends while I was working for her grandfather when I was fifteen. We weren't having some white-girl-colored-boy thing. Her family doesn't understand her."

"Her family doesn't understand her, so I guess you do!" Annie Ruth replied angrily.

"Don't be mad, Annie Ruth." Raymond gestured with his hands. "This whole mess was a mistake. We had a nice friendship that was ruined by dirty lies and prejudices."

Annie Ruth uncrossed her arms. She didn't reply. She just stared at Raymond, not knowing whether to believe him.

Raymond reached out and touched her hand. "You and Curtis been friends since y'all were little kids. You care about him, but does that mean y'all are going together?"

Annie Ruth gazed into his dark brown eyes. She knew she still loved him. "So, you gonna finish school in Jesup?"

"No, I'm going to California to stay with my sister. She's got me a job as a dishwasher where she works. That way I can sit on a stool or something while I work. I'm gonna go to night school."

Annie Ruth allowed her eyes one last feast on his face. She stepped back from the car. "Good-bye, Raymond."

Raymond reached out and caught her arm. "My Lady,

don't go yet. I'm gonna work and save my money, then when everything's cool I'm coming back south to go to college. I'll join you at Fort Valley State. Trust me, My Lady, I'll make up for these bad times."

Lord have mercy, Raymond, I wanna believe you so bad. Oh, how I wanna believe you. "Raymond, are you telling me the truth?"

Raymond stroked her arm tenderly. "Trust me, My Lady."

Annie Ruth pursed her lips. "You expect me to sit around waiting for you?"

"Naw, go on to Fort Valley State like you planned. Like I said, I'll join you there in a few years." Raymond moistened his lips. "You just make sure you save your love for me."

Annie Ruth started feeling hopeful about their relationship. "I expect you to write to me every week."

"I'll write to you every chance I get." He looked towards the door of the beauty shop. "My Lady, I know it's a lot to ask, but I need to borrow fifty dollars."

Annie Ruth's hope fell. "Raymond!"

"I'm sorry about having to ask you." Raymond said hurriedly. "My parents are having to pay off that big hospital bill plus they bought me a bus ticket to California." Raymond tightened his grip on her arm. "I done already asked my mother's family for enough. I need some money for personal expenses until I get settled at my sister's and make a paycheck."

Annie Ruth shook her head. "Raymond, you asking too much."

"Please, Annie Ruth," he pleaded, "as soon as I draw my first paycheck I'm going to send your money back to you."

Annie Ruth tried to pull her arm away from him. He held her arm firmly and spoke in a loving voice. "You always said you loved me, or was that just a big put-on?"

Annie Ruth looked away from Raymond and tried to think about the colored customers who were coming and going from the small Negro-owned store nearby. Raymond's cousin came outside of the store and started drinking a soda. Her mind failed. Her thoughts went back to Raymond. *I love him, but I shouldn't loan him my money. He done hurt me so much. Why should I help him?* She knew the answer as soon as she thought of the question. She still loved him. So she answered him with her heart. "Okay, but I expect you to send my money back before I finish school in May. And, like I said, I also expect you to write to me at least once every week."

Raymond kissed her hand. "My Lady, I will. I'm gonna make all this up to you."

Annie Ruth touched his cheek. Loving him seemed to require so much of her.

"After you get home this afternoon, get the money, and go over to Billie Lee's house," Raymond instructed her. "The two of you make up an excuse about going for a walk or something, and meet my cousin and me at the crossroads." Raymond sighed. "I never thought I'd ever have to sneak in my parents' house, but I do. I'm gonna lay down in the back seat until my cousin parks in our backyard. I'm gonna say good-bye to my parents and get a few more of my things."

Although Billie Lee agreed to accompany Annie Ruth, she wasn't in favor of Annie Ruth loaning Raymond the money. "He shouldn't be asking you to loan him money," Billie Lee said when Annie Ruth told her about it.

Annie Ruth couldn't look her cousin in the eyes. "I love him, Billie Lee. I can't deny him."

So at four forty-five she and Billie Lee were headed towards the crossroads. They arrived at the designated area about the same time as Raymond and his cousin.

"I'll wait here," Billie Lee said as she stopped by a pine tree. "You and Raymond need a little time alone."

Raymond got out of the car and waited for Annie Ruth on his crutches. He expressed gratitude for the loan of the money and made more promises that fueled Annie Ruth's hope for their love. She had so much hope. He had so little time. She tried not to think about how much she was going to miss him.

"Goodbye, My Lady." He demonstrated his old dexterity as he balanced himself on his crutches and kissed her.

Her goodbye was a touch of her finger to his unforgettable mouth and a wave of her hand before she walked away without looking back. Billie Lee fell in step beside her when she passed the pine tree. They walked home silently.

Relieved, Raymond maneuvered himself back to his cousin's car. They drove away. He didn't stare remorsefully at the southeast Georgia countryside. *I can't have Gabrielle. I won't be able to be a professional ball player. I'm not even free to live in my parents' home. The South's too racist for me. California's gotta be better.*

7

Changes

The thrills and excitement of her senior year were lost to Annie Ruth. She wrapped her wounded heart in Raymond's promises and soothed her love-sickness with remedies of her desperate hopes. She continued to study hard, make good grades, do her chores, and to help Aldonia; however, the zest was gone. She heard nothing and received nothing from Raymond. Fighting to prevent her languishment from conquering her, she forced herself to go through the final rituals of her senior year with the rest of her classmates. She went through the motions but her thoughts traveled over a thousand miles away to California. *God, please don't let Raymond betray me. Please God, please make him call me or write to me soon.*

"Annie Ruth, honey child, give me that stapler! This is the third time I done ask you for it," Edwina said.

Annie Ruth adjusted herself on the scaffold. "My mind ain't on decorating for the prom."

"Worrying about Raymond?"

Annie Ruth handed her the stapler. "Do you really have to ask?"

"No, you been trying to act normal, yet I see the pain in your face when you be staring out the window sometimes in class. You just be sitting there stroking that locket he gave you for Christmas. I see how you avoid looking at Dwight and me and other couples here at school." She touched Annie Ruth's hand gently. "I know how I'd feel if something bad broke Dwight and me up."

Annie Ruth tried not to show her envy. "Don't worry, Dwight really loves you."

Edwina stapled a blue streamer to the wire that was strung from the ceiling and outlined the playing area of the gym. "I think he loves me. He's already asked me to marry him this summer."

Annie Ruth nodded. "Yeah, Dwight told me he did. Lucinda said Mark asked her, too."

"Yeah, he did." Edwina looked at Annie Ruth compassionately. "Don't look so sad, Annie Ruth. I know you crazy about Raymond, but you hadn't planned on marrying him until after you got out of college anyway. Y'all still got time to get things back together."

Annie Ruth handed Edwina a gold streamer. "I hope you right."

She kept handing Edwina streamers alternating with blue and gold until they had covered the area of wire near the scaffold. Annie Ruth couldn't help but think about how lucky her friends seemed to be in love and how unlucky she was. She felt like the joy and fun had been drained out of her life. Her sadness started clouding her eyes. She decided to get down off of the scaffold.

"Excuse me, Edwina, I'm gonna get down and go outside for a while. I got to get some fresh air."

"Annie Ruth, I'm sorry," Edwina said. "Did I say something that hurt your feelings?"

Annie Ruth paused. "No, of course not. I'll get Billie Lee to come and help you."

"Child, you got tears in your eyes," Edwina said.

"Please, Edwina, I'll be all right. I need some fresh air, that's all."

Edwina put down the stapler. "I'll go with you."

"No, I'd rather be alone." Annie Ruth climbed down.

Curtis was sitting on a bench outside of the gym. He looked up when Annie Ruth walked out. "Hey, Annie Ruth." He frowned. "You okay?"

Annie Ruth wiped her eyes. "Yes, I'm fine." She cleared her throat. "Curtis, why you sitting out here?"

"I needed a break from the decorating. I been running myself to death trying to help get things together."

Annie Ruth nodded. "Yeah, I know. Everybody, including the teachers, been talking about how hard you been working, and that you been a good class president this year."

Curtis smiled. "Well, I like to do my best."

Annie Ruth sat on another bench. Neither of them said anything for several minutes. Finally, she broke the silence. "Curtis, why you staring at me?"

"I'm sorry. I was thinking about how pretty you are." He paused. "You heard from Raymond?"

"No, I ain't." Annie Ruth didn't want to talk about Raymond anymore. It hurt too much. "Curtis, why ain't you going to college? You a good student."

"I plan to go to college. I'm gonna wait a year or two before I start, though. I wanna get a job at the mill during the winter, and help Dad out on the farm during the summer." Curtis smiled proudly. "Dad's land is his life. A lot of his blood, sweat, and tears have gone into holding on to our land. Once our farm is on firm standing, I'll go on to college."

Annie Ruth thought Curtis seemed older than what he was. "That's good thinking. Curtis, you a real hard working person."

Curtis smiled. "Well, I know you gonna make it at Fort Valley State. You'll be a schoolteacher in no time."

"I sure plan to. I been accepted and everything."

"Good." Curtis cleared his throat and stood up. "Annie Ruth, I was looking at the guest list before I came out. I saw that you still ain't listed your guest's name."

She replied, "I ain't got one."

"Will you be my guest?" Curtis asked.

"Your guest?" Annie Ruth frowned. "What about Elizabeth Collins?"

"Elizabeth and I are just friends. We ain't got any claims on each other. So, will you be my guest?"

Before Annie Ruth could answer, one of their teachers called him. "Think about it," he said as he turned to leave. "I'll call you tonight."

When Annie Ruth sat beside Billie Lee that afternoon on the bus, Billie Lee started talking to her immediately. "I saw you and Curtis talking outside the gym today. He smiled at you when he passed our seat on his way to the back."

Annie Ruth raised her eyebrows. "Child, you been keeping an eye on things."

"Shoot, Annie Ruth, I know you feel terrible about Raymond, but you gotta get back to being your old self." Billie Lee patted her hand. "Curtis is a nice guy. He ain't bad looking. He ain't as striking as Raymond, but he got his good points."

Annie Ruth thought about that. Curtis's smooth dark skin reminded her of black velvet. His narrow moustache made him look older. He had a sincere face enhanced by intelligent eyes. Hard farm work had molded his body into a strong, sturdy physique. Unlike Raymond, who was almost a foot taller than Annie Ruth, Curtis fell short of the top of her head by about two inches. That wasn't so bad, though. "He asked me to be his guest at the prom," she said to Billie Lee.

"Great!" Billie Lee beamed. "I hope you said yes."

"I guess I might as well," she said. "He gonna call me tonight."

Annie Ruth agreed to go to the prom with Curtis that night. Her parents were pleased when she told them she was going with him. Carl's wife, Thelma, sent Annie Ruth a white chiffon gown from Atlanta. Annie Ruth prepared for the prom in a nonchalant manner. Nothing seemed right without Raymond.

When time for the prom came the first Friday in May, Raymond had been gone almost six weeks. Annie Ruth was beside herself with worry about him. When her parents let her drive into town to buy a pair of nylons, she seized the opportunity to visit Raymond's mother.

She felt a little self conscious visiting Mrs. Baldwin, but she had to know about Raymond.

Mrs. Baldwin answered the door. "Annie Ruth, come on in. Please excuse me, I'm cleaning fish for dinner. Come on back to the kitchen with me."

As Annie Ruth followed her through the immaculate house, she tried not to gaze at Raymond's images grinning at her from the maze of photographs on the walls and etageres. His trophies and ribbons were sad reminders of his dreams of a great sports career. Annie Ruth focused her attention on his mother.

Mrs. Baldwin motioned to her to take a seat. "Your mama and daddy doing fine?"

"Yes, ma'am," Annie Ruth replied.

Mrs. Baldwin nodded. "That's good. Lord knows, these are some trying times." She smiled at Annie Ruth. "I bet you gonna get valedictorian this time."

"I hope so."

"Annie Ruth, you a smart girl and pretty, too," Mrs. Baldwin said. "I was so proud when I found out Raymond was courting you. I could see y'all finishing school, going to college, making something of yourselves, and getting married."

Annie Ruth beamed. "You heard from Raymond?"

Mrs. Baldwin turned to the fish. "Yes, he doing fine. Said his knee is healing pretty good." Mrs. Baldwin busied herself cleaning the fish. When she finished, she placed the fish in a pan and wrapped their guts in the newspaper they were laying on.

She turned to Annie Ruth. "I'm gonna tell you this cause if one of my daughters was in your place, I'd want someone to be honest with her." Mrs. Baldwin took a deep breath. "Raymond got to California safely. He got a job washing dishes at the restaurant where my daughter Linda works. He's been working hard and doing good on his job, his sister say. He's going to night school, and he'll get his diploma in June."

Annie Ruth felt a sudden rush of joy. "That's good!"

Mrs. Baldwin's green eyes focused intently on Annie Ruth. "Yes, it is good, but . . ." Mrs. Baldwin paused and then hurried on, "he's met another girl out there, at the night school that he goes to. She's taking up secretary studies. He said she's a pretty little blond, and she reminds him of Miss Gabrielle."

Annie Ruth's head jerked from the invisible slap of Mrs. Baldwin's words. Her heart began to beat faster. In a strained voice she asked, "She a white girl?"

Mrs. Baldwin looked away. "Yes, she is."

Another white girl. Now I know he was lying about he and Gabrielle being only friends. They were going together.

Mrs. Baldwin seemed determined to tell her everything. "Raymond said she smart, too. She already working as a clerk for a chauffeur service. She talked with me on the telephone. She sounded real nice." Mrs. Baldwin lowered her voice. Her next words were still very clear to Annie Ruth, though. "They said they gonna get married. They told me not to worry, cause it ain't against the law for a white person to marry a Negro in California."

Annie Ruth covered her mouth with her hand. She swallowed. A ball of disappointment was in her throat. *Raymond, I thought you said you were gonna come back South and join me at Fort Valley State after things cooled down. I thought you loved me.* She felt hot all over. Somehow she found the strength to keep from bursting into tears.

Mrs. Baldwin started rinsing the fish. "Child, you a good girl. You got a lot going for you." She glanced at Annie Ruth sympathetically. "I love my son dearly, but take my advice, put your love for him away and go on with your education." Mrs. Baldwin cut up the fish and prepared it for frying. "I wanted to finish high school before I got married, but Ballgame said he wanted a wife and he wasn't gonna wait another year. He wanted our children to finish high school, but he didn't want me to. I always wished I had finished high school first." Mrs. Baldwin started frying the fish. She took her attention away from her cooking as if she wanted to make sure Annie Ruth heard every word she said. "You got a chance to finish high school and college. You can follow your own dreams." She gestured with her hand. "Don't let loving a man stop you."

Annie Ruth was too upset about the loss of Raymond to fully comprehend the essence of the older woman's words. She took a deep breath, willing herself not to cry. She'd already cried so much before. Many nights she had lain in her bed with the locket that Raymond had given her pressed to her breast and cried silently as she prayed that he would call or write to her. All of her hoping and praying had been in vain. All along, Raymond had been basking in his new romance with another white girl.

Shrouding the pain that was eating within her like an un-yielding cancer, Annie Ruth managed to muster enough strength to sit and finish her visit.

Slowly, Annie Ruth drove home. Disappointment and sadness drenched her like a sudden hard rain. Raymond didn't love her. He probably never had. He had fooled her, but she still loved him. Now that she was alone, she allowed herself the tears she had previously held back. *Raymond, Raymond, all your promises to me were lies. All my love for you was in vain! Lord, have mercy, I still love you.* She moaned sadly.

That evening, Annie Ruth dressed for the prom without any enthusiasm. Daddy had given her and Billie Lee permission to ride with their dates in separate cars. In spite of Curtis's handsomeness in his tuxedo, Annie Ruth would have quickly turned him into Raymond if it had been possible. She forced herself to smile and act gracious when he pinned on her corsage. If

Raymond had been coming for her, the prom would have been another sweet memory for Annie Ruth.

At the prom she pretended to be having a great time, talking, laughing, and dancing. She thought her act was quite convincing.

Lucinda stopped dancing long enough to say, "Annie Ruth, child, you looking good. I'm glad you ain't moping around tonight about Raymond. He probably having a ball in California." She lowered her voice. "I never told you this before, I didn't wanna hurt your feelings. But he asked me to have sex with him."

Annie Ruth gasped. "When?"

"One Saturday night when I saw him at the Blue Light Inn."

Annie Ruth was suspicious. "You telling me the truth, Lucinda?"

Lucinda cocked her head indignantly. "You know I am. I like to have fun, but I ain't a liar."

"No, I don't believe you would lie about something like that," Annie Ruth replied softly.

"I sure wouldn't. He made me mad anyway. He always acted like he was better than the rest of us. Shoot, I told him, 'Your eyes may shine, your teeth may grit, but none of this you'll get.'" Lucinda paused, listening to the song the disc jockey was playing. "That's *Save the Last Dance For Me* by the Drifters—that's my song. I gotta find Mark so we can dance."

"Okay, Lucinda," Annie Ruth murmured.

Just then Curtis came up and touched her arm. "Let's dance, Annie Ruth."

She danced with Curtis. Strangely, there were no tears. Lucinda's revelation about Raymond's intimate proposal only reinforced what she already knew—Raymond hadn't loved her.

Curtis escorted her off the dance floor, and then went to get them some punch. Billie Lee rushed over. "Child, I'm so glad to see you snapping out of it and having a good time. Curtis look so handsome. You know he crazy about you. I kept from saying anything cause I didn't wanna hurt you, but Raymond's kinda low-down. He got involved with that white girl even though y'all were going together, borrowed your money, and ain't even bothered to write or call you."

When Annie Ruth saw Lenny coming, she seized the opportunity to stifle Billie Lee's criticisms of Raymond. She couldn't bear to hear Billie Lee talk about Raymond even though what she was saying was true. "Hey, Lenny! You looking snazzy."

Lenny grinned broadly. "Billie Lee, your cousin's got good taste."

Lenny's coming made Billie Lee forget Raymond, she slipped her arm through his the moment he walked up. "Enjoying yourself?" she asked.

"Of course," Lenny replied. "The best thing about this night, though, is that we'll be able to spend some time together alone before I take you home."

Lenny turned to Annie Ruth. "I know Mr. Sid and Miss Carrie done gave their permission for Billie Lee and I to get married on the fifth Saturday in July, but it's still hard for me to believe that they gonna actually let me take her home with me after the wedding."

Annie Ruth laughed. "They will."

Curtis came back with the punch and greeted everybody. "Hey Lenny, you and Billie Lee look sharp," he said. "Annie Ruth told me that Mr. Sid and Miss Carrie done gave you permission to marry Billie Lee."

Lenny patted Billie Lee's hand. "That's right, man, come the fifth Saturday in July, this beautiful lady is gonna be mine!"

The way Lenny was treating Billie Lee made Annie Ruth's hurt about Raymond even worse. She still loved him, but the hurt and humiliation that he had caused her made her feel anger and resentment. She wanted to hurt him just as he had hurt her.

"What do you say, Annie Ruth?" Curtis broke into her thoughts. "Would you like to drive out to the Blue Light Inn? Lenny and Billie Lee want us to follow them."

"Oh, okay," she answered.

Leaving the prom was a relief for Annie Ruth. Seeing the happiness of the other couples was beginning to make her feel really bad.

Lenny and Curtis parked in the back behind several other cars. That way no one would see their cars and report them to Daddy. Lenny and Curtis went inside and bought Cokes. Then the four of them sat in Lenny's car and listened to the soulful sounds of Sam Cooke, James Brown, and Chubby Checker flowing from the juke joint. Knowing that Lenny and Billie Lee wanted some time to be alone, Annie Ruth and Curtis didn't stay long in Lenny's car.

As they were getting out of Lenny's car, Melvin Pittman walked up carrying a large bag. "Y'all want some beer?" he asked.

"Yeah, I need something to wash down all that sweet punch and soda water I been drinking tonight," Lenny said, stretching a hand through the open window.

Melvin gave two cans each to Lenny and Curtis, and then went on to a carload of their classmates nearby. Curtis and Annie Ruth said good night to Billie Lee and Lenny and then left.

They drove in silence for a while. Curtis started talking a few miles from Annie Ruth's house.

"Annie Ruth, we still got almost an hour before I have to have you home. We ain't had much time to be alone and talk. Would it be all right if I drove off on a side road?"

Annie Ruth stared out of the window. She was in no hurry to go home to her silent room and be haunted by thoughts of Raymond. "I guess it'll be okay," she said. "But make sure it's some place outta sight. I don't want any problems with Daddy."

"Don't worry," Curtis said. "I know this area. I know a good place." Carefully, Curtis steered the car off the highway and down the dirt road to a clearing where he stopped. They both became silent again. Curtis suggested they drink the beers Melvin had given them.

If you ever get a hankering to taste liquor or beer, be sure you don't do it alone with a boy, or in the company of people you ain't absolutely sure you can trust. Mama's warning echoed in Annie Ruth's head, but she ignored it as the cool liquid slid down her throat.

Within minutes after they consumed the beers, Curtis seemed to become more relaxed. "Annie Ruth, I'm sorry you got hurt by Raymond, but I ain't sorry he's gone and I was able to take you to the prom."

He put his hand on her shoulder. "I've always loved you. Even when we were little children sitting under shade trees by the cotton fields while our parents helped each other with the cotton picking, I'd always share my cookies with you and crack pecans and shell peanuts for you. I loved you even then."

Annie Ruth smiled. "Curtis, we were only three or four."

"Yeah, but even back then I knew you were special. Remember when we were in the seventh grade and our teacher had us to write poems?"

"Yeah, I remember your poem. It was funny and everybody laughed."

Curtis chuckled. "Yeah, it was funny. But it was about love, and I wrote it with you in mind."

Annie Ruth replied with mock seriousness, "So you really love me more than a hog loves slop?"

Curtis laughed. "I'll never forget that poem. It went: *You make my thermometer's mercury sizzle to the top. You make my heart go flip flop. You make my syrup sweeter to sop. And I love you more than a hog loves slop!*"

They both laughed.

"I ain't a poet, Annie Ruth. I was only twelve when I wrote that. I wrote about farm things cause that's what I knew best. And I knew that I loved you. I always been crazy about you," Curtis went on. "But Raymond dazzled you with his good looks and athletic abilities. I wanted so much to be your escort during homecoming, but as usual Raymond took over."

Annie Ruth bowed her head. Yes, she thought, Raymond had always taken over. And now he'd been taken over by a white girl.

"Whistling," Curtis exclaimed.

"What?"

Curtis explained. "That boy, Emmett Till, was kidnapped and lynched in Mississippi a few years ago for whistling at a white woman. I don't understand how Raymond could have been so foolish trying to sneak up to a white girl's bedroom."

I ain't sure about what happened, Annie Ruth thought. I am sure that he loved her and not me, though. And that's what hurts so bad. Annie Ruth started crying.

"Annie Ruth, don't cry, that low-down Uncle Tomish Casanova ain't worth your crying over." Curtis pulled her into his arms and began to gently wipe away her tears. "I love you more than he ever could."

The relaxing effects of the beer and the warmth of Curtis's body began to creep over her. She didn't protest when Curtis pushed back the seat and pushed her gently down. When he began kissing her tenderly, she relaxed in the comfort of his loving caresses. He pushed the thin straps of her gown away from her shoulders and began to stroke her breasts gently.

Common sense said, Sit up. Stop him!

But her broken heart replied, "Wouldn't Raymond hurt if he knew you were doing this with Curtis Lynch?" She wanted to hurt Raymond like he'd hurt her.

Stop him before it's too late, her common sense warned.

But the beer clouded her reasoning. *Ah-ah, go ahead and hurt Raymond. Give Curtis what you didn't give Raymond.*

And so she let him go on. She didn't protest when he removed her dress. By the time he pulled down her panties she had allowed herself to be engulfed in his passionate kisses and caresses. In spite of her virginal pain, she was too caught up in the excitement of their intimacy to stop him. She started crying when it was over. *I done lost my virginity in a car. I should have stopped him. I can't believe I really did it. Lord, have mercy, I did it!*

Curtis pressed his face against hers. "I'm sorry, Annie Ruth. I shouldn't have let things get outta hand. When I started kissing you I just went wild. I only meant to comfort you. I didn't mean for us to go all the way."

Annie Ruth didn't reply. She had wanted to get revenge on Raymond, but she hadn't really wanted to lose her virginity.

Thank goodness it's dark in this car, cause I wouldn't want to have to look at Curtis's face. I'm so ashamed of myself. I done did the very thing Mama's been warning me about. Oh, goodness, I hope she and Daddy never find out about this.

She started dressing herself hurriedly. "Take me home. Take me home," she told Curtis.

Mama and Daddy were in bed and only called out to her when she went into the house. *I'm gonna take a nice hot bath. Oh, how I wish I could wash away what I did tonight.*

8

Nuptials

The following Monday, Annie Ruth avoided Curtis in school. When she got on the bus that afternoon, he was sitting next to Billie Lee. He grabbed her arm.

"Please," he begged. "Let me talk to you."

Annie Ruth looked at the other students. She didn't want to draw attention to herself, so she sat down behind him and Billie Lee. He got up and came to join her. Billie Lee opened a textbook and began to read.

"I'm sorry," Curtis said. "I know we can't really talk here. May I call you tonight?"

"That's up to you," she replied. "You can't do any harm on the telephone."

Curtis looked embarrassed. "I'll call you around eight. I'm gonna go sit at the back so you and Billie Lee can sit together." Curtis reached out to touch her hand, but Annie Ruth jerked it away.

After Curtis left, Billie Lee moved back with Annie Ruth.

"I know you still love Raymond," she said. "But face it, he's no good for you. Curtis seem to love you. In four years you'll be out of college and teaching. You gonna want a good husband." Billie Lee paused. "Curtis is a nice, hard-working person. He's the only child, so you know that big farm will be passed on to him. Plus, he told me he's going to college after a year. A good man ain't easy to find."

Annie Ruth didn't respond. She wondered what Billie Lee would think if she knew what she and Curtis had done last Friday. She wanted to keep that a secret.

That night, Curtis was still apologetic when he called. "I'm so ashamed of myself. I shoulda been man enough to stop. I've dreamed of that happening after we were married. I wanna marry you, Annie Ruth. I'm only gonna wait a year before I go to college. I'm gonna go to Fort Valley State so we can be near each other. I'd like to marry you after we both get our degrees. Will you marry me, Annie Ruth?"

Annie Ruth gripped the receiver. Life could be so strange. She'd been hoping and praying for a marriage proposal from Raymond. And here Curtis was saying the words she'd given anything to hear Raymond say. "Curtis, five years is a long time."

Curtis voice sounded firm. "I'm willing to wait. I love you. I don't want anyone else."

"We'll see," Annie Ruth said. "We need to get our educations first."

"You right," Curtis agreed. "I can wait. I want things to work out for us."

"Curtis?"

"Yes."

"Did you tell anybody about what we did?"

"No, I love you too much. I'd never do anything to embarrass you or hurt you."

May 28, 1961, Sunday evening. Tobacco County High's graduation was a joyful occasion for Annie Ruth. She was valedictorian and was awarded a scholarship.

Her graduation brought a feeling of accomplishment and happiness in her life. She decided it was time to put her love for Raymond aside and go on with her life. *I better get my act together. Shoot, I messed around and had sex with Curtis cause I was so down and out about Raymond. Ain't any sense in me keep thinking about Raymond. I'm gonna get my mind on going to college.*

About three weeks later, Annie Ruth paid Curtis a visit. She watched as lines of worry popped up on his face while he busied himself feeding their cows. "I think you panicking, Annie Ruth. We only had sex that one time after the prom. You wouldn't even let me kiss you on the lips the few times we been together since then."

Annie Ruth attempted in vain to calm the tide of fear that was rising within her. "I'm afraid I was too late being careful. I been feeling tired and drained, and I'm late."

Curtis paused. He spoke nervously. "How late?"

The tide of fear continued to rise. "The last time I saw my period was the last week of April. Today's the fourteenth of June."

Curtis leaned against the fence, staring across the field. "We went to the prom the first Friday in May, didn't we?"

"Yes, May fifth. Curtis we gotta do something. My breasts are sore. I'm beginning to feel sick in the mornings." Her voice trailed off while the tide of fear washed over her. Annie Ruth started sobbing.

Curtis turned and took her in his arms. "Calm down, I'll think of something. Go home. I'll work it out."

Curtis's plan for working it out was revealed to Annie Ruth when Aldonia called her father. She could hear Daddy talking on the telephone. "Well, how long you gonna need to be in Jacksonville, Aldonia? I see. Well, I'm gonna allow Annie Ruth to go since you gonna be with them. Y'all need to get what you need to get done and be headed back this way before sundown. Jacksonville, Florida is a big place. It ain't good for y'all young folks to be there after dark."

After he hung up, he explained to Annie Ruth. "Aldonia said she need to go to Jacksonville to buy some hairdressing supplies. Curtis's got some business to take care of for his daddy, and they want you to ride with them. I told them it'll be okay. Everything's caught up around here."

The next day Annie Ruth stared sadly out of the Lynches' car window. She always enjoyed going to Jacksonville, but the trip that day was one she wished she didn't have to make. *Please, God, don't let me be pregnant,* she prayed. She glanced at Curtis. He looked worried. *If I'm not pregnant we won't be having sex again.*

Aldonia kept trying to make small talk. She gave up after receiving very little response from Annie Ruth and Curtis. Curtis dropped Aldonia off downtown, then he drove Annie Ruth to a doctor's office.

"We used to bring Mom to this doctor before she died. I found his number in her address book, and I called him and made you an appointment," he explained, handing her some money. "This should be enough to cover your bill."

Annie Ruth tried to smile. Curtis was being so considerate and attentive. She couldn't be angry with him. She was disappointed and embarrassed with herself for doing such a dumb thing. The doctor's vaginal examination surprised her. *Good night! I didn't know they did this to you!*

The doctor said, "Yes, young lady, you're pregnant."

Please, God, let it be that I heard him wrong. The doctor repeated himself. "Yes, you're pregnant."

Annie Ruth squeezed her eyes shut and shook her head.

In the car in the parking lot, Annie Ruth and Curtis discussed her pregnancy. Curtis shrugged. "I sure didn't think about this happening. If I could go back to that night, I wouldn't drink any beer, and I'd definitely use some restraint."

Wouldn't we both. But it's too late now.

They were both quiet for a while. Finally, Curtis started talking again. "Neither one of us wanted things to turn out this way, but they have." His voice got a little warmer. "I love you. Will you marry me, Annie Ruth?"

Annie Ruth swallowed. What would Mama and Daddy do when they found out? They'd be so ashamed and disappointed in her. And she certainly didn't want to be an unwed mother. "You didn't have to ask me, Curtis. I ain't got a choice."

Curtis hugged her gently. "I want a yes or no answer."

Annie Ruth held onto him for a few minutes. She could feel herself trembling. *Lord, have mercy, I'm gonna have a baby.* "Yes, Curtis, I'll marry you."

Curtis patted her shoulder. "I figured you were really pregnant. While you were seeing the doctor, I made some plans. We'll get married as soon as we can get our blood tests and license. I'll talk with my cousin, Reverend Phillips. We always been close. He and his wife, Mary Joyce, will help us get things together. They still young. They'll help us get married and keep quiet until we can tell our folks."

Curtis hugged her again. "Don't look so sad, sweetheart. Everything's gonna be all right."

Annie Ruth wiped her eyes. "I'm just feeling foolish. Ain't any sense in me crying. It's done, now."

Annie Ruth told Aldonia about her pregnancy on their way back home. Aldonia was surprised. She was relieved though when Annie Ruth said she and Curtis were going to get married before their parents found out about her pregnancy. Aldonia agreed with their plans and promised to keep everything a secret until they were married and their parents were told.

It seemed like a day for surprises and secrets. Aldonia told them about her secret decision to haul moonshine for a white lady named Miss Della. She said she needed to help pay her brother Walter's college expenses. Annie Ruth and Curtis tried to talk her out of it, but Aldonia believed that as long as her secret was kept, and she hauled for the right folks, she'd be all right.

Annie Ruth was too upset over her own problems to offer much of an argument against Aldonia's decision. *Well, Daddy and Mr. Andrew hauled moonshine a long time ago when they had a few bad years. And they didn't get caught. Everybody know Uncle Bill, Aldonia's daddy, is a poor provider. I know she doesn't really wanna do it, cause she said she doing what she gotta do. Like I don't wanna get married to Curtis right now, but I'm doing what I gotta do.*

June 25, 1961, Sunday evening. Annie Ruth and Curtis were ready to get married at Reverend Phillips's church.

Annie Ruth peered into the small mirror over the sink. She repinned the corsage that Curtis had bought her and touched her cheek nervously. The image in the mirror looked like her. She could smell bleach that someone had used to clean the toilet fixtures. She could feel the heat in the tiny room making her already warm body hotter. She wiped the sweat from her forehead and from around her neck. She wished this was all a fabrication of her imagination and the pregnant person standing in the ladies' room of Elder's Chapel where Curtis's cousin was pastor, wearing a pink permanent-press two-piece dress and white high-heeled shoes, was not her, but it was.

Mary Joyce, Reverend Phillips's wife, opened the door. "Annie Ruth, are you okay?" Her eyes swept over her. "Oh, good, I thought . . ."

"No, I ain't crying." Annie Ruth motioned to her to come in. "I done cried enough. Besides, tears can't change things."

"Don't be so sad," Mary Joyce said. "Everything's going to work out."

"I can't go to college, now," Annie Ruth said remorsefully. "I always wanted to be a teacher like you and Reverend Phillips."

"Well, going to college and being a teacher aren't everything. I mean, I understand how it is between two young folks in love. Moses and I were lucky," Mary Joyce said in a sympathetic voice. "It really was hard to deny ourselves those four years while we were going to college. We came pretty close more times than I care to remember, but somehow one of us always managed to stop."

Annie Ruth bowed her head. "Curtis and I just didn't think

straight. I graduated valedictorian, and Curtis was one of the top ten graduates. You'd think we'd have had enough sense not to get ourselves in this kind of trouble."

Mary Joyce patted Annie Ruth on the shoulder. "Things could be a lot worse. I know Curtis loves you. I'm not saying this because he and Moses are cousins, but he's a nice young man and a hard worker. You're lucky. He could have walked off and left you to face your parents and the world alone. He could have been a lazy playboy . . ."

"Yeah, I know. I done already thought about all those things." Annie Ruth sighed. "I'm feeling bad about getting married like this. I always dreamed of having a church wedding. I never dreamed that I'd tell Mama and Daddy that Curtis and I were gonna attend Sunday evening services at Elder's Chapel and then get married."

"Well, you told them half of the truth. We are having services right after Moses marries you and Curtis in his study. I think that Curtis was right about the two of you getting married before you all tell your parents. It'll probably make things a little easier." Mary Joyce smiled sympathetically. "It's a long way from a pretty wedding, but at least you all are getting married in a church. Elder's Chapel isn't your membership church, but it's a church. You're wearing a pretty dress and that lovely corsage Curtis bought you. I've got a nice supper cooked at my house for you all. It's not so bad."

Annie Ruth nodded. "Thanks for everything, Mary Joyce. Like you said, things could be worse."

Mary Joyce took her by the arm. "Come on, let's get out of this restroom. Curtis and Moses are waiting. One day you'll look back on this day and rejoice. Put a smile on your face. You're getting married!"

The next morning, Annie Ruth was dressed and sitting by her bedroom window when Curtis and his father drove up in their old pickup truck. Her heart began to beat wildly. She was too scared to leave the room. She could hear Mr. Andrew explaining the situation to her parents.

A few minutes later, her mother stamped into the room, "Annie Ruth Watson! How could you shame the family! After all my teaching, you still come up and make a dumb mistake."

Annie Ruth looked at the floor. "I'm sorry, Mama."

Mama sucked in her breath angrily. "A college education was in the palm of your hand. You had good grades and a scholarship and you go get pregnant!" Mama threw up her hands. "I don't know of a better way to spell fool! How could you be so foolish?"

"That's enough, Maybelle!" Daddy walked into the bedroom. "Annie Ruth, get your things packed," he commanded. "Your husband is waiting for you. The Lord knows we tried to teach you the right way." Daddy shook his head sadly. "We were fixing to send you to college and everything, but you chose to do differently. You done made your bed, so now, you lie in it."

Annie Ruth could not bear to look at her parents' faces. She felt so ashamed. *Oh, how I wish I hadn't disappointed them and myself too.* Quickly she finished packing her things. She had already packed most of them the night before and hid the boxes under her bed. Curtis came in and began to carry the boxes to their truck.

Mr. Andrew came into the bedroom and started helping Curtis with the boxes. He paused in front of Daddy, his voice apologetic. "Sid, you know me and you go way back. You and Maybelle and me and Victoria before she died, we were always friends. I'm sorry." He nodded toward Annie Ruth. "I think a lot of Annie Ruth, and that boy of mine is gonna treat her right."

Daddy sighed heavily. "Andrew, it ain't your fault. We done the best we could with these young'uns. They made their bed, let them lie in it." Daddy looked at Curtis, passing him with Annie Ruth's things. "You handled this like a man. You got my daughter in trouble and you married her without any pushing from your daddy or me." His voice became a shade firmer. "Take care of my daughter."

Curtis gripped the box he was holding nervously. "I'm sorry about everything, but I love Annie Ruth."

Mama didn't say goodbye or wish Annie Ruth and Curtis well. She left the bedroom without saying anything. When Annie Ruth was ready to leave, Mama was in the kitchen. She looked at her, but Mama didn't look up from wiping the already spotless table. Annie Ruth wanted to say she was sorry again, but she knew it wouldn't make any difference. She turned and followed her husband and father-in-law out the door.

It seemed almost unbelievable to Annie Ruth that a brief period of rash thoughts and a few passionate minutes had changed the course of her life. The carefree wonders of her youth had slipped away from her overnight. In less than two months, she had gone from a studious college-bound girl to a pregnant farm wife.

Thank goodness Mama had made sure she knew how to cook and clean and sew. There hadn't been a woman in the Lynch house since Curtis lost his mama almost two years ago, and the place really showed it.

Annie Ruth decided to give the house a thorough cleaning. She began by cleaning the kitchen, cupboards, windows, and scrubbing the floor. The Lynches' living room seemed to come alive after her careful dusting and mopping. Curtis helped her to rearrange the furniture in his bedroom and to hang a few inexpensive pictures that they bought to give his room more of a married-couple's appearance.

Both Curtis and his father expressed their appreciation of her work. Seeing that neglect and dust had taken their toll on the drapes and curtains when Annie Ruth washed them, Mr. Andrew told her that she was welcome to make new ones from the material that his late wife had left in their former bedroom. That room and Mr. Andrew's present bedroom which he kept in an almost too-perfect order were the only rooms Annie Ruth had not cleaned.

She started cleaning Curtis's parents former bedroom right after she finished washing the breakfast dishes one morning. Curtis's mama, Miss Victoria, and Mama had been real close friends. Miss Victoria, a short, comely woman, had seemed like a relative to Annie Ruth. But that had been at a different time. Miss Victoria had been alive and the idea of being her daughter-in-law had never crossed Annie Ruth's mind.

As she cleaned the room, Annie Ruth looked through the personal items: clothing, letters, and pictures. She had a comforting feeling as if her presence was welcomed. She sat in a rocking chair to look through an old picture album. The intensity of her activity caught up with her, and she dozed. She was awakened by the sound of Mr. Andrew's voice.

"You all right, Annie Ruth?"

Annie Ruth raised her head and rubbed her eyes, "I'm fine, Mr. Andrew. I sat down for a few minutes to look at this picture album, and I dozed off."

Mr. Andrew was holding several cardboard boxes. He put them on the floor and walked around the room looking at the

array of items that Annie Ruth had scattered while she was going through things. He sat in a nearby chair. "I brought those
boxes so that you can put Victoria's things in them. Please keep
everything you want, I'll give the rest to my sister, Clara." Pride
flickered in Mr. Andrew's eyes. "You our daughter-in-law, and
you carrying our first grandchild."

Annie Ruth blushed when he mentioned her pregnancy.
Mr. Andrew's voice took on a fatherly tone. "Child, don't be
ashamed with me. I know this ain't the way you and your folks
planned things, but life doesn't always go like we want it to."
Mr. Andrew relaxed in the chair. "Victoria and I wanted a big
family, but she was sickly, and we were only blessed with one.
She would have been just as happy as I am about having a
grandchild."

Mr. Andrew waved his hand disapprovingly. "I ain't excusing
Curtis, cause he oughta waited until y'all were married, but he
young and smelling his musk. He love you, though." Mr. Andrew
looked around the room sadly. "Yes, Curtis sure love you, and it
is good to be loved." Mr. Andrew got up to leave. "Thank you,
Annie Ruth, for cleaning this room and taking care of Victoria's
things. I moved outta this room into the other bedroom after
she died. I couldn't take being in here without her."

Annie Ruth thought she saw tears in her father-in-law's eyes
as he left. *Miss Victoria died kinda young. But while she was alive,
she had a husband who really loved her.*

Annie Ruth tried to count her blessings. *I'm pregnant, and I'm
married. I might as well forget about Raymond. He's in the past. He
never loved me anyway. It's all over and done with. I ain't thinking
about him anymore.* In spite of her vow, there were still times
when her thoughts sneaked away from the reality of work and

responsibilities and she remembered the enchanting smile, sweet kisses in her parents' living room . . . Raymond.

That night, Annie Ruth and Curtis had been in bed almost an hour when he reached over and embraced her tenderly. "Sweetheart, you awake?"

"Yes, I dozed a little, and then I woke up. I ain't been able to go back to sleep. I think we went to bed too early."

"Well, I was hoping you'd be able to get some rest first, so we can make love." Curtis began to kiss her.

Annie Ruth didn't respond to his advances. "Please, Curtis, not tonight. Give me a little more time."

Curtis's voice edged with worry. "You sick?"

"No, I'm fine," Annie Ruth replied. "I just need a little more time."

"Annie Ruth, we been married almost a week, and we still ain't made love."

Annie Ruth laughed dryly. "We had sex one time, but I'm sho' nuff pregnant."

Curtis sighed wearily. "I love you, you know."

Annie Ruth pulled away from his embrace. "I know you do. Please, give me a little more time."

Curtis moved to his side of the bed and turned on his side. Annie Ruth gently stroked the tiny locket around her neck—a small reminder of her lost love.

The next morning, Annie Ruth was sitting on the front porch hemming a pair of curtains she'd made; Billie Lee drove up. She got out of the car with a large package in her hand. She started talking hurriedly before she reached the porch. "Annie Ruth, why ain't you called me? Aunt Maybelle came storming over to our house last Monday, ranting and raving about how foolish you'd been."

Billie Lee paused and caught her breath. "I was shocked, then shoot, I got mad. It hurt when y'all got married and didn't tell me anything!"

Annie Ruth felt herself grow warm with embarrassment. She avoided Billie Lee's eyes. "I'm sorry. I was ashamed." Annie Ruth folded the curtains, put them on her sewing box, and motioned to Billie Lee to sit down.

Billie Lee sat and gave her a searching look. "It's hard to believe you pregnant. What happened? You always wanted to go to college."

Annie Ruth looked out at the yard of her new home. "I didn't think straight. Curtis and I drank the beers Melvin Pittman gave us."

"You drank beer!" Billie Lee exclaimed. "Lenny drank both of ours."

Annie Ruth shook her head remorsefully. "I wish I'd used common sense. I was so depressed over Raymond that I didn't think clearly."

"I thought you had accepted the way things turned out between you and Raymond," Billie Lee said.

"I pretended to be doing that." Annie Ruth took a deep breath. "I never told you that I went to visit Raymond's mother the Friday afternoon before the prom."

"No, you didn't." Billie Lee leaned forward.

"She told me a lot more than I was prepared to deal with," Annie Ruth said. "She told me Raymond got to California safely and his sister got a job for him. And he got involved with another white girl right after he started to night school."

Surprise registered on Billie Lee's face. "You mean that

incident down here didn't scare him enough?"

Annie Ruth couldn't cover up the pain in her voice. "Evidently not, cause he's planning to marry this one."

Billie Lee peered at her questioningly. "Marry? I thought you always said he wanted to wait until he finished college and became a big time ball player."

Annie Ruth nodded. "Yeah, that's the line he used to give me. I guess he won't be able to be a ball player because of his knee. And he really love her."

"Hearing about that really hurt you," Billie Lee said sympathetically.

Lord have mercy! Yes, it did, Annie Ruth's heart cried. "Yeah, and I got my thoughts mixed up and call myself getting revenge on Raymond by having sex with Curtis."

Billie Lee looked at the package that she had been holding. "It's done, now. Try to count your blessings and go on with your life."

Annie Ruth nodded. "I'm trying to do that. But sometimes it get hard, though."

"Ain't no sense in crying over spilt milk, Annie Ruth."

Annie Ruth swallowed. "I know."

Billie Lee handed her the package. Annie Ruth thanked her and unwrapped it. "Billie Lee, you always so thoughtful. I'll be needing this material in a couple of months to make some maternity tops." She hugged Billie Lee. "Thanks again."

Billie Lee smiled. "You know you welcome. Polly Brown told me that she and her brothers and sisters have been over here helping Mr. Andrew and Curtis put in tobacco. She said you been working around this house like a maniac."

"She told you the truth," Annie Ruth said. "Working helps me keep my mind off of things."

"Well, you lighten up some," Billie Lee advised. "You need to think about the baby."

"Don't worry, I will."

Billie Lee sat up straight. "Now, we got another matter to get on the ball with."

Annie Ruth put the material back in the wrapping. "What's that?"

"My wedding, you gonna be my maid of honor. Aldonia, Lucinda and Edwina done been measured for their bridesmaids' dresses," Billie Lee said excitedly. "Granny and Aunt Maybelle need to measure you for your dress."

Annie Ruth averted her eyes. "Maybe you should ask someone else."

"Why?"

"Billie Lee, I'm a pregnant, married woman!"

Billie Lee replied firmly. "You ain't showing, yet. You're like my sister. And my wedding wouldn't be right without you. Since you're married, you'll be my matron of honor."

Annie Ruth said slowly. "If that's what you want, okay."

"I'm positive," Billie Lee said. "I'll come back after supper and take you to our house for measuring."

Annie Ruth suddenly felt better. Billie Lee's attitude seemed to brighten her day. "You don't have to do that. I can drive Mr. Andrew's car."

"No, I'll come get you," Billie Lee said. "I don't want you to try to make up some excuse."

When Annie Ruth and Billie Lee walked into Granny's house that evening, Mama was busy sewing. She didn't look up from her work. She just started right in. "Billie Lee been having a fit to have you in her wedding, Annie Ruth. It's her wedding, and if she ain't embarrassed, then I guess the rest of us have to go along with it."

Granny frowned at Mama. "Maybelle, the child done made a mistake, not committed a crime."

Annie Ruth felt so ashamed. *I'm sorry. I'm sorry, Mama. Oh, how I wish I could change things.*

Mama still didn't look up from her sewing. "You would think that a girl who got enough sense to graduate valedictorian would have enough sense not to get pregnant before she's married and finished college."

No one said anything else to Mama. Granny measured Annie Ruth, and then Annie Ruth quickly excused herself saying that she needed to get home early.

Granny hugged her. "Okay, but come back and visit me soon. Billie Lee and Lenny gonna move in the old Parker's house after they get married. Y'all won't be far apart." Granny smiled at Annie Ruth and Billie Lee. "Y'all always been like sisters. I want y'all to stay that way."

Annie Ruth said goodbye to Mama. She didn't look up from her sewing when she mumbled a reply. Granny walked with Annie Ruth and Billie Lee to the porch and stood waving as they left.

Billie Lee tried to make up for Mama's criticisms as she drove Annie Ruth home. "Don't think hard of Aunt Maybelle. She hurt and disappointed cause she always tried to teach us the right way."

Annie Ruth blinked hard. She'd start crying if she kept talking about Mama. "I understand how Mama feel. I ain't mad with her." She swallowed and quickly changed the subject. "I'm gonna can peaches tomorrow. Boy, Billie Lee, being a wife sure is a lotta work. You ready for it?"

Billie Lee nodded happily. "I sure am." She paused for a moment. "Annie Ruth, how is it?"

"How is what?"

Billie Lee glanced at Annie Ruth and then looked back at the road. "Sex, of course! I sure ain't talking about canning peaches."

Annie Ruth looked at the road, too. "Well, the first time is painful." Her voice became serious. "Unless you want to get pregnant on your wedding night, you better use a rubber or something."

"Lenny and I done talked about that. We gonna be careful for about two or three months, then we gonna start our family," Billie Lee said.

"Well, if y'all do, our firstborns won't be very far apart," Annie Ruth said. "That'll be nice."

"That will be nice," Billie Lee said and then moved on to her next question. "Do you climax the first time?"

Annie Ruth giggled. "You and Lenny really love each other. Everything will be all right."

"I hope so," Billie Lee said wistfully. "It's hard to believe that in a few weeks I'll be Mrs. Lenny Wright."

Billie Lee dropped Annie Ruth off at her house about a half hour before dusk. Billie Lee started to drive away and then stopped. "Annie Ruth," she called.

Annie Ruth turned. "What is it?"

Billie Lee leaned out the car window. "I meant to tell you, I went to town this morning after I visited you. Hootie like to broke her neck getting over to me to tell me that Raymond married that white girl last Saturday night."

Annie Ruth shrugged. "His mother said he planned to."

"Yeah, he turned into the marrying-kind awfully fast."

"Yeah, he did," Annie Ruth said. "I guess he love her. He just made a fool of me."

"It's in the past."

"It sure is," Annie Ruth said.

"Bye, Annie Ruth."

"Bye."

Annie Ruth walked into their house. *Good,* she thought, *Mr. Andrew done fell asleep in front of the T.V.* The bathroom door was closed, and she could hear Curtis inside taking a bath. Quietly, she eased into their bedroom and took a cigar box from her lingerie drawer. She reached around her neck and unclasped the locket. The thin delicate chain slipped gently through her fingers and into the opened box. It settled on top of several of Raymond's pictures and a couple of valentine and birthday cards that he had given her. Her steps were brisk as she headed outside. She got a shovel out of the shed and buried the box deep under a chinaberry tree.

Annie Ruth felt relieved. Now, that's over. *I ain't gonna waste anymore time thinking about Raymond Baldwin.* She put the shovel back into the shed and decided to take advantage of what was left of daylight by strolling to a nearby creek.

When she got to the creek, she sat down and inhaled the fragrance of the honeysuckles, custard apples, and coreopsis.

"You okay, sweetheart?"

Annie Ruth turned. Curtis was standing at the end of the path. "I didn't know you were behind me."

"I heard Billie Lee drive up while I was bathing," he said. "I got worried when you weren't in the house." Annie Ruth felt guilty. *Look at him, standing there looking so concerned. He trying so hard to be a good husband.*

Annie Ruth looked at the creek. "I just felt like taking a walk."

Curtis sat down beside her. "It's nice out here. It's so cool under the trees."

"Yeah." Annie Ruth nodded. "And the wildflowers smell so good."

"Uh-huh." Curtis said putting his arms around her.

Annie Ruth relaxed. *It feel good to have someone who really care about me. Curtis say he love me, and he always act like he does. One thing's for sure, he didn't fill my head with lies and run off like Raymond. I'm just as much to blame for my pregnancy as Curtis is. So I ain't got no reason to be mad with him.* She turned and kissed him.

"I love you," Curtis whispered.

They kissed again and in the coolness of their wildflower retreat, on the brink of gentle darkness, they consummated their marriage. Although the fruit of their first time was thriving in Annie Ruth's womb, they experienced for the first time the ultimate in intimate ecstasy.

After the consummation of their marriage, new times came into Annie Ruth's work-filled days: times when she looked forward to their conversations in their bedroom at night, times when she enjoyed Saturday evening rides to town and Sunday evening walks with Curtis, and times when Curtis's loving looks provoked happy smiles from her. There were even moments when Annie Ruth would look outside and see Curtis riding the tractor or doing some other farm chore and a feeling of warm contentment would wash over her growing body.

Billie Lee and Lenny got married on July 29, 1961. Their country church wedding was a lovely lavender and pink matrimonial festivity. Annie Ruth stood happily by her cousin as she took her vows. She was glad that Billie Lee had insisted that she participate.

Curtis was an usher, but being part of Billie Lee's wedding party didn't stop his admiring looks at his wife. Annie Ruth found herself returning his smile. Annie Ruth was glad that he stayed by her side as much as possible after the wedding. His presence made the side glances and smirks of the curious and gossip mongers a lot easier.

Annie Ruth's three brothers and her sister-in-law congratulated her and Curtis on their marriage and gave them a wedding gift of fifty dollars. Daddy greeted her and Curtis warmly; however, his warmth was not shared by his aloof wife. Mama seemed to be making sure that she steered clear of her daughter and new son-in-law during the rehearsal, the wedding, and reception.

Lucinda eased Annie Ruth off to the side during the reception. "Child, I been wanting to talk to you, but Curtis been sticking right under you. I had to get Mark to make up something and get him away from you."

Embarrassment warmed Annie Ruth's face. "I think he was afraid somebody would make a crack about us having to get married."

"And Curtis Lynch ain't gonna let nobody hurt his Annie Ruth's feelings," Lucinda finished Annie Ruth's explanation in a 'baby talk' voice.

Annie Ruth giggled. "Cut it out, Lucinda. I can't help it if my husband love me."

"Well, under the circumstances, it's a good thing that he

does," Lucinda said. "Shoot, Annie Ruth, how in the world did you let this happen?"

Annie Ruth blushed. "I made a mistake."

"Mistake! Foot! When I heard about it, I got mad." Lucinda folded her arms. "Child, you too smart for this, you should be getting ready to go to college in the fall."

"Lighten up, Lucinda," Annie Ruth said. "I shoulda kept my frock tail down like my mama taught me."

"Huh!" Lucinda unfolded her arms. "I ain't taking it that far."

Annie Ruth frowned. "Why did you say that?"

"Child, Mark and I been going all the way for over a year."

"And you ain't got pregnant!" Annie Ruth exclaimed.

Lucinda leaned forward. "Think! A-student, this is 1961. Ain't you heard of rubbers, diaphragms, and foam? There's even some kind of contraceptive pill."

Annie Ruth shrugged. "I never planned to go all the way before I married. Curtis and I lost our heads one time."

Lucinda raised her eyebrows. "You ain't gotta leave the gate to the cow pasture open but one time for the bull to get in."

"Tell me about it," Annie Ruth said. "One time and I got caught."

Lucinda pursed her lips smugly. "See, I never rode no high horses like you, Billie Lee, and Edwina. Think back, when y'all would be talking about being virgins on your wedding nights, you never heard me setting no high goals."

Annie Ruth looked thoughtful. "No, you never did."

"Nope, I didn't waste my time playing those innocent mind games," Lucinda said. "A lot of girls think that preparing and taking precautions before sex means you're whorish. They like to pretend that nice girls get carried away." Lucinda lowered her voice to a whisper. "While I was working for Dr. Avery I had him to fit me with a diaphragm. I ain't having no baby until I'm ready."

Lucinda grinned slyly. "If you and Curtis had taken precautions, you'd still be headed for college and giving Curtis a little to keep him happy while you were away."

Annie Ruth just stared at her friend and shrugged.

Lucinda's grin turned into a giggle. "One time and you got caught. Here I am been dishing it out of both drawer legs!" Lucinda elbowed Annie Ruth. "Child, my wedding dress is gonna be pure white!"

"Lucinda!"

Annie Ruth and Lucinda turned. Billie Lee gestured to Lucinda to come to her. *Thank God,* Annie Ruth sighed to herself. *That dang Lucinda was getting on my nerves. I know I was a fool, but I don't need her to keep rubbing it in.* She looked across the church yard. Her eyes met Mama's. But Mama's face twisted in a disgusted look, and she turned away. Annie Ruth swallowed and bit down on her lip. *I warned you. I told you to stop, and she taught you the safest way,* common sense reminded her. Annie Ruth reprimanded herself silently. *I shouldn't have been so careless!* She raised in her mind her foot and gave herself a swift mental kick. *Fool!*

Edwina and Dwight became husband and wife during a small, but lovely church ceremony in August. Lucinda became Mark's wife on the first Saturday in September. She was as radiant and beautiful as any bride in her delicate pure white apparel as she stood beside Mark in front of the church altar.

9

Motherhood

The month of September brought about a melancholy mood in Annie Ruth. Instead of going to college, she was four months pregnant and busy doing fall canning and freezing. She was thinking about her deferred plans while shopping for a crochet thread for her layette one Saturday afternoon.

"Annie Ruth! Child, you sure are big. Ain't you carrying twins?"

Annie Ruth turned around. Hootie Simpson was smirking at her.

Lord have mercy, everybody's got a cross to bear. It seems like Hootie is mine. "No, I ain't carrying twins," she said. "How are you, Hootie?"

"Just fine. I'm having a good time being a junior in high school." Hootie fluttered her eyelids and gestured to the girl standing next to her. "I been talking to Elizabeth. She's buying some things for c-o-l-l-e-g-e."

Annie Ruth winced at the word. Hootie's gaze swept over Annie Ruth's bulging middle. "I thought you'd be going to college, too. But I guess you got to stay home and be an old married woman."

"Hootie, the only thing I gotta do is stay black and die!" Annie Ruth snapped angrily.

"Huh!" Hootie threw her head in the air and strutted out of the store.

Elizabeth giggled. "Pay her no mind, Annie Ruth. Hootie always talk too much."

"I know," Annie Ruth said. "I shouldn't have said anything to her."

Elizabeth shifted the packages in her arms. "Things are going okay, huh? Aldonia fixed my hair this morning, and she told me you and Curtis are doing fine."

Annie Ruth took a more critical observation of her former schoolmate. Elizabeth's short hair had been attractively pressed and styled. She looked sophisticated and refined in her embroidered short-sleeve white blouse, with a wide patent leather belt around the waist of a straight grey linen skirt. She was slender, yet her figure still had curvaceous hips. And her tummy was so flat (and Annie Ruth's was so big!). Annie Ruth suddenly felt like a tall, clumsy elephant. "Yeah, we doing fine," she said.

Elizabeth waited until Annie Ruth had selected some crochet thread and paid for it. Then she walked with her out of the store.

Elizabeth paused on the sidewalk. "Annie Ruth, I'm glad I got to see you before I left for college. We ain't talked in a long time."

Annie Ruth nodded. "You seemed to not want to have much to say to me."

Elizabeth blushed. "I didn't like it cause Curtis took you to the prom instead of me. It's not like he led me on, though," she quickly added. "I figured you'd forget about Raymond one day and realize how much Curtis love you." Elizabeth averted her eyes from Annie Ruth's stomach. "I just didn't imagine it would happen so soon."

"Things did move pretty fast," Annie Ruth said.

"I better go. I still got a lot to do. I'm leaving for college tomorrow." Elizabeth looked at Annie Ruth shyly. "If you don't mind, tell Curtis bye for me."

Suddenly, Annie Ruth didn't feel so big and clumsy anymore. She felt like a young woman who was pregnant with the child of a young man who adored her. "Sure," she said. "I'll tell him. And Elizabeth . . ."

"Yes?"

"Good luck." Annie Ruth went on. "I hope you have a successful college career."

Elizabeth smiled graciously. "Thank you and good luck to you."

By the time Curtis finished his chores and came in to eat, Annie Ruth had prepared a Saturday evening supper of fried fish, cabbage slaw, baked beans, pear cobbler, and ice-cold lemonade.

Curtis surveyed the table of food. "Wow, I knew you could cook, but I didn't know you could throw-down like you been doing since we married."

Annie Ruth was pleased. "I was a good student, and I wanna be a good wife."

Curtis sat at the table. "Dad said he'll eat later. He went to visit Aunt Clara."

Annie Ruth joined him. "Okay."

They paused as Curtis said the grace. Annie Ruth watched him while he was serving himself. His face shone with an attractiveness that she hadn't noticed until Raymond's striking features had been swept away from her by two white girls.

Curtis looked at her. "Something wrong?"

Annie Ruth started serving herself. "No, I saw Hootie and Elizabeth in town."

Curtis started eating. "You didn't let that Hootie bother you did you? I know she ran-off her mouth."

"She wouldn't have been Hootie if she hadn't." Annie Ruth glanced at Curtis carefully. "Elizabeth's leaving for college tomorrow."

"That's good," Curtis said between bites.

Good. He enjoying his food. I hope he love me as much as he say he does. She got up and poured the lemonade. She put the pitcher in the refrigerator and then turned to her husband. "Elizabeth told me to tell you bye."

"That's nice," Curtis replied. "I'm glad y'all talked. She a real nice person."

Curtis went back to eating as if to make up for the time he'd spent talking. Annie Ruth was still standing. She smiled jubilantly to herself. Elizabeth was *definitely* only a friend to Curtis!

Curtis looked at her questioningly. "Come on, sweetheart, let's finish eating. You wanna go to the drive-in tonight?"

Annie Ruth's heart cut a happy step, and then she sat down. "I sure would."

Annie Ruth was pleasantly surprised when she answered a knock on the kitchen door a few days later and found her mother standing there. She resisted grabbing Mama and hugging her. She did allow her voice to express its joy. "Mama, I'm so glad to see you!"

Mama smiled shyly and walked in. Her arms were full of packages. She put them on the table. "It's good to see you, too. It's so quiet. I thought maybe you were napping."

"No, I was fixing to cook supper. Curtis and Mr. Andrew are in the field." Annie Ruth motioned to a chair at the table. "Have a seat, Mama."

I already cooked the greens. It won't take me long to cook supper. I can take some time to sit and talk with Mama. Annie Ruth sat in front of her mother.

Mama pointed at the packages. "I bought some diapers, flannel material, and crochet thread. Billie Lee told me you done already started crocheting some things."

Annie Ruth felt happiness slide over her like throwing on a sweater on a cool day. "Thanks, Mama. I been crocheting, and I made all my maternity clothes."

"You welcome," Mama said. "Andrew always brag on you about being a good wife. And Sid say you always be working hard when he drop by." Mama looked around. "This house is clean and neat like it was when Victoria was alive."

Annie Ruth stared at Mama. "This is the first time you visited me or we talked since I got married."

Mama looked away sheepishly. "I knew you were okay. Your daddy kept a check on you. I'd sneak a peek at you at church."

Mama looked at Annie Ruth. Her eyes seemed to beg for understanding. "I was so scared for you and Billie Lee. I didn't want y'all to wind up like a lot of Negro girls, being smothered in poverty and raising your young'uns in poor conditions."

Annie Ruth felt a tightness in her chest. She knew Mama had stated a sad truth. Without much thinking, she could name lots of young Negro women living in Tobacco County struggling in poverty. She propped her arm up and rested her head in her hand.

Mama started crying but she kept talking. "Life ain't easy for Negroes. That's why Sid and I always wanted our children to get an education, so y'all could make it."

Annie Ruth took her arm down and touched her stomach. *Being a mama ain't easy. Mama had a right to be scared. Mama ain't pushy. She just a good mother. Like I wanna be.* "I understand, Mama, but things gonna work out. Curtis and I'll make it."

Mama's voice became apologetic. She wiped her eyes with a handkerchief from her purse. "I'm sorry about the way I been acting. I was really mad with myself cause I failed you."

Annie Ruth replied quickly. "You ain't ever failed me. This whole thing was my doing."

Mama gave her eyes a final wipe and smiled mischievously. "I suspect Curtis had something to do with it, too."

"Mama!" Annie Ruth got up and hugged Mama. "I missed you, Mama."

Curtis looked both surprised and pleased when he found his mother-in-law sitting at their kitchen table and talking to Annie Ruth. "Hey, Miss Maybelle, glad to see you."

Mama smiled. "Hey, Curtis, thanks for making me feel welcome. I'm gonna help Annie Ruth make baby clothes."

Curtis sat down at the table. "Good," he said looking at Annie Ruth's stomach. "Ain't much longer. February will be here in no time."

"Yeah, it will," Mama agreed.

Annie Ruth inspected the diapers her mother had bought. "Time may seem to be moving fast for y'all, but it ain't to me. It doesn't seem like I'll ever get back to my regular size."

February 7, 1962. Annie Ruth was struggling in the delivery room of Rail City's Colored Hospital. The room was cool but she was sweating. She had heard so many women talk about how you soon forget the pains of childbirth but she was positive she would never forget the excruciating pain she was enduring.

"Come on, Annie Ruth, push. You a strong, healthy, farm girl," Nurse Vaughn said standing near the delivery table. "You can do it. Push that baby out so your family can stop worrying."

Between gasps for breath, Annie Ruth forced herself to push. She tried to concentrate on the nurse's kindly voice to ease the pain.

Nurse Vaughn must have known Annie Ruth needed her to keep talking because she didn't stop. "I was raised up on a farm like you. I picked a lot of cotton, too." She wiped Annie Ruth's forehead. "Remember how you pick like a maniac in the morning so you can make a hundred and fifty pounds by twelve o'clock? Then you ain't worried cause you know you gonna have over two hundred by 'knocking off' time."

Nurse Vaughn leaned a little closer to Annie Ruth. "Remember how you feel right before 'knocking off time,' hot and tired and sweaty, and you have to push yourself to keep going. Come on, Child, push, then you'll be ready to knock off."

Annie Ruth struggled even more. She wanted to do what Nurse Vaughn said. She wanted it real bad. At that moment, however, she didn't care if she ever had another baby again.

The doctor spoke encouragingly. "Push Annie Ruth, you're doing good, now."

"Yeah," Nurse Vaughn said. "She doing good. She hot and tired and ready to knock off."

The baby's scream sounded like the most beautiful music

Annie Ruth had ever heard. "You and Curtis have got a fine girl." The doctor said, putting the screaming bloody baby on her stomach. *I got a little girl. I'm really a mother!*

"Patricia Victoria Lynch, ain't she beautiful?" Curtis exclaimed, pressing closer to the nursery window.

"She sure is," Billie Lee, Miss Maybelle, and Miss Carrie said unanimously.

"I'm glad y'all named her Victoria for your mother," Dad said.

"She a cute little thing," Aldonia said.

"Yeah, she gonna be another foxy Watson girl," Lenny predicted.

Mr. Sid grinned proudly. "She sho nuff a Watson."

"True, but she a Lynch, too," Curtis said.

"Yeah, but there's one sure sign of a Watson," Mr. Sid said.

"What's that, Mr. Sid?" Curtis asked.

Mr. Sid moved closer to the nursery window and pointed to the baby's hand. "Don't y'all see that tiny survival kit in my grandchild's hand!"

Everybody started laughing. "Okay, okay, Mr. Sid!" Curtis said between chuckles.

Curtis touched the damp collar of Annie Ruth's nightgown. "Miss Maybelle, Annie Ruth's wet with sweat again, and you changed her and the bed less than an hour ago."

Miss Maybelle had just come back from emptying the bedpan. She put the cleaned pan under the bed and then peered at Annie Ruth. She looked just as worried as Curtis felt. "That's a good sign. At least she's sweating the fever out."

Curtis shook his head. "She oughta be back in the hospital."

Miss Maybelle patted him on the shoulder. "I don't feel the best about it myself. But, the doctor keep saying she'll be all right at home, and it's gonna be a few days before the flu wear off."

"She seemed fine when she first came home," Curtis said. "Maybe I didn't keep the house warm enough."

"Curtis, you keep enough wood cut to warm two houses," Miss Maybelle replied. "And I been here taking care of her."

"Then what went wrong?" Curtis asked.

"She had a setback," Miss Maybelle said. "It ain't unusual for a woman to get sick after having a baby."

Curtis was trying to ignore the fear that was trying to take hold of him. "The doctor's right, the flu will wear off in a few days."

Miss Maybelle straightened the covers on the bed. "Uh-huh, we gotta keep praying for her."

"I'm gonna sit with her tonight," Curtis said.

"Curtis, you need to get some rest," Miss Maybelle said. "You done took on that job at the mill, plus you still help your daddy on the farm. It's too much."

"I'll be okay, Miss Maybelle. You gotta stay in the other room with the baby. I'll probably nap a little in the chair."

"Okay," Miss Maybelle said. "I guess you right."

Annie Ruth comprehended only snatches of the whispered conversation between her husband and mother. She felt terrible, didn't seem to have an ounce of energy. She slept, but her body didn't feel rested. If only she could rest . . .

"Annie Ruth, Annie Ruth."

Annie Ruth tried to clear her flu-dazed thoughts in order to identify the gentle voice that was calling to her. She felt herself drifting away from the weakness and infection that filled her body. Slowly, she drifted into a state of peaceful euphoria.

"Annie Ruth, Annie Ruth," the gentle voice called again.

"You look like me; except you a little older, and you so shiny," Annie Ruth said.

Annie Ruth had never heard such a pretty laugh. "Don't look so surprised," the gentle voice said. "You've heard that you are the spitting image of me since you were a little bitty thing."

"Aunt Angela?"

"You are a lot like me; however, you've got a lot more strength to stand up to the meanness of the world than I ever had," Angela said. "You've got to continue to be strong. Don't start giving up now."

"I'm so weak and tired, though," Annie Ruth whispered.

"Hold on, you can make it," Aunt Angela advised. "Look!"

Annie Ruth saw Patricia. "My baby."

"Billie Lee was my baby," Aunt Angela said.

Annie Ruth said, "Billie Lee a grown woman, now."

"I only knew her as a baby, but you'll be able to see your daughter grow up. Look again," Aunt Angela told her.

"That's Curtis and me when we were children." Annie Ruth giggled. "Look at him shelling peanuts for me while I stuff my face."

"You've been married to him for months, and you still haven't told him you love him. Do you love him?"

"Yes, yes, I love him," Annie Ruth replied.

Aunt Angela's voice sounded with authority. "You and Curtis

were destined to be together. Tell him that you love him.”

“I’m so tired,” Annie Ruth said weakly.

“Rest now, you can make it,” Aunt Angela commanded gently. “The Watsons’ strength is in you.”

Annie Ruth left euphoria and went back into her sick body. This time, though, she slept soundly. She rested.

The next morning she awakened abruptly. Her body had returned to its normal temperature, and she could feel the strength easing back into her limbs.

“Curtis.”

Curtis jumped. “Annie Ruth, you feeling better?”

“Yes, much better.” Annie Ruth raised up. “Honey, you shoulda brought the roll-away bed in here.”

“Don’t worry about me. I’m okay.” Curtis looked anxious. “You feeling better for real?”

Annie Ruth sat up straighter in the bed. “Yes, for real. Where’s Patricia?”

“Your Mama got her in the other room.”

Annie Ruth rubbed her eyes. “Oh, yeah, the doctor did say to keep her away from me until I got well.”

Curtis touched her forehead. “Thank goodness your fever done gone!”

Annie Ruth touched his hand. “Curtis, I love you.”

“Huh?”

“I love you. I’m your wife. Can’t I tell you I love you?”

Happiness covered Curtis’s face. “Great! I mean, yes, please, tell me anytime! You know I always loved you.”

Annie Ruth started to get up. “I wanna take a bath and eat a good breakfast. I’m so glad to be feeling better.”

Curtis got up and helped her. “Take it easy, sweetheart. Don’t rush yourself.” Curtis looked at her shyly. “Annie Ruth, do you really love me?"

"I really do love you, Curtis."

Curtis hugged her. "I been waiting so long to hear you say it. It's worth every minute of the wait."

"Y'all keep that up, and I'll soon be a grandpa again," Mr. Andrew said, peeking in the door. "Annie Ruth, glad to see you up, child. You gave us all a scare."

"What you say, Andrew? Annie Ruth up?" Mama called from the other room.

"Yes, I'm up, Mama. Come in here and bring the baby."

Mama rushed over with the baby in her arms. "Thank God, daughter, it is good to have you back from the other side."

Annie Ruth stared at her infant daughter. "It's good to be back, Mama."

10

Hard Times

It was the last of March, Annie Ruth's good health had returned, and she was feeling wonderful. She looked around Billie Lee's small living room. Her mother, grandmother, aunt, cousins, and friends had given her a beautiful honor by celebrating her seven-week-old daughter's birth with a lovely shower.

Mary Joyce, who was sitting next to her, whispered, "Where's that unhappy young lady who was standing in the ladies room at church in June?"

Annie Ruth answered, "I sent her packing."

Annie Ruth could tell Mary Joyce liked her answer by the way she laughed. As though she was saying, "I'm glad! I'm glad!" *And shoot! I'm glad, too,* Annie Ruth thought. *I ain't got time for moping around. I got a life to live!*

Mary Joyce turned toward Lucinda and reached for the baby on her lap. "Lucinda, let me hold Patricia for a while."

"She been holding her the whole time," Aldonia said. "She need to let somebody else hold that baby."

Lucinda gave Mary Joyce the baby. "Well, Edwina's pregnant, and Billie Lee is trying to get pregnant. Excusing Aldonia, I'll be the only one that ain't a mother soon."

"Yeah, but you a married woman, Aldonia ain't," Billie Lee said. "You the one choosing not to be a mother."

"Yeah, I am. And I ain't getting pregnant no time soon."

"She don't want a baby cause she wanna have extra money to buy pretty clothes and wigs," Annie Ruth teased.

Lucinda stood up and modeled her new outfit and wig playfully. "Wigs are the in-thing this year." She touched her long store-bought hair. "See, the Watson family ain't the only Negro women in Tobacco County with hair long enough to sling at the menfolks!"

"Act like a married woman, Lucinda," Mama advised from the kitchen where she, Granny, and Aunt Florence were preparing refreshments.

"That's right. Marriage vows ain't nothing to take lightly," Aunt Florence said.

"Don't get uptight, Miss Maybelle and Miss Florence, I'm just cutting-the-fool," Lucinda said.

"Lucinda, you a woman ahead of her time," Edwina theorized.

Granny started serving ice cream and cake. She glanced at Lucinda mischievously. "She one of a kind. cause I helped her Mama's midwife when she was born. And I know they broke the mold after they made her!"

Lucinda beat everybody laughing. "That confirms it," she said. "I know I'm special!"

After the shower was over, Billie Lee drove Annie Ruth home and helped her take her gifts inside. Annie Ruth sensed that she was in no hurry to return to her house, so she invited Billie Lee to visit with her. Annie Ruth put the bassinet in the kitchen, but Billie Lee wanted to hold Patricia while Annie Ruth cooked supper.

"You got some nice baby gifts," Billie Lee said.

Annie Ruth put on a pot of rice and a pot of blackeyed peas. "Yes, I sure appreciate everything."

Billie Lee looked at Patricia. "This little angel is getting sleepy," she said. Her voice saddened. "Wonder why I ain't got pregnant, Annie Ruth? We been trying four months."

Annie Ruth grabbed a large plastic container of chicken out of the refrigerator as she spoke. "It's gonna happen. Might be good if y'all had time to build your new house anyway."

"I don't wanna wait long. Granny gave us some land, but we still gotta save a down payment." Billie Lee gazed at Patricia. "A baby will keep me from being lonely while Lenny's away working on the railroad gang."

Annie Ruth started preparing the chicken for frying. "Maybe you need a job to help you bide your time."

"I done got one. Miss Helen Bostic asked me to wait on her mother-in-law the other day when I was in their store," Billie Lee said. "She said Miss Gertrude told her about how good I waited on her last winter."

Annie Ruth put on a skillet of grease. "I heard she got cancer."

"Yeah, she real sick. I don't mind, though. I like waiting on folks. If I'd went to college I woulda been a nurse."

Annie Ruth started frying the chicken. "Working will probably help you to relax and stop worrying about getting pregnant. Then it will happen."

"I hope so."

Curtis came into the kitchen for a glass of water. He greeted Annie Ruth and Billie Lee warmly. After inquiring about the baby shower, he kissed Annie Ruth on the cheek and left.

Billie Lee said wistfully, "Curtis is always so easy going and loving to you and the baby. He need to give Lenny some lessons on how to treat a wife."

Annie Ruth turned away from her cooking. "Things okay with you and Lenny?" she asked.

Billie Lee blushed. "Yeah, I'm just being a little sensitive. Lenny get moody sometimes, that's all."

Annie Ruth nodded. "Curtis do, too, sometimes, but I don't let it bother me, cause I know he just be worried about the farm and making a living."

"I know. It ain't the usual worrying about making a living with Lenny, though," Billie Lee said. "He got a lot of anger pent up in him and sometimes he can't handle it."

"Huh?" Annie Ruth asked.

Billie Lee stood up quickly and put the sleeping baby in the bassinet. "Forget what I said, Annie Ruth. I better go."

"I was hoping you was gonna stay for supper," Annie Ruth said.

Billie Lee picked up her purse. "Thanks, but I wanna finish some sewing before I start to work on Monday."

Annie Ruth stood behind the screen door and watched Billie Lee leave. *What is it? Why she jump up and leave like that?*

Billie Lee felt a tightness in the bottom of her stomach as she approached Miss Bostic's house. *Now, I hope this old lady is as nice as her daughter-in-law, cause Lord knows the last thing I need is to have to work for some mean old white woman.*

Miss Helen opened the kitchen door as soon as Billie Lee knocked on it. "Come on in, Billie Lee," she said.

Billie Lee stood in the kitchen and listened to Miss Helen's instructions. "Ruby Walker comes over two days a week and does the major cleaning. And I fix Mother Bostic's meals on weekends," Miss Helen explained. "She'll need you to take care of her and fix her meals during the week." Miss Helen picked up her purse. "I'll be at the store. If you need anything, call us."

Billie Lee walked through the richly furnished house. Miss Bostic was in the first bedroom. She looked very small lying under the lilac bed covers, her white hair fanned over a pillow. She raised her head slowly. "You must be Billie Lee."

"Yes, ma'am."

"I hear you're a good worker. That's good because I haven't had any good help since Gertrude got sick and had to quit."

"I aim to do a good job," Billie Lee said.

Miss Bostic's gaze swept over Billie Lee. "Gertrude told me that you graduated from high school last May and had a lovely July wedding."

"Yes, ma'am, I did," Billie Lee said, smiling.

"That's nice. You're a pretty girl, too."

"Thank you, ma'am."

Miss Bostic sat up in the bed carefully. "Before you help me with my bath, I want you to read to me from the Bible." She pointed to a Bible on the dresser. "My eyes get so tired. It's easier just to let somebody else read."

Billie Lee got the Bible. "What you want me to read?"

Miss Bostic propped herself up with a pillow. "Read Psalm 42. I'm feeling prayerful."

After Billie Lee fixed and served Miss Bostic her supper that evening, Miss Bostic asked her to take her for a ride before she went home. Billie Lee immediately fell in love with her shiny 1959 Cadillac.

"Close that back door, Billie Lee. I'm going to sit up front,"

Miss Bostic said when Billie Lee opened the back door for her.

"You gonna sit up front?" Billie Lee asked.

"Sure, I can talk to you easier if I'm sitting next to you," Miss Bostic said.

Billie Lee felt comfortable and relaxed as she drove Miss Bostic's big fine car. She sighed to herself. *Thank God Miss Bostic is a nice lady. I would've never thought a Southern-reared white woman could be so pleasant to work for. I'm glad cause I got enough unpleasant things to deal with.*

On the third Sunday in April, Annie Ruth kept hoping that Billie Lee would come in during church services. They hadn't seen each other for a couple of weeks. She had been busy with the baby and housework. Billie Lee had been busy with her housework and her job. Granny had told her that Billie Lee was enjoying her job.

Granny had cackled with amusement as she talked about Billie Lee's job when she was visiting. "Annie Ruth, I'm glad Billie Lee's got a job. It helps her bide her time while Lenny's away working." Granny reached for Patricia. "Maybe it'll keep her from worrying about getting pregnant."

Annie Ruth handed her the baby. Granny adjusted Patricia on her shoulder and went on. "I saw her and Miss Bostic out riding the other day while I was downtown. Billie Lee was driving that fine automobile like she was just as rich as Miss Bostic!"

Annie Ruth laughed with Granny and then frowned. "Granny, you ever notice anything different about Billie Lee?"

Granny looked thoughtful. "No, I can't say I have."

"Well," Annie Ruth said, "sometimes, she seem a little sad."

Granny patted the baby on the back gently and spoke in a low serious tone. "Married life ain't always easy. You girls done made your choices. Life ain't always good time and laughter."

"I know, Granny."

"Don't go dipping in Billie Lee's business," Granny advised. "Ever since y'all been young'uns you been protective of her. She a grown woman now."

"Yeah, you right, Granny," Annie Ruth said.

But that third Sunday in April, Annie Ruth was finding that it was a lot easier to say not to worry than to do. The choir didn't even sound right without Billie Lee's talented voice sounding out beside her. *I gotta check on her.* After church, she quickly served dinner, fed the baby, and cleaned up the kitchen. Then she went to visit Billie Lee.

When she got to Billie Lee's house, she sat in the car out front for a few minutes. Everything seemed so still and quiet. It was a warm Sunday afternoon, but none of the windows were open. *Billie Lee probably not home, cause she like to open her windows and doors and let the fresh air blow through the screens.*

She noticed Billie Lee's car. *She and Lenny probably gone off in Lenny's truck. Well, Patricia and I'll just knock on the door anyway and make sure.*

She got the baby out of the car and went to the front door. She was startled when the door opened after her first knock. The curtains were drawn, and it took Annie Ruth a while to focus her eyes in the dim light. Billie Lee was standing in front of her, holding an icepack over her left eye.

Annie Ruth clutched Patricia to her. "Lord have mercy, Billie Lee!" she said, rushing in.

Billie Lee closed the door and motioned to Annie Ruth to have a seat on the couch.

Annie Ruth's mind quickly went to work. *So, that's it. That's why she been acting so funny. Lenny, how could you?*

Billie Lee kept the ice pack to her eye as she sat next to Annie Ruth. She gave a sardonic laugh. "I hope I don't sweat too much wearing long sleeves next week in this spring weather."

Annie Ruth grimaced at the sight of Billie Lee's bruised arms. "How long this been going on?"

Billie Lee leaned back on the sofa. "Just a couple of months. I knew Lenny had a temper, but I wouldn't have ever dreamed he could be so mean to me."

Billie Lee looked at Annie Ruth sadly. "I love him so much, Annie Ruth."

"I know you do, but he ain't got a right to treat you like this," Annie Ruth said. "What y'all argue about?"

"He got mad cause I asked him why he came home so late Saturday night when his gang got into Rail City Saturday morning. I knew they had cause his bossman called around noon to tell Lenny what time they were gonna leave back out Monday morning. So, I asked him what time the men had come in," Billie Lee replied. "Lenny said I ain't got no business trying to check up on him."

Annie Ruth put the baby on her shoulder. "You gotta stand up to him."

Billie Lee shook her head sadly. "He jumped on me one time cause he said I didn't iron his favorite shirt good enough."

Annie Ruth spoke in a firm voice. "Don't let him keep walking over you. You gotta demand respect."

Billie Lee took the ice pack away from her eye. "He even says I don't like to party enough. He says I oughta be more fun-loving like Lucinda."

Annie Ruth tried not to stare at Billie Lee's eye.

How could Lenny beat her when she love him so much?

"Ain't nothing wrong with you, Billie Lee," she said. "I thought Lenny knew that better than anyone else."

Billie Lee put the icepack back to her eye. "Sometimes, I wonder if I deserve to be treated better. Lenny is a good provider. He pay all the bills. We're saving for a down payment on a house. He leave it up to me to decide whether I save my money or spend it."

Annie Ruth shook her head. "No matter what, he ain't got no right to beat you. I wouldn't put up with no man beating me."

Billie Lee tried to make her sore-looking lips smile. "I pity anybody who try to beat you. I gotta learn to be that way, too."

"Ask his folks to talk to him," Annie Ruth suggested.

"No, his mama and daddy and all his sisters think so highly of him. They'd probably blame me for doing something wrong," Billie Lee said.

"Get Daddy to talk to him then," Annie Ruth said.

Billie Lee answered her hurriedly. "No, I don't want Uncle Sid or the rest of the family to know about this. Don't you even tell Curtis. I the one married Lenny. I the one gotta deal with him."

Annie Ruth remembered Granny's advise about not dipping in. "Okay, if that's the way you want it," she said.

The next morning, when Annie Ruth and Curtis got up at their usual 5 a.m., Mr. Andrew was already up and tending to the early morning chores.

Annie Ruth tried to keep her mind on the affairs of her

home and not on Billie Lee's problem. She was glad that Curtis walked into the kitchen as soon as she finished fixing breakfast. She hoped that talking with him would keep her mind off Billie Lee.

She put two plates of food on the table and sat down. Curtis joined her.

"Dad said he'll be in in a little while," Curtis said.

"I'm keeping his food warm," Annie Ruth said.

Curtis said grace and then paused before starting to eat. "Sweetheart, how Dad been acting to you?"

Annie Ruth thought for a moment before speaking. "He been kinda quiet. Lately he just been holding the baby a lot. He ain't even been teasing me or talking to me that much."

Curtis nodded while he was chewing. He swallowed and said, "He been real quiet with me, too. Whenever I ask him what's wrong, he say 'nothing.'"

"Maybe he ain't feeling good," Annie Ruth suggested. "You know how he and Daddy would rather risk death than to admit they sick."

Curtis sighed. "I don't know what's wrong. He been acting like he worried about something for a month or so. Even when we working together he won't talk to me like he used to."

The slamming of the screen door silenced Curtis. Mr. Andrew walked in and headed to the bathroom to wash his hands without saying a word to Curtis or Annie Ruth. Just then the baby started crying, so Annie Ruth went and got her. When she returned to the kitchen, Curtis was trying to talk with his father.

"I think we gonna have a good corn crop. Don't you think, Dad?"

"Maybe."

Curtis kept trying. "Well, the plowing and planting are moving along smoothly."

"Uh-huh."

Curtis gave up and went back to eating. When he finished, he said, "I better go so I can get as much as I can done this morning."

When Mr. Andrew didn't say anything, Annie Ruth said, "I hope you gonna quit the evening work at the mill soon. Y'all got so much to do on the farm."

"I'm gonna quit in about two weeks." Curtis touched Annie Ruth gently on the shoulder and left.

Curtis look so worried. I hope Mr. Andrew is all right.

Mr. Andrew finished his breakfast slowly. When he finished, he looked at Annie Ruth. "Annie Ruth, I love you like my own daughter. I ain't gotta tell you how much I love my granddaughter. I want you to always remember that I love y'all."

Annie Ruth really appreciated how nice Mr. Andrew had been to her. He had shown her and Patricia so much love until it was easy for her to be fond of him. "We love you, too."

Mr. Andrew smiled weakly, got up from the table and went outside. He came back about an hour before noon and went to his bedroom. He went back outside again before Annie Ruth was ready to serve their dinner. When Curtis came in a few minutes later, Annie Ruth had the table set and the food ready.

"Good, you right on time. Go get your daddy, so we can eat. He came in for a while, but he went back out."

Curtis frowned at the sound of her words. "Sweetheart, whatever is worrying Dad, it's eating him up in—"

Curtis's words were cut off by the sound of a shotgun. Curtis ran out. Annie Ruth was right behind. There wasn't anything unusual in the yard, so they hurried to the barn. Mr. Andrew was slumped on the ground. Most of his head had been blown away by the gunshot he'd fired into his mouth. His mutilated body and the area around it was covered with blood.

Annie Ruth started screaming and crying. *Lord have mercy! This can't be happening. God, please keep Mr. Andrew alive!*

"Dad! Dad! Dad!" Curtis dropped to his knees beside Mr. Andrew and began to sob uncontrollably. Annie Ruth put her hand over her mouth and got herself together enough to run back to the house and call the ambulance at the colored hospital. Mr. Andrew was taken there and pronounced dead on arrival.

Curtis found the note in his father's room:

> My Dear Son,
>   I'm sorry to leave you like this. But I got too many bills, and I can't pay them. Take care of your family and do the best you can.
>   I love you,
>   Dad

He read it several times during the night while he sat by the window in his and Annie Ruth's bedroom. Annie Ruth had insisted that he let her leave a small lamp on after she went to bed. The lamp emitted only a tiny amount of light, just enough for him to make out the words of the note. Inside he felt small and weak, like the dim light.

Death wasn't a stranger to him, but he didn't find it familiar. It had taken Mom slowly, and had snatched Dad in a cruel way. *Dad, I love you, too. You were a good father. You always had time to listen to me and help me. You taught me so much, how to catch a baseball, how to ride a bike, how to drive, and how to farm.*

I remember how you, Mom and I used to walk across our fields. You used to be so proud. You'd say, "Son, your mom and I done worked hard to have this farm to pass on to you." I always felt so proud to hear you say those words cause I wanted to be a big farmer just like you.

You were always there for me. When Mom died, you became both my mother and my father. You didn't even get angry when I got Annie Ruth pregnant. You said, "I'm disappointed in you, Son. But, I'll stand by you."

You even went with me to tell Annie Ruth's parents about her pregnancy and our marriage. You never made Annie Ruth or me feel bad about the mistake we made. You gave us your love and your help. That's the way you were, a loving and caring father. Dad! Dad! I still need you!

Suddenly it was morning. Curtis felt Annie Ruth touching his arm. "Curtis, darling, come and eat your breakfast," she said. "We gotta meet Miss Clara so we can plan the funeral."

Hardly knowing what he did, Curtis followed her to the kitchen.

A lot of people came to the wake for Mr. Andrew. Annie Ruth wiped her tears and stared sadly at the coffin. *Mr. Andrew was so nice to me. I loved him like a second father. I know I'm gonna miss him. He and Daddy were so much alike. Both of them so proud to be big time Negro farmers. Daddy's the biggest, blackest farmer in Tobacco County. Mr. Andrew was the second biggest.*

Mr. Andrew's only sister, Mrs. Clara Lynch Phillips, came in and stood by the coffin. "Brother," she said. "You didn't have to do this. The Lord would have seen you through. Oh-oh, Lord." Miss Clara started wailing. "My husband's dead, my parents are dead, and now my only brother's taken his life.

Lord, have mercy! Pray friends! Pray for the Lord to help me stand this burden!"

Annie Ruth felt bad already, but Miss Clara's wailing made her feel even worse. Thank goodness, Billie Lee knew what to do. She started singing. *Father in heaven, help me. Life's done hit me hard, and I'm crying. Father in heaven help me.*

Miss Clara joined in tearfully. *Father in heaven, help me. Father in heaven, help me.*

Annie Ruth and everybody else started singing too. Afterwards, Miss Clara's son, Rev. Moses Phillips, said the Lord's Prayer.

Mama was sitting on Annie Ruth's left, Curtis on her right. Annie Ruth gave Patricia to Mama so she could comfort Curtis. Rev. Moses and Mary Joyce moved closer to Miss Clara to comfort her. Daddy was standing near the coffin. He placed his hand gently at the head of it. Then he turned and walked away slowly, his face frozen in a solemn mourning mask.

Annie Ruth put her arm around Curtis and watched Daddy. He wasn't crying. *Daddy probably done all his crying Tuesday morning. He don't know I peeped in the barn and saw him crying while he was shoveling up the bloody fleshy dirt where Mr. Andrew killed himself. I walked away without saying anything cause I figured Daddy needed time to grieve by himself.*

Curtis moaned and leaned closer. Annie Ruth tightened her arm and took his hand with her other hand. *Life's done burdened me down, and I'm crying. Father in heaven help me.*

The day after Mr. Andrew's funeral, Annie Ruth and Curtis went to the bank to check on their financial affairs. Daddy and Miss Clara went with them. *God, please don't let us lose our farm.* Annie Ruth clutched the baby to her breast and looked at Curtis nervously. But Curtis was staring blankly as the very young white banker flipped through the pages of a ledger. Daddy and Miss Clara, looking on, seemed as worried as Annie Ruth felt.

When the young banker started talking, Annie Ruth thought his voice sounded as if he was clearing the bank's responsibility in Mr. Andrew's suicide. "Andrew is behind five thousand dollars in his payments. He'd been paying well this year, but he had gotten behind too far previously to catch up." The banker cut his eyes at Curtis. "I understand y'all had a good harvest last fall. But, Andrew's financial troubles started four years ago during Victoria's long illness. He had to mortgage his farm in order to borrow enough money to pay her big medical bills." The banker's smile looked like he thought he was being so nice. "We've been trying to work with him, but he had a hard year in '59 and a few setbacks in '60. The banker shrugged. "I tried to tell Andrew that there ain't a cure for cancer. And he might as well just make his woman comfortable instead of running to Jacksonville and up North to those expensive Yankee doctors."

'Make his woman comfortable.' The phrase echoed in Annie Ruth's mind. She didn't like the sound of it.

Daddy leaned forward and looked at the white banker. He spoke in a firm voice. "*Mr.* Andrew loved his *wife, Mrs.* Victoria. He tried to do the best he could, like any man."

The banker made no reply. He just raised his eyebrows and leaned back in his chair. He looked down at the ledger, and when he looked up again he directed his attention to Curtis. "Considering what happened to Andrew and all, we're going to give you ten days to come up with the five thousand dollars. Of course, your next payment will be due at the first of next month."

The banker smiled another of his ain't-I-so-nice smiles. "If you can't make it, Curtis, don't worry. There are several business-men who'd love to buy your farm and let you stay on and work it. You got a reputation for being a hard-working boy."

As soon the banker said "boy," Daddy got up out of his seat. "He'll *have* the money," he said to the banker. Then he beckoned to the rest of them. "Come on y'all."

After they got outside the bank, Curtis began to explain their money situation to Daddy. "Mr. Sid, I appreciate you taking up for me in front of that banker, but I ain't got five thousand dollars. We ain't even got the money for the payment that's coming up on the first."

"We used the little money Dad had saved and the little we had saved from my working at the mill, plus some money Aunt Clara gave us, to pay for Dad's funeral. His insurance wouldn't pay since he committed suicide."

Daddy nodded. "I figured that already. I'll get the money for you out of me and Maybelle's account."

Curtis shook his head. "No, Mr. Sid, I can't let you do that."

Miss Clara touched Curtis's arm. "Please, Curtis, Andrew took his life in fear of losing his farm. Please, let Sid give you the money, and I'll help you with the monthly payments until y'all get on your feet."

Annie Ruth didn't even want to have to think about losing her home. And it just didn't seem right that Mr. Andrew had to almost lose his farm in order to provide good medical care for Mrs. Victoria. "Curtis, Miss Clara's right. We can't let Mr. Andrew's life be lost in vain."

Daddy tried to make Curtis feel better about taking the money. "Most of it is money that I saved for Annie Ruth's college expenses anyway. I done sent all the rest of my children to college. Just look at it as y'all getting the money that was hers anyway."

Curtis stuck his hands in his pockets. "It'll be years before we can pay you back."

"I ain't expecting y'all to pay me back. I'm giving it to y'all."

"Curtis," Annie Ruth said tenderly. "Take the money, please, honey."

Ten days later, Annie Ruth sat beside Curtis and watched him hand five thousand dollars to the banker. Curtis looked so sad. *Curtis told me he feels like a leech, like he done sucked out Daddy's blood and is giving it to the banker.* She shifted the baby in her lap. *I tried to say something positive to him, but Lord, have mercy, I feel that way, too. I feel like we leeches, dependent on Daddy and Miss Clara. Please God, help us to make it to harvest time so we can pay our bills.*

Several weeks after Mr. Andrew's death, Annie Ruth was thinking about how their lives had changed. *Married life had gotten to be pleasant and comfortable after I got over Raymond and started loving Curtis, and had Patricia. Now, hard times done set in, and Curtis and I don't see any relief from our money problems. Curtis and I didn't even use to argue with each other. Now we snap at each other about the least thing. If I don't have a meal on the table when he think I should, he get pissed off, and say I was probably talking on the phone too much to Billie Lee, or somebody else in my family. He even accused me of wishing that I hadn't married him and had gone to college.*

Annie Ruth winced at the thought, because she really had

wished she hadn't. Patricia had started crying while they were arguing about whether she wished she had married him or not. When Annie Ruth picked up the baby, she became ashamed of her thoughts. It seemed like Patricia understood her parents' frustration because she kept right on screaming even after Annie Ruth changed her diaper and was trying to feed her. Finally, Curtis took her in his arms and rested her on his shoulder. Annie Ruth patted her gently on the back. Patricia stopped crying as soon as she was comforted by both of them. *Lord, have mercy, what we gonna do?*

Curtis was also thinking about their money problems that day. *What am I gonna do? What am I gonna do?* That was a question Curtis had no answer for. *I can't even stand to look at the place in the barn where Dad killed himself. How am I gonna stand up and face all these bills and keep our farm? I got more work with Dad gone. I can't work at the mill, now. What am I gonna do?*

Curtis couldn't answer. He just kept working as hard as he could. He could deal with the hard labor, but the constant worry and anxiety over money was more than he could handle. So, he took to drinking a beer on Saturday evenings to help him relax and get ready for the next week of hard work. One beer led to two and two quickly led to three and soon he wasn't counting. He even tried muscatel.

Before he realized it or even took the time to notice, he had slipped into a pattern. He worked diligently from early Monday morning to late Saturday evening. He spent Saturday nights drinking. Sunday was no longer a day of worship, but a day to sleep off his hangover and to stagger through his daily chores.

11

Hauling Moonshine

Annie Ruth squelched the envy she was feeling when she watched her brothers, James and Jerry, get their degrees from Morehouse College in June, 1962.

Next to her, Billie Lee whispered, "This ceremony is so nice. It make me wish I'd gone to college."

Annie Ruth whispered back, "I know the feeling."

Neither Curtis nor Lenny went to the twins' graduation. Annie Ruth, Patricia, Billie Lee, and Granny rode to Atlanta with Mama and Daddy. Annie Ruth tried to cover up her worries and anxieties with the pride she felt for her brothers and her happiness at being with her family. Anxiety had become as much a part of her life as the never-ending house and farm work. Their bills were mounting. No matter how hard she and Curtis worked, they couldn't seem to get caught up.

Annie Ruth glanced at Patricia sitting in Billie Lee's lap. *I'm glad I had her. And even though things ain't so good with Curtis and me, I still love him.* Annie Ruth blinked and willed herself not to cry as she forced herself to concentrate on the graduation ceremony. *Yeah, I love Curtis, but he loving something else now besides me.*

Curtis was thinking about that something else the next Saturday evening while he finished his chores. *Annie Ruth say I love drinking better than I do her. But that ain't true. It's just that I need a few drinks on the weekend to help me relax. I love my wife. God knows I do. But I have to get away from my money worries. She a good wife. I thank God for her. It ain't her. It's me. I feel like a helpless little boy without Dad. All these bills about to worry me to death.*

Curtis finished his last chore—feeding the hogs, and headed to the house. A pint of muscatel was waiting to take him away.

Later that night, Annie Ruth watched him, in a drunken sleep on the sofa. *Oh, Curtis, what gonna happen to us? This drunk man ain't who I married. Where is that smart young man I fell in love with?* Annie Ruth wiped her tearful eyes and covered Curtis with a sheet. After she had taken a bath and gotten ready for bed, she sat on the side of the bed and thought. The night before, she and Curtis had tried to work out a budget, but no matter how careful they were it didn't seem like they'd ever get out of debt.

She thought about what the banker had said, that several business men wanted to buy their farm. *He said they wanted Curtis to stay on and work it. Shoot, that'll make us nothing but sharecroppers. Here we are the second largest Negro farm owners in Tobacco County and we gonna be cut down to sharecroppers. And that young white banker had the nerve to say Mr. Andrew oughta just made Miss Victoria comfortable. Shoot, what he think? He act like Negroes don't matter.*

Annie Ruth got up and snatched back the bedcovers. *Curtis*

and I ain't gonna be sharecroppers. Daddy always say Watsons are born with survival kits in their hands, well, I'm gonna start using mine!

The next day, wanting to avoid Curtis in the last stages of his Sunday hangover, Annie Ruth visited her parents after church. Billie Lee and Granny were there, too, sitting in the kitchen with Mama. She greeted them and sat down with Patricia on her lap. Mama and Granny looked real solemn. Questioning them, she learned the reasons for their gloomy faces. Daddy had decided to allow Mr. Bob to store moonshine in one of his barns. And Aunt Florence had confessed to them over the phone that Aldonia was hauling moonshine.

Mama shook her head sadly. "Even though it's wrong, I understand why Aldonia is hauling moonshine. I know it's hard on them trying to send Walter to college. But Sid ain't hard up for money."

Annie Ruth flushed with guilt. "All that money Daddy gave Curtis and me probably set y'all back."

Mama shook her head. "No, you get that notion outta your head. It cut our bank account down, but we still ain't shooting bad. I don't know why Sid wanna fool with that moonshine."

Granny nodded in agreement. "Anyway, Sid done spent money sending them boys to college. It's only fair that he help you out. Maybelle's right, ain't no cause for him to mess with that moonshine."

"Maybe he need more money to send the twins to medical school," Billie Lee said.

"We got money in the bank," Mama said. "The twins are working at good paying summer jobs in Atlanta, plus we got our fall harvests to count on. Sid ain't got no reason to mess with moonshine."

"You women folks need to let things be." Daddy spoke through the screen door before he opened it and walked in. "No, I ain't hard put for money, but I got good reasons. My barn over in the south field is located in a good position for Mr. Bob to zip in here on his way back from Florida and unload his moonshine. Then a hauler will come and pick it up, and that'll be the end of it as far as I'm concerned."

"The sin is still on your hands, son," Granny said in a solemn voice. "Just like the sin is on Aldonia's hands; Lord, have mercy on her."

Mama seemed to know it was no use in debating with Daddy any longer. "Who gonna be the hauler?"

Daddy sat down at the table. "Mr. Bob gonna haul this load himself later on tonight. Miss Della and Aldonia are hauling the shine he's storing in her barn. He gotta find him a hauler for my barn. He said Miss Della and Aldonia ain't had any trouble. He said women make better haulers cause folks don't suspect them as quickly." Daddy chuckled. "I wouldn't doubt that Mr. Bob and Miss Della being kin to the Sinclairs don't help the situation. The Sinclairs got kinfolks working for the law in Tobacco County and all around it."

Annie Ruth's mind started thinking hard. As she thought about it the words fell from her mouth, "I'll be Mr. Bob's hauler."

"What?" Everybody seemed to say it at the same time.

Mama's voice blared with disapproval. "No, ma'am, NO! NO! Ain't no daughter of mine gonna be hauling moonshine!"

The baby started crying. Annie Ruth covered her breast with a handkerchief and started feeding her. But, at the same

time, she was making up her mind. *I'm sorry to hurt my parents.*
And I can't face God. But I ain't got a choice. "I understand how
you feel, Mama. But Daddy and Miss Clara can't keep carrying
Curtis and me. We outta cash, and we over our heads in debt
for our farm supplies and operating expenses."

Daddy sighed wearily. "What I do is one thing, but what
you do is another. You don't need to be hauling moonshine."

Annie Ruth wasn't about to give up. "I know it's risky business, but y'all don't seem to realize what bad shape we in. Curtis
and I are just as desperate as Aldonia is—even more so."

She paused to catch her breath. "We spent hours Friday
night trying to set up a budget. It was impossible, no matter
how much we sacrificed and saved. If something don't give, we
gonna be sharecroppers."

"Sharecroppers make an honest living," Granny said. "I
rather see y'all sharecroppers than in jail."

"That farm ain't worth getting in trouble about," Mama
added.

"I gotta try to save our farm," Annie Ruth said. "I just can't
give up. I'll quit soon as we pay off some bills and get some
money ahead."

Daddy frowned. "You right. Ain't no way you and Curtis
can keep on like you going. It take money to keep a big farm
going."

"Annie Ruth probably won't get caught," Billie Lee said.
"Just like Aldonia ain't. Curtis done lost both his parents. He
lose their farm, I don't know if he can take it."

Granny sounded real sympathetic. "He a might young man
to carry the burden he carrying."

"Being helpless is a bad feeling," Billie Lee said. "I understand
how Annie Ruth feel."

Annie Ruth kept trying to get Mama, Daddy, and Granny to see her point, but they refused to agree. Finally, she just told them pointblank, "I'm a grown woman, the decision is mine. And I'm gonna do it."

"I'll go with her," Billie Lee said suddenly. "Lenny and I could use some extra money to save for our house."

Mama threw up her hands in frustration. "Mother Watson, we better start praying longer, cause we got several family members headed to hell!"

Later that Sunday afternoon, Mr. Sid was feeding his hogs when Curtis walked up. "Mr. Sid, I can't believe you gonna let Annie Ruth haul moonshine!"

Mr. Sid turned around. He looked tired and sad. "I can't believe it either. We tried to talk her out of it, but she just as determined as Aldonia is."

"I ain't gonna let her do it," Curtis said.

"I wish you wouldn't." Mr. Sid sighed. "I hate to admit it, but it might be better if y'all just go on and sell off your farm."

"No . . .no . . .I can't." Curtis's shoulders drooped. He sat down on a log by the fence. "I don't know what to do. I feel like it's my fault—you having to store moonshine in your barn. I know giving me that money set y'all back."

Mr. Sid sat on another log nearby. "No, I ain't that hard up for money, but I got good causes." Mr. Sid regarded Curtis carefully, and then said, "Your Aunt Clara didn't want me to tell you, but I'm gonna anyway. She borrowed the money to help with your daddy's funeral and she been borrowing the money to make your mortgage payments."

Curtis bowed his head. "I shoulda known. She just a widowed school teacher. She ain't got much money, plus she in debt for sending my cousins to college."

Curtis felt like crying like a little boy. "I hate to sell, Mr. Sid. I don't think I can take losing the farm on top of everything else. But what else am I gonna do? I'm drowning in a sea of debts. And no matter how hard I try I can't swim to shore."

Mr. Sid and Curtis just sat there for a long time with their heads down, looking at their hands. Finally, Mr. Sid raised his head and looked out across the field. He said in a hushed voice just loud enough for Curtis to hear him. "Well, right or wrong, my daughter is determined to throw you a rope."

So, although his manhood was shaky and he was burning with shame and guilt, Curtis let Annie Ruth haul moonshine. To make himself useful and to improve her safety, he overhauled the engine in his father's car and always made sure that the car was in excellent working condition for her runs. He also adjusted the rear springs so the car would not sag when loaded and cause the police to suspect she was hauling moonshine.

Now, Curtis needed his weekend drinks not only to take him away from money pressures, but to steady his quaking manhood and cool his burning shame and guilt about letting his wife haul moonshine. Also he found no peace in the state of national affairs. The civil rights struggle continued as persistently as his personal struggles.

In July, 1962, he read and heard about Rev. Martin Luther King, Jr. being convicted in Albany Georgia's Recorder Court of violating street and sidewalk ordinance by leading a parade without a permit on December 16, 1961. The month before that he had become irritated by the report that James Meredith's application for enrollment at the University of Mississippi had been rejected solely on racial grounds. Those events, like many other events of the civil rights movement, disturbed Curtis. He expressed his thoughts to Annie Ruth one Sunday afternoon while she was getting ready to leave to haul moonshine.

"Annie Ruth, I love farming, but sometimes I wish I could be more involved in the Civil Rights Movement."

"Don't get so worried about civil rights." Annie Ruth picked up her purse. "Things gonna get better for Negroes. You doing what you need to do, and that's working and holding on to our farm." She kissed him and headed to the door. "See you later. Take the baby to Mama if you decide to go anywhere."

Annie Ruth was irritated with herself as they waited for the car ahead of them to get gas at the country store right outside of Gator Town. She usually took care of filling her tank on Saturday, but she'd gotten busy and forgotten to do so. A county sheriff drove up as they were being served. It took only a few minutes for the white store clerk to pump their gas and accept payment, but to Annie Ruth it was an eternity. She swallowed, feeling her nerves become a tight knot in her stomach. She glanced at Billie Lee, hoping their appearances gave no sign of their fear. They both kept their eyes averted from the sheriff as he got out of his car and walked up to the store entrance. Annie Ruth adjusted her hat. Billie Lee straightened the collar of her white linen suit and picked up the Bible on the car seat and began to read.

"Where you gals headed all dressed up?" The store clerk asked after he took the money from Annie Ruth's gloved hand.

"We headed to church services, sir," Annie Ruth replied.

"That's nice." The store clerk grinned, showing tobacco-stained teeth. "I can see y'all are decent colored women."

Annie Ruth drove away.

The sheriff barely glanced at the 1952 black Ford. His mind was on the beautiful well-dressed mulatto in the front seat by the not-so-bad black wench.

The store clerk looked at him knowingly. "That one on the other side looked almost like a white woman."

The sheriff was not a man of pretense. "Damn sure did. And just as pretty."

After they got out of sight of the store, Annie Ruth felt the nerve knot in her stomach relax. "Got kinda hot back there, didn't it, Billie Lee?"

Billie Lee patted her face with her powder puff. "I see why Uncle Sid always insist that we do our runs on Sunday afternoons. I hope everybody think we just two dressed-up Negro women headed to church service."

"Well, after this month, we'll only be making one run a month and we alternated between Gator Town and Swampville, so I don't think anybody's gonna pay us much mind," Annie Ruth said.

"And you say you only gonna do it for a few more months."

Annie Ruth shrugged. "I said that, but we got so many bills. I'll probably be hauling a long time. Don't you feel obligated, though. You quit when you get ready."

Billie Lee rolled up the window a little to keep the wind from blowing her hair. "I'm gonna keep riding with you until I get pregnant. This extra money is helping us save for our house."

"I was surprised when Lenny let you ride with me. I thought he'd hit the ceiling."

"I wasn't," Billie Lee said. "I knew how he felt about Negroes hauling moonshine. He always said that white folks gonna sell moonshine no matter what, so us Negroes might as well try to get some of that fast money, too."

"That's one way of looking at it."

When she arrived home a few hours later, Annie Ruth patted her purse and smiled to herself. Her phone was ringing.

"Hello."

"Thank goodness, you back."

"Aldonia, what is it?"

"Come to the jailhouse," Aldonia said. "Curtis is in a little trouble."

Annie Ruth gripped the receiver, "Trouble! What is it?"

"Calm down, Annie Ruth. It's for speeding and drinking. Bring twenty-five dollars, too."

Aldonia was waiting outside of the jail. "You look mad enough to spit fire."

"I am," Annie Ruth said.

"Well, humble that attitude," Aldonia advised. "We don't wanna get on the wrong side of these white policemen."

As soon as Annie Ruth paid his fine, Curtis was released. Seeing that he was still too drunk to drive, Annie Ruth told Aldonia to drive their truck home.

Curtis stumbled into the car. "Man, I'm glad to be free again."

"I hope you remember this, cause you just made us twenty-five dollars poorer. We coulda used that money to pay bills!" Annie Ruth's voice snapped whips of anger at Curtis.

"Annie Ruth, you might as well call Miss Maybelle and tell her you gonna pick up Patricia in the morning."

Annie Ruth guided the car out of the parking lot before she answered. "I did that before I came to get you, *dear* husband."

"Shoot, woman, don't get uppity with me. Ain't a man entitled to a mistake?" Curtis growled. "You can afford the twenty-five dollars. You such a good runner. Mr. Bob told Mr.

Sid the other day when I was helping them unload some shine, 'Sid, your gal can sure run that shine.' Mr. Sid told him that you ain't a gal, you his daughter and my wife." Annie Ruth could sense the shame in Curtis's voice. "How you think that made me feel having to listen to some white man talk about my wife being a gal and running moonshine? So what if I made you spend twenty-five dollars? You can afford it, Miss Shine Annie!"

Annie Ruth choked back the tears that sprang from her own personal well of guilt and shame. "I know I'm wrong, but I'm trying to save the farm that your daddy, Patricia's grandfather—died because of."

Her words seemed to stifle Curtis's anger. "I'm sorry, sweetheart. I'm really pissed off with myself. Thanks for getting me out of jail."

Annie Ruth left Curtis at their house and then took Aldonia home.

Aldonia glanced at Annie Ruth. "Don't be too mad with Curtis," she said sheepishly.

"I'm angry about the money and his drinking. I wish he'd stop drinking. I don't know why he got drunk tonight. Usually he get drunk only on Saturday nights."

"You gotta talk with him about his drinking. Encourage him to stop," Aldonia said.

"I done that. I do it all the time, but he say I be nagging."

"Well, just keep being as supportive as you can."

Annie Ruth took a deep breath. "I'm doing all I can. That's why I'm hauling moonshine to help us get out of debt."

Aldonia patted her on the shoulder. "Hang in there. We Watsons don't give up easily." Aldonia paused. "Tonight was probably my fault."

"Why you say that?"

Aldonia sat up straight. "I went out to the Blue Light Inn with Lucinda."

"Where was Mark?"

"He had to drive a truck outta town for his bossman. Harold met me out there. We stayed in the parking lot and talked. I told him about how lonely I get for him. I'm so tired of waiting for him to get a divorce."

Aldonia hesitated. Annie Ruth suspected she was trying to keep from crying. "I can't take it much longer. Child, I get to longing for that man so bad sometimes."

Annie Ruth frowned. "You sure you love him, or do you just wanna take him back cause Natalie got pregnant and married him?"

"I love Harold. I can't even imagine loving anybody else. When I think about him being with Natalie, I almost die from the pain."

Life is so hard. Sometimes I wish I was back home being Mama and Daddy's little girl. I never dreamed loving somebody could be so hard. "Love is something else, ain't it?" Annie Ruth said softly.

"Tell me about it," Aldonia said. "After Harold left, I kept standing out there in the parking lot. Ray Charles's record called 'I Can't Stop Loving You' was playing on the juke box." Aldonia lowered her voice. "That's the way I feel about Harold. I can't stop loving him. Curtis saw me standing out there with my head down and came over and started trying to cheer me up." Aldonia's voice lightened a little. "You know how kind he can be, sometimes."

Annie Ruth smiled. "Yeah, I know."

"Curtis asked me why I was acting so down. I started crying and told him I was feeling low about Harold. He told me that y'all were married and had had Patricia before you told him that you loved him."

Yeah, it took me a while, but when I started loving that man, it sure was for real. "That's true," she answered Aldonia.

"Curtis told me sometimes you have to wait on the person you love, but he thinks I oughta give up on Harold, cause he don't think he'll ever leave his wife."

"What did you say to that?" Annie Ruth asked.

"I told him that I can't give up Harold. Curtis just looked at me and said, 'Then stop letting it drag you down.' 'Twistin' The Night Away' by Sam Cooke was playing on the juke box. Curtis asked me to go inside and dance with him. We did, and then Curtis offered to drive me home."

"What happened to Lucinda?" Annie Ruth asked.

Aldonia paused. "I don't know. With Mark outta town, she was flirting with the menfolks worse than the single women. I couldn't find her, so I took Curtis's offer. Curtis kept trying to convince me to give up Harold. He thinks somebody gonna get hurt. I got a feeling he right, but I can't give up."

Annie Ruth understood her cousin's feelings. "It's hard to give up someone you love. Curtis could be right, though. Somebody may eventually get hurt."

"It's a chance I gotta take," Aldonia said.

"How did Curtis get picked up by the police?"

"Curtis drank several beers at the Blue Light Inn. After he stopped talking about Harold and me, he started talking about how he doesn't like to see us haul moonshine, and how he wish he could participate in the Civil Rights Movement. He got real upset. I guess the truck was weaving, cause the next thing I knew the police was pulling us over."

Annie Ruth shook her head sadly. "It's a mess. Curtis is

drinking, and I'm out hauling shine." Suddenly Annie Ruth was very scared. "Suppose we get caught, Aldonia?"

"Relax." Aldonia seemed sure. "As long as our family keep it a secret and we haul for the right folks we'll be all right."

Their family kept their secret, and it appeared that Annie Ruth and her relatives were definitely hauling for the right folks. The summer of '62 ended and none of them had had the slightest trouble with the law.

This ain't the life I dreamed about! Annie Ruth would often cry to herself after she and Billie Lee had finished a run and were headed home. She'd look at the setting sun. Her eyes would sting with tears of disappointment and shame for wrong doing. *God forgive me. If I don't help Curtis, we gonna lose Mr. Andrew's blood-stained farm.* She would think about the young white banker's words: make-his-woman-comfortable, several-business-men-ready-to-buy-your-farm, Curtis, you-got-a-reputation-for-being-a-hard-working-BOY! Then she'd get angry. *I ain't gonna let the white folks get our farm.* When her anger eased, she'd get ashamed again. *Lord, have mercy, I'm hauling moonshine. I ain't nothing but a Shine Annie.* She'd grasp the steering wheel and say to Billie Lee, "Billie Lee, life doesn't always turn out like we want it to. Does it?"

Billie Lee must have been thinking along those same lines, because her voice always sounded like she was trying to keep from crying.

"No, it doesn't, cousin. Life doesn't always turn out like we want it to."

12

Trials and Tribulations

The bright sun shone through the picture window. Annie Ruth followed Billie Lee through the rooms of her new home. Patricia toddled along beside them.

Billie Lee pointed toward an empty room. "This is gonna be my nursery. Hopefully, 1963 will be my year to begin the joys of motherhood."

Annie Ruth looked around admiringly. "Billie Lee, this house is lovely."

"Thanks. Hauling moonshine with you helped me to pep up our budget. We were able to make the big down payment we needed."

After they finished the tour of the house, Billie Lee invited Annie Ruth and Patricia to visit with her for a while. They went into the kitchen so Billie Lee could fix some tea. Annie Ruth sat at the table and held Patricia firmly on her lap. Billie Lee gave Patricia a cookie. When she finished eating it, Annie Ruth wiped her hands and made her stay on her lap.

Billie Lee noticed her restraint. "Why you making her sit on your lap?"

Annie Ruth's eyes swept over the beautiful modern house. "Everything look like a picture in a magazine. I don't want her messing up."

Billie Lee took Patricia, put her on the floor, and gave her the toy Annie Ruth had with her to play with. "I be glad when I have some little ones to mess up things."

Annie Ruth saw a flash of sadness in Billie Lee's eyes before she went back to fixing the tea. "I hope living in this pretty house will make things better with Lenny and me."

Annie Ruth felt a pang of anger toward Lenny. "Billie Lee, you gotta stand up to him."

Billie Lee put two glasses of tea on the table. "I wish I could be like you," she said, sitting in front of Annie Ruth. "You always stood up for me and you when we were little."

"You can. You ain't gotta let anybody walk on you."

Billie Lee took a sip of tea. "I was thinking the other day about you, Lucinda, Edwina, and me. It seem like I got the worst deal for a husband. Lenny's a good provider, but he so mean at times. Dwight adores Edwina and their little boy. Everybody know how Curtis love you." Billie Lee looked thoughtful. "Sometimes I envy Lucinda. Except for moving up North, Mark does what she says. You shoulda seen them at the Blue Light Inn a couple of weeks ago."

Annie Ruth swallowed some tea. "You went *into* a juke joint?"

"I just went to be with Lenny," Billie Lee said. "Lucinda was as sharp-as-a-tack in a red cardigan coatdress and matching spike-heeled shoes. All of the men were looking at her, and she was flirting all around them." Billie Lee drank some more tea. "Mark just sat watching her like a doting puppy. If I had acted like that, Lenny woulda jumped on me in that juke joint."

Annie Ruth traced a finger around her frosty glass. "You gotta stop him from pushing you around."

A little later, while she was driving home, Annie Ruth thought about what Billie Lee had told her. *I wonder if that fancy red dress and shoes and flirting with the men was Lucinda's way of making her lemonade-of-life sweeter. She talked about doing that last year that cold Saturday morning in November when she came to the house.*

It had been a cold Saturday morning in November 1962. Annie Ruth was washing clothes when she looked up from a boiling wash pot of diapers and saw Lucinda drive into the backyard. Annie Ruth peered through the smoke and frowned. Lucinda looked more like a tacky housewife than her usual fashionably dressed self. Her hair was braided, and she was wearing a faded sweater and dungarees.

"Love," Lucinda said. She got out of her red '55 Ford and slammed the door. She passed the boiling pots without noticing the blue smoke that gushed suddenly in her face when the fire flared up. She repeated the word. "Love, Annie Ruth, is like they say. It ain't nothing but a monkey on your back."

Annie Ruth laughed and started putting clothes through the wringer. "Good morning, Mrs. Jones," she said. "If love is a monkey on my back, I wish it would get its behind down and help me with my washing!"

Annie Ruth's joke seemed to find a little bit of Lucinda's old self. Lucinda laughed, put her purse on the back porch, and started helping Annie Ruth.

"I was cutting-the-fool, Lucinda. You ain't gotta help me."

"I don't mind," Lucinda replied. "I think better when my hands are busy, anyway."

Annie Ruth glanced at Lucinda questioningly. "Where's your wig? Why ain't you sharp today?"

Lucinda began to feed the clothes through the wringer. "I left my sharp clothes in Rail City. That's gonna be my home it looks like until I die."

Annie Ruth picked up speed. Lucinda was working so fast she was afraid it would look like she was putting her work off on her. "Why you talking like that? Sure, that's your home. Why you say it like you don't like it?"

They finished sending the clothes through the wringer from the washing water, adjusted the wringer over two tin tubs of clean water and started rinsing them.

Lucinda shrugged. "I like my house. I'm proud of Mark for buying it and fixing it up. He even plans to fix it extra nice later on." Lucinda grabbed several of Patricia's dresses, rinsed them and put them through the wringer. "What I wanna do is lock up that house and move to New York."

Annie Ruth rinsed several blouses and put them through the wringer. "Yeah, Curtis told me he saw Mark last Sunday evening. Mark told him about you wanting to move to New York. He said Mark doesn't wanna go."

Annie Ruth accidentally splashed water on herself. She looked down at her wet shoes. She couldn't imagine her feet being contented anywhere else except on the Southern ground that she was willing to haul moonshine to save. "Why you wanna move up north?"

Lucinda stopped rinsing clothes. A faraway look gleamed in her eyes. "I been dreaming about moving up north since I was a little girl."

Annie Ruth frowned. "Why you married if you wanted to move to New York?"

"I love Mark. Plus, I thought I'd be able to convince him to move after we married."

Annie Ruth continued rinsing the clothes while Lucinda explained her reasons for wanting to move north.

"Annie Ruth, you remember how good I was at typing and shorthand in high school. I wanna move up north so that I can go to trade school and become a secretary." Lucinda's voice was filled with discontentment. "You know an educated Negro woman ain't got a chance of becoming anything down here but a teacher in a segregated school or a nurse in a segregated hospital."

"Racism is up north, too," Annie Ruth replied.

Lucinda nodded. "I know. There are more opportunities for Negroes, though." She added wistfully. "Child, I wanna follow my dreams."

Annie Ruth put a shirt through the wringer. "Everybody had childhood dreams. Life is made of reality, not dreams. Sometimes, dreams and reality don't jive."

Lucinda responded irritably. "Dreaming, what's wrong with dreaming? Living without dreams is like having half a life. You need dreams to keep going."

A dusty memory of her naive love for Raymond Baldwin came to Annie Ruth. Quickly she shoved it back—to a road no longer traveled in her mind. "It's okay to dream; however, some dreams are for dreaming only, not living."

Annie Ruth's words seemed to cast a quietness on both of them. Neither of them spoke again until they were hanging the clothes on the clothesline. Then Lucinda said, "My mama told me she gave up on dreams when I was a baby and my daddy ran off with another woman. She said all dreaming ever got her was four children fathered by different men. She said a colored woman ain't got time for dreaming. She said a colored woman is better off with her mind on God and her hands and feet in work."

Lucinda took a deep breath. "Mama got mad when I told her I wanna move to New York. She agrees with Mark. She thinks we oughta stay down here, and I oughta be thankful I got a good husband."

Annie Ruth pinned several shirts on the clothesline. "Curtis said Mark is scared he wouldn't be able to make a good living up there like he does down here, since he ain't ever done anything but drive trucks and work on farms."

Lucinda's voice was edged with anger. "Fear! Mark's letting fear hold him back. He a high school graduate. He got carpentry skills, and he can fix anything." Lucinda paused and caught her breath. "Mark always try to please, but he won't give in on this."

Annie Ruth looked around their farm. It seemed like part of her. Patricia was sleeping in her crib near the back door. Curtis was doing his morning chores. Her cupboards were full of canned fruits, vegetables, preserves, and jams. Her freezer was almost overflowing with meat and vegetables. She and Curtis still owned their farm. "Living in the South ain't so bad," she said. "You and Mark doing good. Y'all own your own house, some pretty furniture, and a good car."

Lucinda handed Annie Ruth a clothespin. "That's what Mama said." Lucinda shook her head sadly. "Annie Ruth, I'm so tired of southeast Georgia. There's a great big world out there. Honey child, don't you want some excitement in your life?"

Annie Ruth winced. Hauling moonshine was a lot *more*

excitement than she wanted. She smiled to keep the shame of her secret business from showing on her face. "The fair gonna be here next week."

Lucinda nodded. "That's all we have to look forward to: 'big days' at church, the fair, house parties, cane grindings, and going shopping every now and then in Jacksonville or Savannah. I want more outta life." Lucinda eyed here intently. "You don't really understand, do you?"

"I'm your friend. I'm willing to listen," Annie Ruth replied. She answered Lucinda more directly in her mind. *No, I don't understand. I love living in southeast Georgia. I wanna take care of my family and be here near my parents.*

Annie Ruth got a pair of tongs off the back porch and took the simmering diapers out of the wash pots. Lucinda helped her put them through the wringer.

Lucinda went on to her next subject while they were hanging the diapers on the clothesline. "You better take care of homework, that's what Mama told me. She said I'm not taking care of my homework cause I ain't had a baby for Mark." Lucinda laughed dryly. "She said there's a time for catching-it-in-the-headrag, but when a woman's gotta good loving husband like Mark, who's begging for a baby, that ain't the time."

Annie Ruth paused from hanging diapers on the clothesline. "What she mean by catching-it-in-the-headrag?"

Lucinda giggled. "Child, please, you know a lotta Negro women sleep with headrags on their heads, so if you get caught up in a passion cloud, you might have to let you man grab the nearest thing to protect you from the *love* rain!"

Annie Ruth blushed and then spoke carefully. "You think it's fair to deny Mark a child? He really is a good husband."

Lucinda took the last diaper and hung it on the line. "He

denying me my dream of moving to New York. So, I ain't studying about being in a hurry to start a family."

After they finished the washing, Annie Ruth invited Lucinda inside. She fixed her some coffee and served her some home-roasted pecans. When Patricia woke up, Annie Ruth changed her diaper and started feeding her.

Lucinda ate a few pecans and took a sip of coffee. "Half-sweet lemonade," she said. "I remember one time when I was little, Mama made my brothers and me some lemonade. She didn't have enough sugar, but we drank it anyway. That's the way my life seem now without my dream of moving to New York, like my life is only half-sweet."

Annie Ruth flinched at the sadness in Lucinda's eyes. "I hope you ain't thinking about leaving Mark. Don't throw away your marriage for a dream."

Lucinda gazed out of the kitchen window. "No, I love him too much to leave him. I'll find other ways to make my life sweeter, though."

Annie Ruth followed Lucinda's gaze out of the window. In her mind's eye she saw her yard in the spring: pretty marigolds, petunias, zinnias, and azaleas. Southeast Georgia's winters were mild. Spring would come soon. She believed she and Curtis could make it. She'd learned in school that the colony of Georgia didn't prosper until after the legalization of slavery. To Annie Ruth, that meant that Negroes had a right to the South, too. And she didn't want to or intend to leave it.

She looked away from the window and went back to feeding the baby. As she reached for a napkin to wipe Patricia's mouth, Annie Ruth was almost startled by the unhappy looking young woman sitting at her kitchen table.

Good night! Look at Lucinda sitting there, so down and out cause she gotta stay down South to save her marriage. There are a lotta Negro women around here who'd love being married to Mark, living in their cute house, driving that car, and wearing her pretty clothes. I know cause I done heard their jealous gossip at the beauty parlor. And I done seen their envious glances at church and social functions. Yeah, they'd love to be in her shoes. Yet, Lucinda's got what they jealous of, and she ain't happy. Maybe her mama's right. Maybe a colored woman is better off not dreaming.

June, 1963, brought the second anniversary of Annie Ruth's and Curtis's marriage and the first anniversary of Annie Ruth's moonshine hauling.

Annie Ruth's anniversary gift to Curtis was a nice wrist watch. Curtis bought her an expensive anniversary clock with a glass dome. A clock should have been the appropriate gift for the first wedding anniversary. At that time, though, they had been too broke to afford anything except I-love-yous and a night of passionate lovemaking.

Curtis was sitting in their living room the Sunday morning after their second anniversary. Annie Ruth and Patricia had gone to church. He wasn't nursing his usual hangover because he'd drank only a couple of beers the night before. The elegant anniversary clock drew his attention. He got up and walked over to the table.

Man, we done made it to our two-year anniversary. If anybody had told me when I was back in high school that I woulda been married to Annie Ruth for two years by now, I wouldn't have believed them. I figured ole Casanova Raymond was gonna slip up eventually, and I'd be able to start going with Annie Ruth. But I sure didn't expect it to happen so soon.

Man, I really love her. I gotta get my act together, though, cause

I know she getting tired of me drinking. She won't even let me make love to her when I'm drinking. She always say she don't want no drunk man blowing in her face.

Curtis stared at the clock's swirling chimes. *I love Annie Ruth and Patricia. I need my family. If I keep drinking I might lose them. What am I gonna do?* Curtis looked up at their family portrait on the mantel. The picture was taken on their anniversary day. The smiling images told him what he had to do. He had to stop drinking. His first step would be to visit Reverend Phillips.

Reverend Phillips and his family had just gotten back from morning church services. When Mary Joyce and their children went into the house, Curtis got out of his truck and walked over to Reverend Phillips.

Reverend Phillips frowned. "What's wrong, Curtis?"

Curtis put his hands in his pockets. He saw no reason to beat around the bush. "I gotta stop drinking."

Reverend Phillips stared like he couldn't believe what he had heard.

"Curtis, I've been praying for you to say that!" He reached out and hugged him. He got so excited he could hardly invite Curtis inside. "Co-co-come on in!"

They went into the living room. Mary Joyce and their children were in the kitchen.

Curtis started talking again as soon as they sat down. "It seemed like I had to start drinking in order to deal with Dad's death and all our bills."

Reverend Phillips's eyes were compassionate. "I know everything's been hard on you. That's why I've been reluctant to get on to you about your drinking."

Curtis looked at his hands. They trembled. "I gotta start

dealing with my problems without drinking. I'm scared it's gonna cause me to lose my family."

Reverend Phillips seemed glad to hear that. "Praise God, Curtis, you're getting your thoughts straight. Drinking could cause you to lose everything: your family, your farm, and yourself."

Curtis felt a tightness in his throat. He forced himself to say the next thing he needed to say. "I still can't face that place in the barn where Dad killed himself."

"Really?" Reverend Phillips looked thoughtful.

"Yes, I go in there, get what I need, I do chores, but I keep my eyes away from that spot."

Reverend Phillips didn't reply. He kept looking at Curtis like he was thinking about something.

Now that he'd gotten started, Curtis wanted to tell all he could about his drinking. "I read a few articles on drinking. You know you can still be considered an alcoholic even if you only drink on weekends."

When Reverend Phillips nodded, Curtis kept talking. "Reverend Phillips, I don't wanna be an alcoholic. I don't want my wife and child thinking of me as a drunkard."

Reverend Phillips stood up. "Let's go to your house. The first thing you need to do is face that place in your barn."

Curtis didn't get up. "I don't know if I'm ready for that."

Reverend Phillips spoke firmly. "Get up. It's time you got yourself together, Curtis."

Curtis got up. His legs were trembling.

When they got there, Curtis and Reverend Phillips went directly to the barn. Curtis went inside slowly. His eyes took in everything: the storage bins, the corn, the hay, the farm equipment, everything except that place. Reverend Phillips gave him a gentle nudge. "Mr. Sid told me that he shoveled out the bloody soil and filled in the hole with clean dirt. But Uncle Andrew's suicide is still on that ground. As long as you allow it to, it's going to scare you and grieve you."

Reverend Phillips's voice rose. "Face that place, Curtis, then give your burden to God. You're a young man. You got too far to go to carry such a load."

Curtis closed his eyes and walked by memory to the spot. When he opened his eyes, the pain of Dad's suicide seem to flare up like a fire being doused with gasoline. The pain felt like it was burning from his head to his toes. He heard himself crying. "Dad! Dad! I miss you! I miss you! Dad! Dad! Dad!" When he finally calmed down, he was still staring at the spot. It no longer frightened him, but tears were streaming down his cheeks.

Reverend Phillips wiped his own eyes and put an arm gently around Curtis's shoulders. "You've been walking in a dark alley, Curtis, but the light's started to shine for you."

That Sunday night Curtis sat in his pajama bottoms by the opened window of his and Annie Ruth's bedroom. He looked out at the silhouetted frame of the barn. At last he felt at peace. The warm June night air blew against his bare chest. Annie Ruth came into the bedroom from the bathroom and sat on the bed behind him. He glanced at her and then looked back out the window. "Today I faced that place in the barn with Reverend Phillips."

Annie Ruth got up and peered out the window. "What place in the barn?"

"The place where Dad killed himself. I been going in and

out of the barn since his death, but I never looked at that place." Another breeze blew against him. Its coolness felt good. "Reverend Phillips told me that if I wanted to stop drinking I had to face that place."

Annie Ruth touched his shoulder. "You think it's gonna really help you to stop?"

Curtis could hear the hope in her voice. "I hope so. I can't keep hiding in drunkenness on weekends while you wear the pants and haul moonshine."

Annie Ruth moved back to the bed. "We were so desperate for money. I had to do something. It's a lot safer for a woman to haul shine than a man."

"We got our bills caught up," Curtis said. "You can stop, now."

"We caught up, we ain't got much money saved, though. I don't wanna be desperate for money again."

"You gonna quit," Curtis said flatly.

Annie Ruth spoke anxiously. "Curtis, we need to plan." She waited a while. "How about I quit next June. That'll give us a year to save money." She hesitated. "And it'll give you time to beat your drinking."

Suddenly, Curtis felt anxious. Keeping himself sober every weekend wasn't going to be easy. Maybe he'd better not rush things. "Okay, one more year of hauling moonshine. After that, you quit no matter what."

Annie Ruth seemed relieved. "That's fine with me."

Curtis went to sit by Annie Ruth on the bed. "I promise you, by then I'll be quit drinking."

Annie Ruth looked him in the eyes. "I don't like broken promises."

She looked so soft and sexy. He kept his eyes on her. "I gotta quit drinking, so you'll like being married to me again."

Annie Ruth blushed. "I love you, Curtis."

Curtis embraced her. "I wanna keep it that way."

The coming of each weekend reinforced the fact that giving up drinking wasn't going to be easy for Curtis. But in spite of his yearning for alcohol, he struggled from Saturday evening to Monday morning without drinking anything stronger than a cup of coffee. Some Saturday nights he chewed sticks and sticks of chewing gum while he feverishly read the Psalms in the Bible. Sometimes he visited Buck Miller, a reformed alcoholic and a friend of Reverend Phillips. Through their long talks he found the courage to stay sober.

He started going to church again. He held on to every word that the minister said about God's forgiveness and understanding. He prayed in church and out of church for the strength to deny himself the consolation of alcohol. And he stayed sober all summer.

September brought fall and melancholy thoughts. Curtis's thoughts became so dreary, even his good farm harvests didn't stop them. It was as if the change of the season had frightened the little boy inside of him. The little boy cried out for Dad. His shrill cry startled Curtis's sober mind. A can of pain seemed to re-open in Curtis. It was too much. So, one September Saturday Curtis took again the soothing drinks he knew would quiet the frightened little boy in him.

Some weekends he made it without drinking and rejoiced on Sunday in church. Other weekends he just barely made it to Saturday evening before he was resting in the arms of alcohol. He spent those Sundays remorsefully nursing his hangover at home. Lying on the sofa one Sunday morning in November

Curtis remembered the night he'd been picked up by the police. The memory turned his stomach. He stumbled to the bathroom. He threw up, but what was really making him sick wouldn't come up, because it was the thought of what he would become if he didn't stop drinking.

He flushed the commode and got up. He walked slowly out of the bathroom and looked straight at the door to his father's bedroom. His hands trembled as he opened the door and entered the room he hadn't been in since the day he'd found his father's suicide note.

The room was the same: toast brown bedspread, Dad's dress shoes under the dresser, Dad's clothes hanging on nails on the wall, and Mom's picture on the little table by the bed.

Curtis got Dad's suit down off the wall. He tried on the coat. He went over to the dresser to look in the mirror. When he saw himself wearing Dad's suit coat, he felt a sudden rush of relief. The little boy in him had grown up. Now he felt only Dad's love.

Curtis started sorting Dad's clothes and personal items. There were some things he would store, some he would give away or throw away, some he'd keep. *Dad loved me. I know he did. I still love him. I won't ever stop missing him. But it's time for me to go on with my life.*

After he cleaned out his father's bedroom, Curtis remained sober. Annie Ruth decided to give him a party for his twenty-first birthday. And Billie Lee agreed to have the party at her house on December 7.

While they were dressing for the party, Curtis got into one of his talking moods. "President Kennedy done been assassinated, Medgar Evers was killed, and Dr. King delivered his 'I Have

A Dream' speech at the march on Washington. And here I am getting ready to go to my birthday party."

Annie Ruth was determined for them to relax and enjoy the evening. "Let's not talk about civil rights now, Curtis. You trying to get your life together. I think that's a lot."

Everybody else was already at Billie Lee's when Annie Ruth and Curtis got there.

"The man of honor, you finally bless us with your presence," Lenny teased, playing the warm host to the hilt.

When everybody started singing happy birthday, Annie Ruth was thinking how she hoped Curtis would stay sober. *Two things for sure. I'm gonna stop hauling moonshine next year. And I don't like being married to a drinking man.*

Billie Lee led them to her elegant dining room. The cake Annie Ruth had purchased was sitting on the lace-covered mahogany table.

"This is terrific," Curtis said looking at everybody. "I really feel happy tonight. We all together. And we all still friends."

"May God bless us all," Reverend Phillips said.

Billie Lee lit the candles. "Curtis, close your eyes, make a wish, and blow out the candles."

Silently, Annie Ruth wished he'd remain sober.

"Yeah, blow them candles out and wish for a boy the next time Annie Ruth has a baby. Excusing Reverend Phillips, I'm the only one of us who has fathered a son," Dwight bragged. "All right, you other cats, one of y'all gotta give me some competition."

"You don't need any competition." Edwina blushed and went on. "I'm already six months pregnant, and Dwight Jr. ain't even two years old."

"Don't get too confident, man. I'm just lying low in the beginning, letting you speed ahead like a hare. I'm like the old tortoise, slow but steady. In a few years," Lenny predicted, "Billie Lee and I will have enough boys around this house to start a basketball team."

Curtis spoke in his defense. "A man need a son to carry his name. I'm gonna get one eventually, but a man also need a daughter to cherish and protect."

"You right, man," Mark agreed. "I want a son, but I'll be proud of all the children that Lucinda and I have."

"That's right," Lucinda added. "Girls are important, too."

Dwight seemed determined to have the last word. "Ah-ah, go on and blow out your candles, Curtis. I'm gonna let you off the hook since it's your birthday. Of course, any man know it don't take as much to make a girl. Shoot, you gotta pattern lying right under you!"

Everybody laughed. Curtis closed his eyes like he was making a wish and blew out the candles. Annie Ruth served the cake, and they all went into the den. Aldonia wanted to dance, so Lenny put "Another Saturday Night" by Sam Cooke on the record player and he and Aldonia lead the dancing. They partied until late that night. *I'm so glad I gave the party for Curtis. He looked so happy. And everybody said they had a good time. Curtis and I been having so many hard times, we really needed a good time.*

The following Monday, Annie Ruth was making Christmas decorations when the telephone rang.

"Hello."

"Annie Ruth, that you, My Lady?"

Raymond! Annie Ruth grasped the receiver. "Raymond?"

"Yes, it's me."

"I didn't know you'd come back."

"I slipped into town for a couple of days to visit my parents. I been thinking about you and how nice it would be to see you. What about meeting me somewhere?"

"No, I'm married, and I got a child."

Raymond laughed. His laugh made Annie Ruth want to throw off her responsibilities and dance down memory lane.

"I know you married. I'm married, too. I just wanna see you for old times sake. What harm could that do? Annie Ruth, don't go silent on me. I need to see you."

He right. What harm could us seeing each other do? "Okay, I'll meet you over in Gator Town around five o'clock at the first store on the right as you go into town from Rail City."

Raymond was waiting when Annie Ruth arrived. He was leaning against his new Cadillac dressed in a navy blue suit with matching accessories.

When she saw him, Annie Ruth could feel her heart pick up its pace. She got out of the car cautiously. She closed the door, but she didn't walk away from the car. Raymond walked over to her with a slight limp.

Annie Ruth tried not to stare. *Raymond looks so manly, now.* "The years must been good to you. You look real successful."

"I ain't shooting bad. My wife and I own a chauffeur business." Raymond's eyes swept over her. He smiled. "I hear you and Curtis inherited that big farm, and he works like a fool."

"We gonna make it," Annie Ruth said.

"I don't doubt it," Raymond said. "With you at his side a man can do whatever he wants to."

Annie Ruth remembered how Raymond had rejected her and all the pain it caused her. "Really?" Her voice was tinged with sarcasm.

Raymond took a deep breath. "I'm sorry, My Lady."

Annie Ruth swallowed hard and looked at Raymond's expensive shoes. "It doesn't matter anymore. It's all over and done with."

Raymond raised her face gently to his and kissed her lips. "You sure it doesn't matter anymore?"

Annie Ruth backed up and reached for her car door. *You done made a fool of me once, Raymond. I ain't gonna let you do it again.* "I'm positive."

Raymond dropped his hand and shook his head. "I don't believe this. I once had your nose wide open!"

Annie Ruth dropped her hand from the car door. "That's in the past. I love Curtis and respect our marriage." She folded her arms. "Why should I matter to you, anyway? I'm a black country woman. You got your white city woman."

Raymond shrugged. "Old Curtis always did have a crush on you." His eyes narrowed. "Why did you let him beat my time? When Mama wrote me and told me you'd gotten pregnant and married Curtis Lynch, I wanted to come back down here and 'tell your head a mess,' the nerve of you to go all the way with that country workhorse. You wouldn't even let me touch the rim of your panties!"

Annie Ruth smiled. *Thank God I didn't. I would've been a fool if I had.* "You got *who* you *want.*"

Raymond raised his eyebrows and spoke with his old confidence. "Yeah, I love my wife. Ain't anything wrong with her being white."

"No, it ain't. Love ain't got anything to do with color. Who you marry is your business." Annie Ruth was suddenly curious. "What happened to Gabrielle Sinclair?"

Pain surfaced in Raymond's eyes. "I heard she in college at

Emory and engaged to a bigtime lawyer."

Annie Ruth understood his pain very well. "First love ain't easy to forget."

Raymond replied sheepishly, "It sure ain't." He shrugged and returned to his seductive manner. "This ain't how I planned things. I thought we'd slip away somewhere and put a little loving on each other."

Annie Ruth laughed. "Daydreams are good for the soul."

"My soul wasn't on my mind, but that's the way it is, sometimes." Raymond reached into his pocket, pulled out a roll of money, and peeled off a hundred dollar bill. "Here, Annie Ruth, I think this will make up for the money I borrowed from you."

Annie Ruth took the money. "The extra fifty will cover the interest. Your loan been long overdue." She smiled. "Raymond, don't look so shocked."

"You really have changed."

Annie Ruth put the cash in her purse, got into her car, waved good-bye, and drove away. She smiled to herself as she headed back to Tobacco County. *I needed to see Raymond again to prove that I ain't been lying to myself all this time. Now, I know without any doubts that I don't love him anymore. He was still as good-looking and sweet-talking as ever, but I'm OVER him!*

Curtis was putting Patricia to bed when Annie Ruth got home. "Hey, sweetheart, did you find the material you were looking for in Gator Town?"

Annie Ruth held up the material she had hastily purchased after leaving Raymond. "Yes, I did. Thanks for taking care of Patricia." She undressed and dimmed the lights. Curtis looked mesmerized. Annie Ruth smiled. "We ain't ever took a bath together."

Curtis started unbuttoning his shirt. "There's a first time for everything."

The air in Aldonia's shop was still heavy with the scent of hair-dressing pomade. Annie Ruth wished she could get up, walk outside, breathe the fresh March air, and everything would be all right.

She gazed at Patricia playing with her toys on the floor and bent her head. Her mind and heart clasped hands in disapproval. "Please, Aldonia, don't force me to get involved."

Aldonia moved closer to Annie Ruth on the vinyl sofa. "It's still early in my first trimester. I ain't hardly two months."

"Maybe you ain't pregnant," Annie Ruth said.

"You wanna bet?" Aldonia said sadly.

Annie Ruth sighed. "No, I don't. I know how it was with me. You pregnant."

"Yeah, I done been to a doctor."

God, why this had to happen to me and Aldonia? "You told Harold?"

Aldonia looked across the room. "Yeah, his wife is pregnant, too." Aldonia's voice sounded angry. "Natalie always had perfect timing when it comes to keeping Harold and me apart."

Annie Ruth stared at Aldonia. "Was this pregnancy an accident?"

Aldonia cringed. "I had my diaphragm with me, but I didn't use it." Aldonia's voice dropped. "Deep down I was hoping that a pregnancy would push Harold into divorcing Natalie and marrying me."

"Well, you need to think about your baby, now."

Aldonia stood up. "I ain't gonna have a baby. I'm gonna end

this thing before it's too late."

Annie Ruth shook her head. "I'm sorry, but I can't help you. I don't believe in abortions. Two wrongs don't make a right."

"Hell! Annie Ruth, don't preach to me. I ain't got some nice single man to help me through this like you did." Aldonia sucked in her breath. "Curtis love you. If you told him to jump, he'd say how high, sweetheart?"

Annie Ruth blushed. "Don't get nasty, Aldonia."

Aldonia sat back down quickly. "Please, forgive me. I'm about to go crazy. I ain't able to provide for a baby."

Annie Ruth began to plead. "Don't worry about money. Just think about doing right by your child. Very few people can afford a baby, but they make it, though."

Aldonia sighed. "I can't help but to worry about money. You know how it feel to need money, but you don't know how it feel not to have enough to eat. Uncle Sid always been a good provider. I wish my daddy was like him."

Aldonia stared at Annie Ruth. "How many times have you had to eat cornbread and pot licker for supper? You ever had to wear your shoes until they were almost bottom-less?" Aldonia shook her head. "I don't want a child of mine to have to experience poverty the way I did."

"Your child won't. You too strong to let that happen. I know you don't want the guilt of an abortion on your conscience," Annie Ruth said. "You got one year of college and cosmetology training. You could make it up north." Annie Ruth was trying to think fast. "Call Cousin Fannie. I'm sure she'll let you stay with her until after you have your baby."

"No, even if I went up north, I still wouldn't want to have an illegitimate baby," Aldonia said. "You know how they do girls in our church when they have a baby and they not married."

Annie Ruth waved her hand. "Ah-ah, that ain't nothing. You just confess your sin and renew your membership. You go up north and you won't have to be bothered with that."

Aldonia was quiet for a while. Annie Ruth hoped she was thinking about not having an abortion. *Lord have mercy, I always heard people live to regret those things. I know I wouldn't want to have one.*

Aldonia propped her head in her hands and stared across the room. "When I was a little girl and use to see those girls stand up in front of the whole church and apologizing for having a baby, I always said I'd never have a baby and not be married." Aldonia sat back up straight. "Look at Juanita Bates and Ethel Combs. They both graduated from high school the same time I did. Juanita's got three children—all by different men, and she ain't ever been engaged. Ethel is pregnant with her second illegitimate baby by Pete Ways, and he done skipped town on her. I ain't gonna wind up like them."

"Don't keep talking about *illegitimate,*" Annie Ruth said. "It's a lotta Negro children whose parents weren't married and those same children are *somebody* today." Annie Ruth pointed to Patricia playing on the floor. "A baby just a baby. It ain't got anything to do with how it got here." Annie Ruth touched Aldonia's stomach. "That baby you talking about getting rid of could be your pride and joy. Just cause you have one baby and ain't married, it doesn't mean you gotta have two."

Aldonia stood up and walked over to the window of the shop. "No matter what you say, I ain't going through with this pregnancy. Harold can't leave his wife. My daddy is a poor provider. I can't depend on him. If it wasn't for Mama and me, we'd be living from hand to mouth in a shack somewhere."

Aldonia turned her back to the window. "I ain't gonna break

my mama's heart by having an illegitimate baby."

Annie Ruth remembered how Mama had acted when she got pregnant. "I understand how you feel about that."

Aldonia folded her arms and looked directly in Annie Ruth's eyes. "I'm gonna get an abortion. It's my decision, not yours. I just want you to go with me."

Annie Ruth rubbed her forehead nervously and sighed. "How you gonna get an abortion? They illegal."

Aldonia sat back down on the sofa. "I gotta friend in Savannah who works for a doctor who will give me one this Friday night. I'll ask Curtis if you and Patricia can go with me to visit Aunt Geechee."

"So, Aunt Geechee knows."

"Yeah, but you and her are the only ones in the family who know. I want y'all to keep it a secret."

Annie Ruth nodded. *Lord have mercy, we about to be a family of secrets.*

Aldonia went on. "Aunt Geechee don't believe in abortions, but she ain't judgmental. She said I can recuperate in her house." Aldonia squeezed Annie Ruth's hand. "You and Patricia can come back Sunday after you sure I'm all right. Aunt Geechee is getting old. I'll feel better if you be there."

Annie Ruth tried to ignore the sick feeling in her stomach. "Okay, you ask Curtis. Seem like you gonna do this, no matter what."

Aldonia nodded. "I'm gonna do what I gotta do to survive."

The next Saturday morning, Annie Ruth was pushing Patricia in the swing in Aunt Geechee's yard, her conscience clouded with guilt. She felt like an accomplice to murder. *No, I ain't gonna allow myself to feel like that. Aldonia was gonna have an abortion whether I came or not. I'm here cause I didn't want her to bleed to death or something. It was her decision not mine. I don't agree, but I guess she did what she had to do to survive.*

Aunt Geechee came out into the yard. "It's a pretty day, ain't it?"

"Yes, ma'am," Annie Ruth said. "How's Aldonia?"

"That doctor knew what he was doing. She gonna be okay. Harold with her. So, I came out to visit with you and Patricia."

Annie Ruth shook her head. "Aunt Geechee, I don't feel good about Aldonia's decision, cause I ain't proud of how I got Patricia, but I'm sure glad I had her."

Aunt Geechee took a seat in a lawn chair. Annie Ruth left Patricia on her own in the swing and sat down beside her. "Yeah, I know what you mean. Being a midwife, I ain't ever wanted to do anything but save babies lives." Aunt Geechee turned to Annie Ruth. "When I was a young woman like you, and my husband was alive, I got up early one morning to use the slop jar. I felt a sharp pain. When I got up. I saw what would be my only child—bloody and dead." A painful look covered Aunt Geechee's face. "I still had almost five months to go. I cried for the longest. My husband did everything he could to try to comfort me. Some nights I'd dream about it and wake up screaming, 'My Baby! My Baby!'"

Aunt Geechee sighed. "We can't judge poor Aldonia. The whole matter is between her and God."

Aunt Geechee looked at Patricia in the swing and started talking baby talk to her. "Her such a cute thing. Her be two years old, now. Ole Aunt Geechee sure love for her to come to visit."

Patricia grinned and blew her ancient aunt a kiss. Annie

Ruth and Aunt Geechee laughed. "That child sure looks like Angela did," Aunt Geechee said. "Well, that's to be expected, cause you look like her, Annie Ruth."

"Yeah, I know," Annie Ruth said.

Aunt Geechee kept talking about Aunt Angela. "She was a pretty thing. She had the Watsons' smooth black skin, tall stature, and thick hair." Aunt Geechee shook her head in awe. "Angela had a head on her shoulders. She was a schoolteacher and had a master's degree. Everybody figured she'd end up a principal or something, but that no-good Ray Rodgerson sweet-talked her into marrying him. It was just like the poor child had married Satan's brother."

Now I can find out why Mama, Daddy, and Granny are so tight-lipped about Aunt Angela and what happened to her. "Aunt Geechee, tell me what happened to Aunt Angela. All I ever heard was that that Ray Rodgerson caused her to be raped by a white man."

Aunt Geechee's many bracelets jangled as she folded her arms across her breast. "Nobody like to talk about what happened cause her life ended so badly."

"If she was a teacher and all that, how she get involved with a person like Ray Rodgerson?" Annie Ruth asked.

Aunt Geechee seemed to get angry just talking about Ray Rodgerson. "Ray was a schemer. He knew how to put on a big front and make people think he was a lot more than he was," she said. "He was a sharp dresser and a smooth talker."

"Oh, he was a handsome man," Annie Ruth said.

Aunt Geechee smacked her lips in disgust, "No, he was a good dresser, real clean and neat, but he was short and round with narrow eyes and an arrogant manner."

"I wonder why Aunt Angela fell for him?"

"He was a smooth talker. He could talk as smooth as owl's shit," Aunt Geechee said. "Angela was always a hard working, bookworm type of person. I doubt she'd ever kissed a man before she met him. She was a very sweet person, and always tried to live the right way."

Annie Ruth could tell that Aunt Geechee had a long story to tell, so she relaxed and listened.

"I don't really know where Ray grew up. His mother moved here when she inherited Sally Dale's house. Ray showed up a few months later. I distrusted him from the beginning. He was always putting on airs and talking like he was a 'bigtime' man. He'd brag, 'I go to Atlanta and New York frequently.' He could always tell somebody else how to handle their financial affairs and business transactions, but he didn't seem able to do much with his own. He was l-a-z-y. That man could come up with more excuses to keep from working than Van Camp's got beans! The whole family, her friends, and even some of the other people around here who had dealings with Ray tried to tell Angela not to marry him, but she already had fallen in love with him. In less than a year, that roach of a man had ruined Angela's life.

"I'll never forget it. It was raining hard on the third Sunday in June, and I was up early getting my things ready to go to Sunday School at my church. I heard a soft knock on the door. When I opened it, Angela was standing there. Her appearance was straight heart-wrenching. I could hardly believe that the messy, red-eyed woman in a wrinkled dress was her. I said, 'Angela, what in the world is wrong with you?' She said, 'Aunt Geechee, please, let me in.'

"She collapsed on the floor. I got her up and put her in bed. Then I bathed her, put her on a clean nightgown, and braided her hair. After she had rested and came to herself, she told me about the horrible thing that had happened to her. 'Aunt Geechee, I should have listened to you and the rest of the family when you all tried to warn me about marrying Ray. I was so in love with him until I didn't see the kind of person that he really is.'

"Tears streamed down her face. She said he had spent all her savings and run up her credit accounts. He never helped pay any of their bills and was always asking for money. 'He's arrogant, pretentious, bossy, mean, and lazy,' she said. 'Angela,' I said, 'I don't know what all them big words mean, but I sure know that he mean, bossy, and lazy.'

"'Yeah, and you sure tried to warn me,' Angela said. 'In spite of everything that I know about him now, I would never have believed that he would have done the low-down nasty thing that he's done to me.'

"'Child, what he do?' I asked.

"Angela put in to telling me. 'Ray likes to try to live like a big shot.' 'Yeah, but he works like a no-shot,' I said.

"'That was one of our biggest problems,' Angela said. 'He wouldn't work to help me pay our bills, but he was always making bills. After he got our credit in such a mess until he couldn't get any loans, he started borrowing from Mr. Ned.'

"I said, 'Mr. Ned! Didn't that foolish Ray know that if you don't pay that evil white man, he'll have you killed?'

"Angela shrugged. 'Well, Ray is such a crook himself until he doesn't have common sense. Apparently, Mr. Ned had other plans for Ray if he didn't pay. Ray left home yesterday morning and he didn't come back until about ten o'clock last night and Mr. Ned was with him. Ray told me to fix them a glass of wine. Seeing that I had only poured two glasses, Ray told me to fix myself one, too. I told him he knew that I didn't like to drink and I said I was going in our bedroom to read. Ray was acting strange and nervous.

"'He shouted at me, "Hell, woman, can't you get off of your high-and-mighty horse and have a drink with your husband and his company? Pour yourself a drink!" His outburst startled me. Ray can be so mean. I didn't feel like arguing with him. Plus, I didn't want to make a scene in front of Mr. Ned. I poured myself a drink. Before I could take a seat, Ray told me to go to the kitchen and get Mr. Ned a slice of cake. When I returned, Ray told me to go ahead and drink my wine before it got warm. I just wanted to go to my bedroom, so I drank the wine quickly. It tasted funny. and then I started feeling light-headed, like I was moving in slow motion and my vision got so blurred I could barely see Ray and Mr. Ned. I blanked out. When I came back to, I was lying naked on our bed.'"

"Angela was sobbing. 'Aunt Geechee, it was awful. Mr. Ned was on top of me. He was naked, too. He was doing things to me that I've only let my husband do.'

"Lord have mercy!" I said to Angela.

"She said, 'Aunt Geechee, Ray just stood by the bed and watched. He had a disgusting grin on his face. I heard him say, "She good, ain't she, Mr. Ned!" I was screaming and I was so humiliated and sick to my stomach that I threw up. Ray quickly cleaned it up, and said, "Don't worry about that, Mr. Ned. She just biggity. Thinks she too good to get a good screwing. Go on and take care of business."'

"Angela told me she kept blanking out and when she come to she tried to fight and scream but it done no good. She said she thought Mr. Ned had sex with her three times and then after he left Ray got on top of her. She said she begged Ray to leave her alone but he slapped her and shouted, "You high society black bitch. I gotta right to fuck you if I want to. I'm your husband!"

"Angela began to cry even harder. 'Aunt Geechee, what am I going to do? I feel so dirty and used. I can't face other people after what has happened to me.'"

"I told her, 'Angela, you ain't done nothing wrong. It wasn't your fault.'"

Annie Ruth frowned sadly. "How could a man do that to his own wife?"

Aunt Geechee twisted her face in disgust. "He wasn't a man. He was a roach of a person, a self-righteous, wanting-something-for-nothing bum!"

"What happened after that?" Annie Ruth asked.

Aunt Geechee sighed. "In a way, Angela died that night, cause her spirit was gone. Mr. Ned and Ray murdered her spirit that night. Angela sank into a deep depression. She barely ate, and she just stayed here in my house. She resigned from her teaching job and told me to take care of her business. Ray had made a mess of their money matters. I called the creditors and told them to repossess everything. They had so many bills until there was no other way. Angela didn't want any of their things, anyway. That low-down Ray Rodgerson had the nerve to come over here after he found out that Angela was letting everything get repossessed."

"'I wanna see my wife,' he barked at me.

"'You ain't got a wife, cause you ain't been acting like a husband,' I snapped back.

"'I ain't studying you old woman.'

"'You need to be studying something,' I told him. 'How could you drug your wife and then let a man rape her?'

"That sorry Ray claimed he had no choice. He owed Mr. Ned $500 plus interest and he couldn't pay it but Mr. Ned would give him another month to come up with the money if Ray could fix it so he could lay up with Angela. Otherwise, he going to have Ray killed. 'You know how he like to mess with colored women. He just took advantage of me in order to get to Angela,' Ray told me.

"I told him, 'Seem like you still alive and well and over a month done passed.' Ray said, 'My mama mortgaged her house and borrowed some money for me.'

"Then I told Ray off. 'Ain't nothing you can say that will excuse you for what you did. If you had taken your lazy behind to work, and not went around spending so much money, buying expensive cars and clothes on credit, and trying to act like you a big shot, you wouldn't have needed to borrow money from Mr. Ned! If you had really loved Angela, you would have taken her and run out of state until you got the money. You could've done something, but you didn't care about anybody but yourself.'

"'Go to hell!' Ray said. I told him, 'Don't invite me to go with you, cause you already writing your ticket.'

"Then I heard Angela say, 'Don't argue with him, Aunt Geechee. He's not worth your breath.' She was standing in the doorway holding my sawed-off shotgun with a mad look I had never seen on her before. 'Ray, you get away from here. I never want to see you again as long as I live.'

"Ray smiled like he didn't believe her. He said, 'Aw, Angela, I'm sorry about what happened. Come on, let's go home. We can stop the repossessions. I know that you ain't spent the money from your summer checks. We can get the Cadillac back and pay some on the bills. I heard about you resigning from your teaching job. As good a teacher as you are, they'll hire you again if you ask them.'

"Angela said, 'You still looking for the easy way in life, Ray. After all the terrible things that you've done, you still don't want to take any responsibility. Well, you've used me for the last time.'

"'I am your husband,' Ray said.

"'In name only.' Angela kept the gun pointed steady at Ray's head. 'You get away from here, Ray, before I do something that we both will be sorry for. Nothing matters to me anymore, Ray. You took all the beauty out of my life.'"

Aunt Geechee laughed sadly. "Ray got the message. That scoundrel ran back up the lane and onto the street faster than a young'un."

"What happened then?"

Aunt Geechee sighed. "Angela stayed around here with me. Talk got around town about what Ray had done to her. Angela stayed in my house most of the time cause she couldn't stand the stares and whispers. She was always the soft one. She wasn't strong like Sid and Florence."

"The family made plans to send her up north, so that she could start a new life and get back into teaching. She seemed to feel better. She started back to going to church and reading." Aunt Geechee frowned. "But then she missed her period. I took her to a doctor in South Carolina, cause folks around here had talked so much. She was pregnant. I think that was the burden that broke what little spirit the poor child had left."

"When we got back from the doctor, she said to me, 'Aunt Geechee, I don't know what color this baby is going to be. It could be Ray's, and it could be Mr. Ned's. We'll wait and see.'"

"I knew a doctor who'd done an abortion on a white girl

who'd been raped. I told Angela that I was sure that the same doctor would give her an abortion. But she said, 'Aunt Geechee, I don't believe in abortions, so I have no other choice but to have this baby. I pray that it will take its character traits from me and only take from its father the little goodness that's said to be found in even the worst human beings.'

"Angela just existed from then on. She didn't talk much or do much of anything. I used to beg her to eat. She was frail and sickly the whole nine months. Like she said, when the baby came, we knew. Billie Lee looked as white as any white baby I done ever seen.

"Sid, Carrie, and me were standing by Angela's hospital bed, when Ray burst into the room. 'I wanna see my wife,' he said, rolling his eyes at Sid and me.

"'You see her, now get out of here,' Sid told him.

"'She my wife.'

"'Then why you treat her like a dog? The only reason she ain't divorced your no-good ass is cause she found herself pregnant.' Sid was so mad his voice trembled. Ray started acting biggity. 'She ain't nothin', herself. That's a white baby down there in that nursery.'

"Sid was furious. 'Nigger, you know damn well why that baby is white. Your chicken-ass let her be raped by a white man in order to save your hide! I shoulda been killed you!' And Sid grabbed Ray and started choking him while Carrie was crying and begging him to stop. Angela herself pleaded with him. 'Please, please, Sid, let him go. He's not worth going to jail for. Think about Maybelle and your children. What will they do without you?'

"Sid looked at his sick, weak sister and dropped his hands. Ray stumbled backwards gagging for breath.

"Angela was so weak, but she kept talking. 'Sid, killing Ray won't change a thing. We all need you. I want you to help Ma raise my baby. I know I'm not going to live.'"

"Carrie started crying. 'Don't talk like that, daughter.'

"'It's my time, Ma. Take care of my baby. I named her Billie Lee—boy names so maybe she'll be strong. She needs to be strong.'

"A nurse came in and made everybody except Carrie leave. We went to the waiting room and Ray was in there. 'Why did y'all have Watson written as the baby's last name?' Ray asked. 'Angela and I are still married. Legally, she's a Rodgerson.'

"'Legally, you oughta be in jail, but you ain't,' I told him.

"Sid added, "That baby's name is Watson cause Watson blood is in her veins, and that's all that matters.'

"Ray's mother come into the room about then. She looked like she could hardly catch her breath she was so upset. 'Ray! How could you do such a nasty thing? I just saw that white baby! Folks told me you had let Mr. Ned lay with Angela. I didn't believe them. Now, I see it's true. And they say Angela ain't gonna live.'

"Ray's mother pointed her finger at him. 'Ray, you killed that child, and she was a good wife to you. You done made her lose everything. You my son, Ray, but the Lord don't like your ugly ways. You gotta stop cheating and using people, cause if you don't, the buzzards are gonna peck your eyes out.'

"Ray's mother was crying when she left the hospital. Ray left the hospital without saying anything else to Sid or me. Angela died an hour later. After her death, Ray left Savannah and went up North. He did time in prison for stealing. I think he was found dead in '49 or '50. They said he borrowed money from his girlfriend and wouldn't pay her back. Nobody was ever sure if she killed him herself or had him killed. Anyway, his body was found on the roof of an apartment building. Just like his mother prophesied, the buzzards had pecked his eyes out."

Annie Ruth took a deep breath. "Aunt Geechee, I'm glad you told me all about Aunt Angela. Now I understand why Mama was always preaching to me about not letting some sweet-talking man fool me."

Aunt Geechee nodded. Her bracelets jangled when she uncrossed her arms.

"How's Billie Lee?"

"She okay," Annie Ruth said.

"She still enjoying that pretty new house?"

"Yes, ma'am." Annie Ruth thought about Lenny beating Billie Lee. *I wish he wasn't so mean to her.* "Lenny ain't nice to her sometime. I tell her she gotta stand up to him."

Aunt Geechee nodded. "She easy-going like her mama was. And she love Lenny just as much as her mama loved Ray."

Annie Ruth went over and started pushing Patricia in the swing again. "Aunt Geechee, love is a strange thing."

Aunt Geechee's bracelets jangled again as she shifted in her chair. "It sure is. It can be like a comforter on a cold night. It can be everything. It can be the best thing, and it can also be the worst thing."

Harold walked out of the house and over to them. "Aldonia is asleep," he said. He smiled. "Aunt Geechee, you're still going strong. You're going to outlive all of us."

Aunt Geechee laughed. "I might. The Ogeechee River is definitely long, and that's what I was named after."

"Thank you for your help. Thank you, too, Annie Ruth," Harold said, heading to his car.

Aunt Geechee sat staring as he left. "Love can be like a

wound that never heals. Love can be like a haint—it keeps coming back."

That year the month of May brought a bountiful harvest from their spring garden. Annie Ruth had just finished putting some fresh squash in the freezer when Mama called her and said Billie Lee was in the hospital. Annie Ruth grabbed Patricia and rushed over there.

Daddy and Lenny were standing in the parking lot of the hospital arguing when Annie Ruth drove up.

"It don't make any sense. Being married to a woman don't give you a license to beat her!" Daddy shouted.

"Mr. Sid, I just got hot and flew off the handle too much. I done told Billie Lee that I'm sorry about hurting her," Lenny replied.

"Yeah, but this ain't the first time you done beat her," Daddy accused.

Lenny looked surprised. "I ain't a fool. I seen the signs," Daddy said.

Lenny looked Daddy squarely in the eyes. "I run my house, Mr. Sid, and you run yours. I'm the man of my house. If Billie Lee need to be set straight, then I gotta right to set her straight."

Daddy looked straight back. "Billie Lee a grown woman. Me, Mama, and Maybelle done a good job of raising her! She don't need you to try to raise her again. She being a good wife. A couple oughta talk and try to work things out."

Lenny responded sarcastically. "Thanks for the advice. Now, I gotta go take care of some business."

Daddy hadn't finished. "Lenny, Billie Lee's like my daughter. It hurts to see her being treated badly. Divorce her if you can't stop beating her." Daddy took a deep breath. "I don't cater to divorce, but I rather see y'all break up than see you keep beating her."

Lenny snarled. "Divorce! Shit! I ain't about to let Billie Lee go. The moment I let her go, every single man in Tobacco County will be trying to get her. I love her! She my woman!" Lenny pointed his finger in Daddy's face. "Mr. Sid, get off my back and outta me and Billie Lee's business. Y'all Watsons are the damnest bunch of Negroes I ever seen. You have a little gripe with one, and here come the whole blame clan!"

Lenny pushed Daddy aside, jumped in his truck and sped away. Annie Ruth got out of the car and ran over to Daddy.

Daddy glared in Lenny's direction as he drove away. "Daughter, thank God I don't have the temper I done once had, cause that's one Negro woulda been meeting his maker right along now!"

A few days later, Annie Ruth was sitting on Granny's porch helping her shell garden peas. Patricia was playing in the yard.

"Lord, June ain't even here, and it's already hot!" Granny exclaimed as she emptied her pan of shelled garden peas into a large dish pan.

Annie Ruth threw some pea hulls into a basket. "Yeah, and it seem like you and I been shelling peas forever."

"Well, I'm glad to keep busy—keep my mind off things."

"I know what you mean, Granny." Annie Ruth frowned. "You reckon Billie Lee gonna ever learn to stand up for herself?"

"I don't know."

"I don't either. Lenny done took the 'rag off the bush' this time, though. He got better sense than to beat his wife until she miscarry."

"Annie Ruth, people done always had better sense than to

do stupid things, but that ain't ever stopped some of them."

Annie Ruth shook her head sadly. "Billie Lee been wanting a baby so bad, then when she finally get pregnant, her own husband beat her and make her lose it."

"Lenny said she slipped and fell," Granny said.

Annie Ruth couldn't keep the anger out of her voice. "Yeah, running from him cause he was beating her."

"Well, neither one of them knew that she was pregnant," Granny said. "I know he wouldn't been beating her if he'd known she was pregnant."

"Well, he ain't had any business beating her in the first place."

"You right about that. And what they were fighting about ain't worth a dime—Billie Lee burned the biscuits. Shoot," Granny said, "Lenny ain't the first man who had to eat burned biscuits."

"Ha! If I was Billie Lee, anything he eat if I had to cook it would be burned," Annie Ruth said.

"You ain't Billie Lee, Annie Ruth, and I suspect she gonna head right back to Lenny as soon as she can."

"After all he done to her!" Annie Ruth cried.

Granny filled her pan with more peas and began to shell rapidly. "She getting her strength back, and she been fretting about going back to work for Miss Bostic."

Annie Ruth put her pan down and rescued Patricia from being attacked by ants, and put her on the porch.

"Lenny seem to love Billie Lee, but why in the world you reckon he beat her?" Granny asked.

"He just mean, Granny." Annie Ruth looked in the direction of an approaching truck. "Speak of the devil, here come Lenny."

Annie Ruth and Granny busied themselves shelling peas. Neither of them said anything as Lenny got out of his truck and headed to the porch.

"I know the cat ain't got either one of y'all's tongue," Lenny joked, "cause Miss Carrie would preach it to death. And Annie Ruth would beat it to death first."

Granny looked up. "You mighty sharp and neat, Lenny."

"Thanks, Miss Carrie. I wanna see Billie Lee."

Granny didn't say anything.

Lenny seemed irritated. "Miss Carrie, don't go getting silent on me. I'm trying to be respectful."

"It's all right, Granny. Come on in, Lenny," Billie Lee said coming to the door.

Granny shrugged and continued shelling peas. A while later, Lenny and Billie Lee came out together.

"Granny, I got all my things," Billie Lee said. "I'm going home. Lenny gonna take care of me."

Annie Ruth stood up. "Yeah, I bet he will!"

"Annie Ruth, sit your black ass down and finish shelling them peas with Miss Carrie," Lenny warned.

Annie Ruth turned toward Billie Lee. "How can you trust him?"

Lenny replied angrily. "Mind your mouth, Black Beauty. This ain't none of your business. I know Curtis worships you, but you don't get nothing here, cause I'll slap you back into your black place, quick!"

"Sit down, Annie Ruth!" Granny commanded.

Annie Ruth sat down.

Granny put her pan in a chair and stood up. "Don't you make any more black insults on my property, Lenny!" she warned. "Billie Lee love you to death. I don't want that love to be the death of her." Granny put her hands on her hips. "Billie Lee a good wife, and you better stop beating her."

Lenny responded in a subdued manner. "Okay, Miss Carrie. Come on, Billie Lee, before I have to hurt Annie Ruth." Lenny went to the truck with Billie Lee's things.

Billie Lee leaned down and hugged Patricia. "Bye y'all. I'll call."

"Bye."

Annie Ruth stared at them as they left. *I don't see how Billie Lee can trust Lenny. How can she be loving toward a man who made her lose her baby?* Annie Ruth looked at Granny and shook her head.

Granny picked up her pan and sat down. "Lenny her husband. She gotta make her own decisions."

13

Maturity

The last Saturday in May, Annie Ruth witnessed an unusual event in Aldonia's beauty shop. She could hear arguing before she opened the door. Patricia clutched her hand.

Aldonia and Lucinda were standing near the door arguing. Edwina was sitting quietly in the styling chair watching. All three of them looked surprised to see her.

"I got an appointment. Sorry, I'm disturbing y'all?" Annie Ruth asked cautiously.

"No, have a seat, Annie Ruth," Aldonia said. "I done finished Lucinda's hair, and she was just leaving." Aldonia walked away from Lucinda and started straightening Edwina's hair.

Annie Ruth sat on the sofa and pulled Patricia onto her lap. "I sleepy, Mama," Patricia said. Annie Ruth gently pressed her head against her breast.

Lucinda grabbed her wig and slipped it into its carrying case. "I sure was just leaving," she snapped. "And if certain folks don't learn to tend to their own business, I'm gonna find another hairdresser to fix my wigs and wash and press my hair." She glared in Aldonia's direction.

Aldonia blew the smoke from a hot straightening comb and replied, "One less head to fry!"

Lucinda turned angrily. "You need to sweep around your own door, Aldonia. Tell me, does the dog that's chasing your cat belong to you?"

Aldonia stopped straightening Edwina's hair and looked directly at Lucinda. "No, he doesn't. I ain't saying I'm perfect. I'm saying even a cat can cover its shit!"

"Huh!" Lucinda threw her head in the air and stormed out of the door.

Annie Ruth gasped. "Lord have mercy! What's wrong with y'all?"

Edwina said, "Let it be, Annie Ruth." Annie Ruth started to say something else, but Edwina gestured to her to be quiet.

By the time Aldonia finished Edwina's hair, Patricia was sleeping soundly. Annie Ruth laid her on the sofa so she could get her hair done. Now, that Edwina was gone she tried to get Aldonia to tell her what the argument between her and Lucinda had been about.

Aldonia refused to discuss it. "Let it go," she said.

Aldonia stared at Patricia. When she saw Annie Ruth looking at her, she quickly looked away and went to the storage cabinet. Annie Ruth had seen the sadness in her eyes, though.

"I know you glad you had her," Aldonia said bending to get clean towels.

Annie Ruth sat in the shampoo chair. "Yes, I am."

Aldonia got the towels and started washing some combs in the shampoo bowl behind the chair. Annie Ruth wondered if she was beginning to regret the abortion. "You sorry you had the abortion?" Annie Ruth said glancing back at her.

Aldonia finished washing the combs. "I regret having sex with Harold and getting pregnant." Aldonia combed Annie Ruth's hair in preparation for shampooing.

Annie Ruth was glad that abortion wasn't among her own sins. "But do you regret the abortion?"

Aldonia looked at her. Annie Ruth looked up. Aldonia's eyes were sad and stern. "I did what I had to do in order to survive. I'd make the same decision today."

"You still going with Harold?"

Aldonia adjusted the chair. Annie Ruth leaned back on the shampoo bowl.

"I seen him a few times, but I'm fixing to quit him. After the abortion, my love for him ain't seemed so sweet."

Annie Ruth thought about what Aldonia had said while she shampooed her hair. *I told Aldonia to be careful a long time ago. Curtis and I were both scared that she was gonna get the short end of the stick. I be dog, if it didn't work out like we feared. I wish she hadn't had to get that abortion. Everything's been so hard on her.*

It's so hard being a woman. I see why Mama was always preaching to me when I was growing up. It seem like no matter what, the burdens always seem to fall on our laps.

Ain't no telling how these menfolks gonna treat you. You don't ever know when they might two-time you like Raymond did me or like Harold did Aldonia. They might go weak on you (like Curtis) and you gotta wear the pants. They might get to have things their way, just cause they the man (like Mark). They might keep you pregnant and at home (like Dwight). Or they might beat you (like Lenny). But we still love them, cause they the men and we the women.

They can give you beautiful children. And then you just about work and worry yourself to death trying to be a good mother. God,

*is there anything EASY about being a woman? If there is, then,
please, Jesus, shine the light on it, cause I can't see it.*

Curiosity simmered slowly in Annie Ruth's mind while she
drove home. Both Lucinda and Aldonia were so out-going and
generous-hearted. What could possibly cause the anger she'd
witnessed between them a few hours before?

Her curiosity about the argument suspended when she arrived home and found Curtis sitting on the front porch reading. The sight of him reading a farm magazine with a stack of
newspapers beside his chair reminded her of his sobriety. Annie
Ruth let Patricia play in the yard while she sat with Curtis on the
porch. He picked up some papers off the stack of newspapers
and handed them to her. Annie Ruth took them. They were
calendar sheets. She looked at him.

Curtis answered her before she asked what the sheets meant.
"Each sheet represents a month that I ain't took a drink."

Annie Ruth looked through the sheets. November, 1963,
December, 1963, January, 1964, February, 1964, March, 1964,
April, 1964. The phrase "Praise God" was written on all the
weekend dates. The pages were like sheets of gold to Annie Ruth.
Curtis was beating his drinking problem, Praise God, indeed!

Curtis told her that he would give her the calendar sheet for
the month of May after the weekend was over. They decided
that her next moonshine run would be her last. *One more run
and no more Shine Annie*

Curtis had another present for Annie Ruth that Saturday
evening. He handed her a large envelope. When she opened
it, she found an application for Savannah State College and
other information.

She looked at Curtis questioningly. Curtis smiled. "It's time you went to college and got that degree you always wanted. I wanna help you go to pay you back for all the sacrifices you made for me."

Annie Ruth's hands trembled with excitement. "How can I go to college? What about you and Patricia?"

Curtis seemed to have already thought everything out. "You can go to college during the regular term and be home during the summer to help with the canning and freezing. Aunt Geechee will probably let you board with her. We can see each other on weekends."

I can't believe I gotta second chance to go to college. It's gonna be a lotta work, but I can do it. "Your plans sound good. Mama will probably be glad to keep Patricia while I'm away at college."

They decided that Annie Ruth would begin college the next year, fall, 1965. They talked about their future plans for the rest of the evening.

Annie Ruth was still awake that night after Curtis had gone to sleep. He had embraced her after they made love, and she was still in his arms. She knew she was strong. Yet, it felt good to be able to walk at her husband's side and let him be the man. Annie Ruth snuggled closer to Curtis. He stirred, tightened his embrace and started making love to her again. *Yes! Having Curtis act like the man of the family feels wonderful, and it's just as good as his most passionate midnight loving!*

The next day, Annie Ruth and her family went to Mama and Daddy's house for dinner after church. They were having a small family get-together. Granny, Billie Lee, Lenny, Aldonia, Aunt Florence, and Uncle Bill were there. Everybody was happy about

Annie Ruth's decision to stop hauling moonshine. Billie Lee and Aldonia quickly agreed that they were ready to quit, too.

The women were sitting on the porch when the men came out of the house from watching a wrestling match on television. When Daddy came out, he paused by Mama, put his hand on her shoulder, and leaned down and kissed her on the cheek Mama patted his hand and smiled up at him. Annie Ruth blushed at her parents' unexpected display of affection. She stared at Daddy inquisitively. What had happened to Daddy while she had been so wrapped up in her and Curtis's money problems and other troubles? What had caused him to lose weight and look so weary?

Daddy said that he and the rest of the men were going out to look at his new tractor. The other men quickly stepped down off the porch. Daddy followed them more slowly. *Lord have mercy! Daddy's health is failing him!*

Mama watched Daddy as he walked away. She started talking when he was too far away to hear her. "Don't y'all let on to Sid what I'm gonna say, cause he don't wanna worry nobody. He going down. He be so sick some nights he can hardly rest." Mama started crying. She wiped her eyes and went on. "He just been waiting for Annie Ruth to stop hauling shine, so he could stop keeping it in his barn."

Granny looked like she was about to cry, too. She reached over and patted Mama on the shoulder. "He sure prayed hard in church today."

Mama wiped her eyes again and nodded sadly. "I think he trying to get his soul right."

Annie Ruth felt a lump of fear in her throat. "Mama, Granny, please, don't talk like that!"

Annie Ruth and Billie Lee completed their last moonshine run the next Sunday evening.

I felt so good when the last load of moonshine was unloaded and Billie Lee and I was headed back to Tobacco County. I felt like screaming hallelujah! Then I felt bad cause we'd been sinning by hauling moonshine, and it was like God had protected us in spite of our wrong doing.

I shuddered when I thought of what could've happened. We could've been arrested or worse we could've been shot or killed in a revenuer raid.

It seemed like Billie Lee was thinking about the same thing cause she said, "Annie Ruth, I'm sure glad we through hauling moonshine."

"I'm glad, too," I replied.

"I'd already decided to quit before you told me you were quitting."

I nodded and said, "I expected you to quit right after y'all built your new house."

Billie Lee shifted in the car seat. "I kept hoping having more money would make Lenny happier, and he'd be nicer to me."

I understood quite well how money can affect a relationship. "Money can make things easier sometime," I said.

"Maybe so, but it ain't made Lenny any nicer to me." Billie Lee turned toward me. "Annie Ruth, I ain't ever gonna do anything illegal and risk my safety and loyalty to God ever again like I did hauling moonshine."

My hands gripped the steering wheel. Billie Lee had voiced my exact feelings. I remembered how I felt that afternoon when I drove out of my yard. Patricia was by a bunch of pampas grass waving to me as I drove off. She looked so sweet and innocent. I don't want folks whispering behind her back one day, "Her mama used to haul moonshine." (I sure hope our family continue to keep our secret).

I love our farm. And God knows it woulda almost killed Curtis and me to have to sell it, but it wasn't worth hauling moonshine for.

Billie Lee must have been thinking about that, too, cause she said, "Annie Ruth, ain't anything, ain't a love, ain't a man, and ain't any land worth disobeying God for."

I relaxed my hands on the steering wheel and said, "AMEN!"

Later that Sunday night, Annie Ruth was sleeping peacefully when she was awakened by the telephone. Curtis got up and answered it.

She couldn't believe her ears when Curtis came back and said that Mama had called to tell them that Mark had killed both Lucinda and Lenny. They got dressed and went to Granny's house, because Mama had said that was where Billie Lee had gone after she heard the news.

The whole family, including Reverend Phillips, Mary Joyce, Edwina, and Dwight, was at Granny's house. Curtis went with the men to the jail to see Mark.

Aldonia explained to Annie Ruth that she had found out about Lucinda and Lenny's year-long affair from Hootie Simpson. She and Lucinda had argued the week before because Aldonia had warned Lucinda to break off the affair.

Billie Lee was in her old bedroom. Annie Ruth went to her as soon as she could. She opened the door and stood.

Billie Lee was lying on the bed. She looked at Annie Ruth.

"May I come in?" Annie Ruth asked.

Billie Lee wiped her tearful eyes. "Come in."

Annie Ruth closed the door and went over and sat on the side of the bed. "I wish I could say something to make you feel better."

Billie Lee dropped a wad of tissue in the waste basket near the bed and got several more out of a box on a nearby table. "I wish you could, too. But ain't anything to say, though."

Annie Ruth and Billie Lee were quiet for a while. Billie Lee seemed to be in deep thought. Finally, she said, "Remember that joke they use to tell about the Negro woman who went to heaven and asked Jesus why he had given her such black skin and kinky hair."

"Yeah, I remember it," Annie Ruth said. "I always hated that joke."

"I did too," Billie Lee said. "I always thought it was disrespectful of Jesus and Negro women."

"It was."

Billie Lee wiped her eyes. "Sometimes, I think about seeing Jesus."

"You will. Your heart is pure."

"I mean now, not after death. I'd like to ask him why I wasn't given dark skin and kinky hair like my mother. Why I had to look like my evil white daddy?" Billie Lee sighed. "I'd also ask him why a good person like my mother had to be betrayed and hurt."

I'm glad Billie Lee ain't expecting me to answer her, cause Lord have mercy, I couldn't answer her in a million years.

Billie Lee kept talking. "Annie Ruth, you and Aldonia are my friends, but y'all are also relatives. If anybody had asked me who was my closest non-relative friend, I woulda said, 'Lucinda.'" Billie Lee shook her head sadly. "She betrayed me. She grinned in my face and stabbed me in the back."

Annie Ruth replied carefully. "I don't think Lucinda intended to hurt you. I think she had a lotta resentment against Mark cause he wouldn't move to New York. I really think her affair with Lenny was a way to get back at Mark."

Billie Lee started crying again. "Lenny's betrayal hurts me more than Lucinda's. I love him so much." Billie Lee's voice got higher. "How could he beat me and be sweet to her? That ain't fair."

Annie Ruth took a cloth out of a wash basin sitting on the nearby table and began to bathe Billie Lee's face. "Cry, honey child, cry it all out."

Later that night, while waiting for the men to come back from the jail, Annie Ruth sat at Granny's dining room table with the other women.

"I tried to warn Lucinda," Aldonia said rubbing her sleepy eyes. "She said she loved Mark. Everybody know how crazy he was about her. Seem like she oughta been trying to keep her husband."

Aunt Florence looked at her work-roughened hands. "That girl had a good provider. A lotta women woulda been glad to be married to a hard working man like Mark."

Granny had been keeping busy all night doing one thing or another. She'd already served coffee and was now serving pound cake. "Billie Lee always thought of Lucinda as a friend. I don't see how Lucinda coulda went with her own friend's husband."

Mama picked up a piece of cake and then paused to preach her little sermon, "Lucinda forsook her marriage vows, and she didn't live to repent. That's why we gotta be careful about what we do."

Edwina sounded like she thought Lucinda had acted like a fool.

"I love Dwight and my boys too much to even imagine another man. I don't know what Lucinda coulda been thinking."

"I know Lucinda's mother real well," Mary Joyce said stirring her coffee. "She didn't raise Lucinda to be like that."

"Uh-huh," Mama added. "I feel sorry for her, too, losing her only daughter in a mess like this."

Annie Ruth offered the same explanation she'd given Billie Lee. "I think Lucinda was just trying to get back at Mark for not moving to New York." *They don't see what I mean, cause they like me, they happy living in the South. They think Lucinda had everything a woman could want—a good husband and material things. But Lucinda didn't think like we do. She wanted more. I know cause I remember how she looked that cold Saturday morning in '62 when she talked about wanting to move to New York and having to stay down here and live without her dreams. Poor thing, she'd still be alive if she hadn't had dreams.*

After the men returned from the jail that night, Annie Ruth and Curtis went home. Curtis had gotten ready for bed and was sitting by their bedroom window by the time Annie Ruth finished getting ready for bed. She knelt down beside him and placed her hand in his.

Curtis squeezed her hand. "It was a hard time at the jail, sweetheart."

"I know it was bad seeing your friend locked up."

Curtis nodded. "They put us in the cell with Mark and locked the door. He was sitting on a dirty cot like he was in a trance. We all squatted down. At first nobody said anything. Finally, Mr. Sid spoke, 'Mark, we ain't here to judge you. We sorry about what happened, but we still your friends.' 'Yeah,' we all agreed. Dwight said, 'I called Mr. Tucker. He said your parents done already called him, and that he gonna help them get you a good lawyer.'

"Mark's lips moved several times before any sound came out. 'Ma and Pa told me. They were here earlier. Before they left, Ma asked me why I didn't walk away and say to hell with both of them. I been sitting here thinking about why I acted so hastily. I was to drive a truck outta town, but it broke down, so Mr. Tucker told me to go back home. All I could think about was taking a warm bath, making love to Lucinda, and getting a good night's rest.' Mark paused. 'I felt like something was wrong when I walked in the door. I felt kinda like folks whose houses done been robbed say they felt—like somebody invaded my privacy. All the lights were out except for a small lamp in Lucinda and my bedroom. I walked to the door.' Mark stifled a sob. 'They were both naked. Lenny was on top of Lucinda. They were loving each other so hard until they didn't even realize that I had walked in. I always leave a loaded pistol in the dresser drawer for Lucinda to protect herself when I have to drive a truck outta town.'

"Mark started crying while he talked. 'I couldn't control myself. It was like I had gone mad. I snatched open the dresser drawer, grabbed the gun, and started firing. I didn't stop until the gun was empty.'

"Mark looked like he was begging for understanding. He went back to talking after a few minutes. 'Men, y'all know how it is down here for us Negroes. We get treated like second-class citizens. We can't even drink water out of a decent water fountain in town or use a decent restroom. There ain't a white-owned restaurant that'll let a Negro go in and sit down and eat a meal. No matter how much education we get the best job we can hope for is to be a teacher or at the most a principal in a segregated school. If we get hired at a factory or a mill, it's always as a janitor or some other hard, dirty, low-paying job that the white men don't want.

"'My cousin, Henry, y'all remember him and how smart he was. He worked his way through college and became an engineer. He got hired by a company in Atlanta. One of his older white co-workers told him, *I hate to see a nigger with a job like you got. Some young white man ought to have your job so he can take care of his family.* You see, it was as if Henry didn't deserve anything for all his hard studying and work. It was like Henry's family didn't matter.'

"Mark looked at Mr. Sid. 'I done heard my parents talk many times about the way you done had to tell-off some of the whites around here about calling you and other Negro men *boys*. There ain't a white man around here who done worked any harder than you have or provided for and stood by his family any better than you, yet you had to make them call you by your name instead of *boy*.'

"Mr. Sid nodded sadly.

"Mark kept talking. 'Negroes around here still have to deal with *nigger knocking*—groups of white males riding around looking for Negroes to beat up.' Mark turned to Reverend Phillips. 'Reverend Phillips, you know you told me how when you were younger a group of rednecks caught you out on the road alone and were fixing to beat you up.'

"'You're right about that, Mark,' Reverend Phillips said. 'Mr. Tolbert happened to come along, and he made them leave me alone, because he said he knew my mama and daddy.' Reverend Phillips smiled. 'I've never in my life been as glad to see a white man as I was that day.'

"Mark had more to say. 'Dwight and I do the work of four

men, and Mr. Tucker get richer and we get by.' Mark glanced at me. 'The white banker made Curtis's daddy mortgage everything before he'd loan him money to pay Miss Victoria's medical bills.'

"Mark started talking louder. 'All a Negro man's got is his wife, her love, and maybe some children. If a Negro man ain't got the love of his family, then he ain't got much, cause his home is the only place he can be somebody. Lenny had a good wife, yet he still took mine. I love Lucinda. I tried to give her everything she wanted.' Mark looked like he got angry. 'I been wanting children since the first day we married, but I went along with her decision not to have them. I didn't matter though to her or Lenny. So, you see, I had to chastise them both!'"

Curtis put an arm around Annie Ruth's shoulders. He sighed and finished telling her about the jail scene. "Mark shouldn't have killed Lenny and Lucinda, but a lotta what he said was true. Annie Ruth, it took all the willpower I could muster to keep from bawling like a baby. I felt so bad. It was like we were all helpless—hardworking, humbled, Negroes, like we were all victims of circumstances. Finally, I said, 'Reverend Phillips, please, read some scriptures from your Bible, and then, please, pray. Pray for us *all*.'"

It's Wednesday. Lenny's funeral was today. We all been doing everything we can to comfort Billie Lee and make things easier for her. Mama and Granny helped her plan Lenny's funeral. I went over to her house and packed her clothes and moved them to Granny's house, cause she said she didn't wanna go home.

We all feared she wouldn't be strong enough to attend Lenny's funeral. So, I was glad when I visited her a couple of hours before the funeral and found her calmly getting dressed in her old bedroom.

She told me she'd dreamed about her mother last night.

She said at first she was a baby and Aunt Angela was singing to her softly. And then she was grown again and Aunt Angela was sitting beside her bed telling her that she loved her and she wanted her to be strong. Billie Lee said the dream had made her feel better and stronger.

"Annie Ruth, you reckon I'm wrong to believe in a dream?" she asked, handing me the beautiful black hat she'd bought to match her suit.

While I was putting the hat on her head and fixing the veil, I thought of the dream I'd had about Aunt Angela when I was sick. "No, honey child," I told her. "You ain't wrong."

Friday. Lucinda's funeral was today. All of the family except Granny and Billie Lee went. People were talking about Mark killing her and Lenny, even at her funeral. Some people thought Mark was forced to commit the crime due to Lucinda and Lenny's betrayal. Some people acted like it was just good gossip. But, a lotta people thought it was an unfortunate situation wherein everybody lost. I agree with those people. Lenny and I had our differences cause I didn't like the way he treated Billie Lee. But I ain't ever wanted to see him dead. Yeah, Lenny, you long, lean, mean, Negro, Mark shouldn't have killed you. And Lucinda, I don't like the way you betrayed Billie Lee. But, Mark didn't have to kill you. Child, you good-timing, sharp dressing, pretty heifer, you oughta still be alive.

After the funerals were over, Annie Ruth and Curtis concentrated on harvesting their crops. Mark's fate was determined in September. Reverend Phillips came by to tell them the verdict. The three of them were sitting at the kitchen table when he told them.

"Not guilty by reason of temporary insanity." Curtis repeated the verdict as though he was trying to make sure he'd heard it correctly. "I know Mark was wrong," he said. "But I still hated to see him be in jail."

Annie Ruth felt let down. "Lucinda and Lenny both deserved a second chance."

Reverend Phillips nodded. "You're right. Killing them didn't solve a thing."

Curtis shook his head sadly. "We all gotta start living our lives according to God's teachings."

Curtis said his next words in a low voice. "I done heard the Lord's warnings and his call."

Annie Ruth started to speak, but Reverend Phillips motioned to her to be quiet. He gave Curtis a searching look and then said, "Curtis, how many times has the Lord called you in his service?"

What? The Lord done called Curtis? Annie Ruth stared at her husband.

Curtis seemed shocked by Reverend Phillips's intuition. "I heard him first when I was at a prayer meeting before I finished high school. But, I thought I was too young." He smiled at Annie Ruth. "Then Patricia was on the way and Annie Ruth and I got married." His eyes saddened. I lost touch with God when Dad died and we found out about the farm being in debt. I heard him the second time that night we were in the jail with Mark."

"How many more times does he have to call you, Jonah?" Reverend Phillips exclaimed.

Annie Ruth shook her head in amazement. *Curtis a preacher, ain't life full of surprises?*

Later that day, Annie Ruth had fixed supper and was feeding Patricia when she heard a soft knock on her kitchen door. "Billie Lee, come in. You look terrific!"

Billie Lee turned around to show off her new outfit. She was wearing a mint green lace-trimmed cotton sheath with a matching belt.

Billie Lee sat at the table. "I came to tell you that I sold my house, furniture and all."

"That's good," Annie Ruth said. "But I didn't know you were gonna sell the furniture too."

"Two newlywed teachers at the high school wanted to buy everything. Uncle Sid went over the paperwork with me. He thought their offer was very fair." Billie Lee threw up her hands. "Shoot, Annie Ruth, I need a fresh start. That house and every stick of furniture reminded me of Lenny."

Annie Ruth nodded and continued feeding Patricia. "Well, you still real young. You got time to remarry and buy another house and furniture."

Billie Lee laughed dryly. "Lenny been dead only a few months and men already calling me. I turned them all down. I ain't ready to start keeping company with another man."

Annie Ruth smiled. "I ain't surprised. You an intelligent, beautiful woman and the men folks know it."

Annie Ruth finished feeding Patricia. Billie Lee handed her a napkin to wipe her mouth. "You'll feel differently as time goes by."

"Maybe." Billie Lee looked around. "Where's Curtis?"

Annie Ruth hesitated. "He ate his supper early and went to see Mark. You heard the verdict for his trial?"

"Yeah, Uncle Sid told me about it while we were at the lawyer's office getting the papers ready to sell my house. I'm glad he gonna be free. He was wrong for killing Lenny and Lucinda, but I didn't want to see him go to prison. His conscience will probably be prison enough."

"That's true. He gotta terrible burden to bear," Annie Ruth said. "I was kinda surprised at the verdict, though. I think he shoulda served some time."

Billie Lee spoke with a calmness that Annie Ruth admired and was glad to see. "They say he had a dynamite lawyer. Mark had a good reputation of being hardworking and a devoted husband." Billie Lee started tracing a flower on the table's oilcloth with her finger. "Let's face it, Annie Ruth. Lenny didn't have the best reputation. They said Mark's lawyer had more than enough witnesses to verify the fact that he and Lucinda had been going together for almost a year."

Having completed tracing the oilcloth flower several times, Billie Lee moved her manicured finger to an oilcloth vase and started tracing it. "We liked Lucinda, and we were friends to her, but a lotta people thought she was too fast and flirty."

Billie Lee stopped tracing the oilcloth pictures and looked thoughtful. "I wish Mark had just walked away that Sunday night and let Lucinda and Lenny have each other. We woulda all been better off divorced and going our separate ways."

Annie Ruth put Patricia down to play. *Thank God, Billie Lee is dealing with everything well.*

A few minutes later, Miss Bostic's son called. He asked to speak to Billie Lee, explaining that Granny had told him to call Annie Ruth's house. When Billie Lee hung up the phone she asked Annie Ruth to go with her to Miss Bostic's house.

Miss Bostic's son opened the door for them. "Y'all girls come in. Billie Lee, I appreciate you coming back. Mother has been asking for you."

Miss Bostic was writhing in pain on her bed. Her daughter-in-law was standing by her bedside with tears in her eyes.

Annie Ruth stood near the door with Patricia in her arms. A lamp near the bed was the only light that was on. It illuminated the room with a golden glow.

"The doctor has done all he can. Bless her heart, she's having a hard time, Billie Lee," the daughter-in-law said.

Miss Bostic struggled to focus her pain-filled eyes on Billie Lee. "Billie Lee, folks around here say you're half-white. I wanted to tell you that I've known some good people in every race." The old lady paused as if her will to talk and her pain were struggling against each other. "I've seen the good of two races in you. The Lord has smiled on you." The old lady gasped in pain.

Billie Lee took Miss Bostic's right hand in hers. The old lady continued to writhe. Her daughter-in-law took her left hand. Billie Lee began to sing softly and sweetly. Follow Jesus to your heavenly home. Follow Jesus. Follow Jesus. He know the way from earth to heaven. Follow Jesus to your heavenly home. He knows the way from earth to heaven. Follow Jesus. Follow Jesus.

Annie Ruth turned Patricia's face away from the bed and the dying lady. The writhing stopped. Miss Bostic's cooling lips froze in a smile.

Annie Ruth was in bed that night when Curtis got back from seeing Mark. He undressed in the bathroom and got into bed without turning on the bedroom light.

"Is Mark outta jail?" Annie Ruth asked.

Curtis turned towards her. "Yeah, he went to see all his family and packed his clothes."

"What he packed for?"

Curtis hesitated. "He, ah, he going to Savannah to visit his oldest sister, then he going to New York. His brother is gonna rent he and Lucinda's house."

Anger flared in Annie Ruth. "He going to New York?"

Curtis spoke carefully. "Sweetheart, you know he probably couldn't stand to stay in that house and in Rail City after what happened."

Annie Ruth exhaled loudly. "He wouldn't move to New York for Lucinda. But, now he done killed her, he go running up there."

"Well, Annie Ruth, you know Mark was a good husband to Lucinda. Everybody said it. Everybody talking about how he gave her everything she wanted."

"I think he gave her what *he* wanted her to have," Annie Ruth said. "The only thing Lucinda ever told me she wanted was to move to New York."

"I'm like everybody else, I don't see how she had an affair with Lenny if she wanted to be a good wife." Curtis's voice lowered. "Annie Ruth, you know people always called her fast. And Mark's folks never thought she was any good."

Annie Ruth's anger at Mark suddenly turned to sadness and sorrow for Lucinda. She pressed her face against Curtis's and cried. "Lucinda wasn't like they said. She made a mistake. Everybody makes mistakes. She deserved a second chance!"

Lucinda, I'm still your friend. I know you were just an out-going, fun-loving person. I wish you were still alive, living in New York, making your dreams come true, with or without Mark.

14

High Time

Time moved on. Life settled into work and easier times. It didn't seem like long before Curtis had given Annie Ruth calendar sheets representing his sobriety that ran from November, 1963, to March, 1965.

Curtis ain't drinking anymore. I'll be starting to college in the fall— Mama and Daddy so happy about that. Our financial situation is stable. Curtis is involved with voter registration. He even made a good speech to the all-white school board about giving more supplies to the Negro schools. Things are getting better. I believe we can make it.

One evening during the month of April, Reverend Phillips stopped by and asked Curtis to be the speaker for the men at the Women and Men Day Program at Elder's Chapel. Reverend Phillips told Curtis that a lot of people were impressed with the way he'd been handling himself with voter registration and with the way he had spoken to the all-white school board.

Annie Ruth smiled. *I'm so proud of Curtis.*

"I wish I could do more," Curtis said. "What do you want me to speak about?"

"Speak about men," Reverend Phillips told him. "And let it come from your heart."

Reverend Phillips also invited their church choir to sing. Annie Ruth sat in the choir stand in Elder's Chapel that fourth Sunday in May and smiled proudly at Curtis. She glanced at Mama, Daddy, Granny, and Miss Clara. They were all looking proudly at Curtis, too. Granny and Miss Clara were sitting next to each other. Miss Clara dabbed at her eyes several times. Granny reached over and patted her hand. *I know Miss Clara probably thinking about how she wish Mr. Andrew was still alive. I do, too.*

The spirit was high in the church. The speaker for the women finished. Reverend Phillips introduced Curtis.

"I present to you my first cousin, my close friend, my brother in Christ, Mr. Curtis Lynch."

Curtis walked over to the podium and placed a small stack of index cards neatly in front of him. He looked at the audience and stood up straight. His voice sounded warm and sincere.

"Reverend Phillips, pulpit guests, members, and friends, I am very thankful to be able to speak to you. It is with pleasure that I say the things that I have prepared to say. I asked Reverend Phillips what I should speak about. He told me to speak about men. He also told me to let it come from my heart.

"When I was in school, my teachers would sometimes tell me to be more specific whenever I answered questions, so I am going to speak about being a black man. I know that some of you are probably having trouble adjusting to the word 'black.' I'm truly sorry if you are, because if you are, in my opinion, that means that you have succumbed to the brain washing that has plagued our race and caused some of us to think that there is something bad or ugly about being black, and that a person should be ashamed of being black.

"Some of you would probably feel better if I said 'colored,' but, you see, my brothers and sisters, I was born this way. I was born with skin darker than mahogany, with hair that doesn't lie flat on my head, but prefers to rear up and kink, and with eyes that are not blue or green, but brown. My little daughter likes to use crayons to color pictures in her coloring book. When she finishes, she has colored pictures. I don't feel colored.

"Our ancestors were brought to this country as slaves from Africa. Research tells us that one of the first conditions of beauty in Dahomey, which was an ancient West African Kingdom, was blackness. Through 244 years of slavery and one hundred years of oppression, poverty, segregation, and overt prejudices, we have forgotten the beauty of blackness. So, I say to you, black? Yes. Negro? Yes. Colored? No."

The congregation applauded. Curtis seemed to relax.

"Romans 13:11 states, 'And that, knowing the time, that now it is *high time* to awake out of sleep: for now is our salvation nearer than we believed.'" Curtis paused and then said, "The title of my speech is High Time."

"High Time," the congregation repeated.

Annie Ruth felt her smile broadened. *Go head on, husband.*

Curtis went on. "The dictionary defines high time as being the time just before it's too late."

"Explain it to us, brother," was the response from the Amen Corner.

"On February twenty-first of this year, Mr. Malcolm X was assassinated. Reverend King and other civil rights leaders are still leading civil rights demonstrations. civil rights workers are still being murdered, beaten, and humiliated. I say to you, on this day, the fourth Sunday in May, 1965, in Rail City, Tobacco County, Georgia, it is high time!"

"A-a-amen, brother!" The audience responded.

"It is high time that the black man be called a man. God made two sexes—male and female. How can a white boy grow up to be a man, yet, a black boy grows up to be a boy? If the black man humbles himself enough and smiles the right way, y'all know what I'm talking about."

"Yes, we do. Lord have mercy," was heard from the deacon pew.

"I say, if he drops his eyes at the right time, grins, and belies his intelligence, steers clear of trouble, and remembers to say 'yes, ma'am' and 'yes, sir' to whites half his age and younger, then he'll get the distinguished title of 'uncle.' It is high time. It is high time that the black man be called a man!

"It is high time that the black man—the black race—obtains equal rights. It is high time that we are allowed to attend schools, colleges, and training institutions of our choice. It is time that the 1955 ruling that states must desegregate their schools with all deliberate speed be adhered to.

"It is high time that the black race be given equal opportunity to work on jobs with good salaries and benefits, to live in nice homes and neighborhoods, and to participate in a society without being plagued by 'white only' signs and 'colored' places that should be called unfit and humiliating. It is high time that we have equal opportunity to live like the proud human beings that we are, and be able to enjoy the greatness of this country. It is high time for the black man—the black race—to be set free from the modern bondages of poverty, prejudice, discrimination, and segregation.

"It is high time that we love ourselves, be proud of who we are. Remember the Dahomein's first condition for beauty—blackness. Let's remember the blackness. It does not matter if you are as dark as the pitch that is used to make pavements, or as light as the cream that our mothers use to make butter, remember the blackness, remember Africa, remember, and be proud!

"It is high time that we love each other. It is high time that we act like brothers. It is high time that we treat each other right, stand by each other and help each other. It is high time!

"It is high time that we stop being Uncle Tom and start being Mr. Black Man. Stop telling the white people what we are saying at the voter registration meetings. Stop saying bad things about Dr. Martin Luther King and other civil rights workers to the white folks. Stop 'talking down' another black brother just to try to make yourself look good in some white person's eye. Stop acting like crabs, when another black tries to get up and do something, don't pull him back down.

"It is high time that we not just be called men, but that we are men. Some say that the benefits of the Civil Rights Movement are going to materialize like a storm in this society. Some say that it's going to be a revolution. Revolution or storm, it is high time that we make ourselves ready for it. How can we be ready for the revolution if we are— Now, Church, I'm going to sweep around my own door first. How can I be ready for the revolution if I'm drunk on alcohol and letting it control my life? How can I be ready for the storm if I'm not standing up and being the man in my family. I cannot, and neither can you.

"It is high time that we get ready for the revolution. How can we be ready for the revolution if we're busy being baby makers, siring children by several women and fathering none of them? How can we be ready for the revolution if we walk away and leave the total support and nurturing of the black race's future—our children—solely in the hands of our women? How can we be ready for the revolution if we let alcohol and drugs cripple our brains and convert us to careless shadows? How can we be ready for the revolution if we are walking around, doing nothing, and talking about 'we've got to find ourselves'? Go to school, learn a trade, work on whatever job that you can find until you can do better, start your own business, volunteer for a charity organization, do something to help somebody, and then accept Jesus Christ as your Savior. He will help you to find yourself, because then you won't be lost! In the Bible, the Third Epistle of John, the second verse, says, 'Beloved, I wish above all things that thou mayest prosper and be in health.' God wants us to have a more abundant life. It is high time that we claimed a more abundant life. And when high time is over, and there is no time, and it is God's time to call, and our time to answer, we want Him to be able to say, 'Well done, my good and faithful servant, well done.' The Lord's going to give us eternal peace!"

The church exploded in applause. Billie Lee rose and began to sing. The choir and audience joined in jubilantly: "Lord, it's high time, and I done changed. I done accepted Jesus Christ as my savior and changed my ways. I'm going to praise his name all of my days. Lord, it's high time, and I done changed."

Applauding all the way, Miss Clara went up and hugged Curtis. Granny, Mama, and Daddy followed her.

Annie Ruth was standing with the choir. Her lips were singing, but her mind was saying, *Curtis you spoke so well. I'm so proud of you. You are becoming the man you're meant to be. I love you.*

Billie Lee nudged her. "Go congratulate your husband. You

gotta start acting like a preacher's wife."

Annie Ruth found her feet in her state of euphoria and went and hugged her husband. Reverend Phillips followed her. He told Curtis, "As soon as you're ready to heed the Lord's call, notify your pastor. He'll make all the necessary arrangements."

Curtis smiled and nodded. "I will."

Annie Ruth hugged him again and went back to the choir stand. *Curtis is really gonna be a preacher. Curtis got the strength to stay sober, now. I been thinking he did, but after today I know he gonna make it.*

The spirit was still high in the church. Annie Ruth looked at Aldonia in the congregation. *Lord have mercy. She crying up something. I know she feeling sad about how things turned out with Harold. She called me last night and told me she done quit him. I know she hurting, but I'm glad she done let him go, cause it was high time.*

The July heat wasn't troubled by the large fan blowing in Mama and Daddy's bedroom. Annie Ruth wiped her brow with her handkerchief and then started reading the paper Daddy had just given her.

One of these days, just like the sun sets, my life will be over, and I'll meet death. All worries will be over, and troubles, too. Going to put on a long white robe, and be like new.

Going to meet my heavenly father. Going to see those pearly gates. No sorrow, no worries about tomorrow, I am going to be filled with joy. One of these days, just like the sun sets, my life will be over, and I'll meet death.

Annie Ruth stifled a sob and folded the paper gently. "Daddy, I didn't know you could write poems."

Daddy smiled. "I ain't ever tried to write any before. Them

words come to me this morning while I was praying. I just finished scribbling them down when you walked in."

Annie Ruth sat in a chair near the bed. "Why you keep your illness from us for so long?"

Daddy shifted his failing body in the bed. "I didn't see any sense in worrying everybody. The doctor said there ain't any cure for cancer. I figured I'd live as long as I could and not worry anybody."

Annie Ruth got up and looked out of the window. She felt like a little girl inside. "You always been there for me, willing to do whatever you could to help me. Even when I was hauling moonshine, I knew you'd do everything you could to keep me outta trouble."

When she turned around, the love showing in Daddy's eyes poured over her. "Life is filled with changes," he said. "My love for you will always be with you. I may not be here in person, but you, Maybelle, your brothers, and all of my family know I'll always love all of you."

"I don't wanna give you up, though," Annie Ruth said.

"You gotta. You a grown woman, now. You got your own family. I wish I could stay, but my fate is in the most powerful hand."

Annie Ruth tried to smile through her tears as she walked over and hugged him. "I love you, Daddy."

"I love you, too, my Baby Ruth."

Billie Lee walked in Uncle Sid's room that day, timidly.

"Why you acting so scared, Billie Lee?" Uncle Sid asked. "Have I ever bit you?"

Billie Lee laughed softly. "No, you ain't, Uncle Sid. You the closest thing I ever had to a daddy."

Billie Lee sat in the chair next to the bed. Uncle Sid turned to her. "I wish things had been different, but I love being a father to you. I promised your mama on her death bed I'd help raise you."

Uncle Sid seemed to have a lot to say to her. "Billie Lee, I want you to quit letting the way you were conceived bother you. You here. We all love you. That's what matters."

Uncle Sid sighed heavily. "In spite of all the low-down things Ray Rodgerson done to your mother, he had the nerve to ask why we gave you 'Watson' for a last name. I told him cause Watson blood was in your veins, and that was all that mattered. Like I told you, you here, and that's what matters."

Billie Lee wiped the tears that were beginning to flow steadily. "Thank you for being so good to me, Uncle Sid."

Uncle Sid smiled broadly. "When you and Annie Ruth were little bitty things, some folks used to try to be funny and say, 'Sid, are both them girls yours?' I wouldn't even bat an eye. I'd just say, 'They sure are both my girls. I got an ebony girl and an ivory girl. Now, ain't both of them pretty?'"

Uncle Sid chuckled softly. Billie Lee took his hand in hers and joined his laughter with tears and all.

Later, when Curtis went into the room neither he nor Mr. Sid said anything. They just smiled at each other and Curtis took a seat next to the bed.

Finally, Mr. Sid said, "How long you gonna sit there and not say anything, son?"

"I was trying to give you a little time to rest," Curtis said. "The whole family been in and outta here all morning."

"How they taking this?"

Curtis thought for a moment. "The women seem to be

taking it better than James, Jerry, and Carl."

"They'll be all right. All three of them told me they felt guilty about going away to college and building their careers. They blame themselves for not staying on the farm and helping me with the work." Mr. Sid took a deep breath. "I told them that I wanted them to get their educations. I didn't wanna stand in the way of them trying to do things that they wanted to do."

"Yeah, they needed to do what they wanted to do," Curtis said. "I'm glad Carl done moved back here, though."

Mr. Sid nodded. "I am, too. Since he gonna be teaching, too, he hired a man to help with the farming. I want you to help keep an eye on things also."

"I will," Curtis said. "You can count on me."

Curtis looked down. "Mr. Sid, sometimes, I get so ashamed of myself, cause Annie Ruth couldn't count on me when I was drinking and letting her haul moonshine."

Mr. Sid's voice was sympathetic. "Don't look back to the past. I feel bad about all of us . . . Annie Ruth, Billie Lee, Aldonia and myself. All I can tell you is pray and let it go."

"I love Annie Ruth so much. I wanna be a good husband to her."

Mr. Sid sat up straighter in the bed. "She love you, too. And she ain't expecting you to be perfect." Mr. Sid looked across the room thoughtfully. "Remember what Mark said about a Negro man and his family that night at the jail?"

Curtis remembered well. "He said a Negro man ain't got much if he ain't got the love of his family."

Mr. Sid nodded. "He sure told the truth. I think that's why your daddy took his life. He and I both went through a lotta struggles. There were some hard years when I felt like giving up. But Maybelle would bolster me up. She'd tell me she loved me and treat me like I was special. Somehow, I'd find the strength to go on. Andrew loved you and your little family, but I think he needed that special attention to keep him going. Unfortunately, Victoria had already passed on."

A burden Curtis hadn't realize existed was suddenly lifted. "I'm glad you told me that, Mr. Sid. Dad probably did feel alone without Mom."

Mr. Sid looked directly into Curtis's face and spoke firmly. "Promise me two things."

"Yes."

"Number one, don't you ever let my daughter take a risk like she did hauling moonshine ever again. Number two, you make sure she finishes college."

"I promise."

"Curtis, I'm counting on you."

"Yes, sir."

Mama said Daddy told her that day in July that death was in the corner waiting for him, but he didn't go until August. It was as though he wanted to make sure we would all be okay without him. That's the way he was, always trying to look out for his family. He finally confessed to us that he stored moonshine in his barn because he wanted to make sure Mama wasn't hard-pressed for money after he died.

His funeral was last week. A lot of people went to it just like they did to Mr. Andrew's. At the funeral, they talked about how kind and generous Daddy was. And how he'd always try to help people. The preacher told us not to worry about Daddy because we still have his love. The preacher also said "Y'all, the biggest, blackest farmer in Tobacco County just gone home." I believe Daddy is just gone home. And I ain't worried. But Lord have mercy, I'm missing him. I'm missing him.

Mama knocked on Annie Ruth's kitchen door and then walked in. "Coming in, my goodness," she said. "Annie Ruth, it look like you done peeled and sliced two or three bushels of pears!"

Annie Ruth wiped her brow with her apron. "I'm trying to get as much as I can done before I got to college." She checked a large pot of pears cooking on the stove. "How things been going?"

"Oh-oh, so, so, I miss your Daddy," Mama said.

Mama's sadness about Daddy's death had settled on her like a sudden hush in a once animated room. *I lost a father. And that's a lot, but Mama lost more. She lost her husband of thirty-five years, her companion, her best friend, and her lover.* "How's Granny?" Annie Ruth asked.

"She okay. She misses Sid, too."

"We all miss him," Annie Ruth said. "It will be a long time before this family get used to Daddy not being here."

"Uh-huh." Mama changed the subject. "You got everything ready for college?"

"Yes," Annie Ruth said. "Aldonia called me last night and told me she got everything ready, too."

"That's good," mama said. "I'm glad Sid convinced her to go back to college before he died. Hopefully, Billie Lee will follow y'all after a while."

Annie Ruth stopped Patricia from playing in the pear peelings. Mama smiled at her. "Little lady, you gonna be spending a lotta time with me when your mama goes to college."

"Yes, ma'am," Patricia said, heading back to the pear peelings.

Annie Ruth pulled her away again.

"Annie Ruth, I'm gonna help you with your college expenses," Mama said. "Sid had two life insurance policies and they both paid well. Plus, I got the money he made storing moonshine."

Annie Ruth felt very lucky that she had such a helpful and generous mother. "Thank you, Mama. I appreciate everything."

"Patricia!" In the few seconds that Annie Ruth had taken to respond to Mama, Patricia had seized the opportunity to topple over a bucket of pear peelings. *My goodness, Patricia is as strong-willed as I was. I'm gonna need to preach to her just like Mama used to preach to me.*

That afternoon Annie Ruth had finished canning pears and had cleaned up the kitchen when Billie Lee drove into the backyard.

Annie Ruth was surprised to see her in Mrs. Bostic's car. "What you doing in Mrs. Bostic's car?"

Patricia ran to the door. "Hey, Billie Lee!"

"Hey, Patricia," Billie Lee said getting out of the car. She touched the shiny Cadillac. "Miss Bostic left it to me. Her son brought it to me about an hour ago."

Annie Ruth looked at the car admiringly. "That was really nice of her," she said as she went on the porch and got two chairs for them to sit in. Patricia went into the yard to play with a toy wagon.

Billie Lee went onto the porch and sat next to Annie Ruth.

"Miss Bostic was really a nice lady. She also left me some money for college tuition. Her son done already contacted a school in Augusta. Hopefully, I'll get all my paperwork completed in time to be able to start in January."

Annie Ruth felt a pang of disappointment. "I'm glad you gonna go to college, but we all been hoping you'd join Aldonia and me at Savannah State."

Billie Lee shook her head. "No, I wanna be a nurse, and Savannah State doesn't have a nursing program." Billie Lee smiled. "Anyway, I need to be on my own. If I were to go to school with y'all, you and Aldonia would be trying to protect me like y'all always do. I gotta grow up. I can't depend on y'all and Granny forever."

Lenny had been dead over a year. In spite of his harsh treatment of Billie Lee and his final betrayal, there were still times when his name would come up during the course of a conversation or Billie Lee would mention the good things about their relationship, and her love for him would shine on her face as bright as the midday sun. Yet, his death hadn't left her bitter and self-doubting, but strong and self-confident. *This will be the first time that we haven't lived near each other,* Annie Ruth thought sadly. "I'm gonna miss you."

Billie Lee nodded. "I'm gonna miss you, too."

"We always been like sisters," Annie Ruth touched Billie Lee's hand. "I hope your going away won't change things."

Billie Lee grabbed her hand and squeezed it. "It won't."

Annie Ruth felt like crying.

Billie Lee smiled knowingly. "Don't start crying, cause I ain't fixing to die. I'm just going to college."

Annie Ruth forced a smile and then started talking about their college plans so she'd stop feeling sad. "In a few years, you, Aldonia, and I will have college degrees."

"Yes, we will, and it sounds great to me," Billie Lee said. "Edwina will probably decide that she wants to go to college."

Annie Ruth shook her head. "No, they visited us Sunday. She's pregnant again. Edwina loves being a housewife and raising children."

"Yes, she does."

"Billie Lee!" Patricia pointed to the Cadillac. "Let's ride."

Billie Lee stood up. "Okay, come on, Annie Ruth."

When they returned from their ride with Billie Lee, Annie Ruth put Patricia down for a nap and then walked back outside. Everything seemed so quiet after having Mama and Billie Lee visit.

So many things done happened and changed since I was that seventeen-year-old girl head over heels in love with Raymond Baldwin. I'm a wife and a mother, and I'm gonna soon be a college student.

Bigtime black farmers like Daddy and Mr. Andrew are becoming rare. More and more people are moving from the country into town. Although a few better jobs are opening up for Negroes, a lotta black people are still moving to the North for more opportunities. It seem like Georgia's schools are gonna probably be integrated in a few years. Yeah, it's like Daddy said, life is full of changes.

Annie Ruth looked out across the field and saw Curtis plowing with the tractor. He was wearing a straw hat, but she knew he had to be sweating in the sweltering August heat. She went inside and made a pitcher of lemonade, put it and two glasses on a tray and carried it out to the field. She placed the tray on the stump of a tree and waited for Curtis to return to that end. When he returned, he stopped the tractor, got off and walked over to her. "My sweet wife must have read my mind. I was just thinking about how good a cool drink would taste."

Annie Ruth felt her love for him stirring. Suppose my going to college destroys our marriage? The thought caused her to wrinkle her brow.

Curtis looked at her questioningly. "Why the frown?"

"I don't want us to break up." Annie Ruth said. "Maybe I shouldn't go to college. Four years is a long time."

Curtis didn't appear worried. "Four years ain't forever. We got the rest of our lives to be together. We survived a lotta hard times. We gonna make it."

"What about your preaching?"

"I'm gonna heed the Lord's calling. And I'm gonna get an education." Curtis took out his handkerchief and wiped his face. "After you start teaching, we'll be able to hire someone to help me out. That way I'll be able to take some college courses at night over in Albany or Jacksonville."

"That's all gonna take a long time," Annie Ruth said.

"Yes, it will. But we both always wanted to go to college. You can still achieve your goal of being a teacher, and I can still hold on to our land and get an education, too."

Annie Ruth filled two glasses with lemonade and handed one to Curtis. "Let's promise to achieve our goals and keep our marriage together."

They both smiled.

"I promise."

"I promise."

A beam of sunlight shined through their cool glasses as they touched them together in a toast.

About the Author

BETTY PAYNE, a native of rural Georgia, is a schoolteacher and writer in Union City, Georgia. She has been published in *Ebony Junior Magazine, True Story, Black Romance,* and *Jive Magazine.* This is her first novel.

CPSIA information can be obtained
at www.ICGtesting.com
Printed in the USA
FSHW011643050321
79214FS